THE PICASSO HEIST

For a preview of upcoming books and information about the author, visit JamesPatterson.com or find him on Facebook, X, Instagram, or Substack.

THE PICASSO HEIST

JAMES PATTERSON
AND HOWARD ROUGHAN

LITTLE, BROWN AND COMPANY
NEW YORK BOSTON LONDON

The characters and events in this book are fictitious. Any similarity to real persons, living or dead, is coincidental and not intended by the author.

Copyright © 2025 by James Patterson
Excerpt from *The Invisible Woman* © 2025 by James Patterson

Hachette Book Group supports the right to free expression and the value of copyright. The purpose of copyright is to encourage writers and artists to produce the creative works that enrich our culture.

The scanning, uploading, and distribution of this book without permission is a theft of the author's intellectual property. If you would like permission to use material from the book (other than for review purposes), please contact permissions@hbgusa.com. Thank you for your support of the author's rights.

Little, Brown and Company
Hachette Book Group
1290 Avenue of the Americas, New York, NY 10104
littlebrown.com

First Edition: October 2025

Little, Brown and Company is a division of Hachette Book Group, Inc. The Little, Brown name and logo are trademarks of Hachette Book Group, Inc.

The publisher is not responsible for websites (or their content) that are not owned by the publisher.

The Hachette Speakers Bureau provides a wide range of authors for speaking events. To find out more, go to hachettespeakersbureau.com or email hachettespeakers@hbgusa.com.

Little, Brown and Company books may be purchased in bulk for business, educational, or promotional use. For information, please contact your local bookseller or the Hachette Book Group Special Markets Department at special.markets@hbgusa.com.

ISBN 9781538758434 (hc) / 9780316596961 (large print)
LCCN 2025933219

Printing 1, 2025

LSC-H

Printed in the United States of America

FOREWORD

THIS IS A true story.*

How James Patterson even heard about it in the first place is still a mystery to me, although I guess that's what a lot of his books are—mysteries—so, yeah, there you go. Still, it's not like I was scurrying around door to door and hawking my tale to the highest bidder. Or any bidder, for that matter. That's one of the rules of the Witness Protection Program. You're not allowed to profit off the very reason they stick you in it.

Somehow, some way, Patterson must have had access to somebody awfully high up and with a badge, because that's the only way to explain how he ever got hold of me. Of course, that's mere speculation. I'll never know for sure, and I'm more than fine with that. Just because Patterson wanted to know my secrets didn't mean I needed to ask about his. As for why I ultimately said yes to him, I think it's because I had every reason to say no. Someone near and dear to me

---

* Except for the parts that aren't.

FOREWORD

once explained that the secret to life was learning how to zig when the rest of the world zags. Otherwise, what's the point of it all?

So what more can I tell you before I let the storytellers take over? Well, maybe this. There's a reason none of what you're about to read ever made it into the press. It's complicated. Not so much the reason but the story itself. When you combine organized crime, power-hungry federal officials, and filthy-rich people with a hell of a lot to hide, the results are never neat and tidy. Especially in New York. Go figure, right? If it ain't extra-messy, it ain't Manhattan.

As you turn these pages, you might think you know what's going on, and you might think you know what's going to happen next. And maybe some of you will.

Most of you won't.

—Halston G.

PROLOGUE

SERIOUS AS A HEART ATTACK

"So can we trust her?"

"What if she can't pull it off?"

"How smart?"

"What do they call that, again?"

"That's right."

"What do you mean?"

"So?"

"She could've taught that class."

"Can we afford not to?"

"She's pretty damn smart."

"Second in her class at Columbia."

"Salutatorian."

"She should've been the valedictorian."

"She got all As until her last semester. Then got a C in one course."

"The course was Twentieth-Century Art History."

"How do you know?"

"What about her? Did she admit it?"

"Why not?"

"It is if we intend to trust her."

"He's not the one I'm worried about."

"Of course he would say that. He's her brother."

"I understand. But their motive . . . "

"Sometimes people get blinded. Emotions — "

"We're not shrinks."

"Exactly. She tanked the final on purpose."

"The professor's convinced."

"I didn't ask."

"Because it's not relevant."

"Remember, she's not working alone."

"And he says she can handle it."

"He's not just some guy, though."

"Can you blame them?"

"That's what we're here for."

"This is personal for them."

"That's what I'm saying."

"So you're okay with that?"

"Because it's so personal?"

"Some people would call that crazy."

"Because that's the risk if things go sideways."

"Are you really, though?"

"I want you to say it out loud."

"As a heart attack."

"Yes. What happens to this girl, Halston, if she gets caught?"

"I know."

"Very personal."

"How can it not be, though?"

"It's why I trust her."

"Because she's willing to risk her life."

"I'm well aware."

"Well aware of that too."

"What do you want me to say?"

"You serious?"

"You mean, if she gets found out?"

"Fine what? Let me hear the words."

"Fine."

"She's as good as dead, that's what."

ACT I

GAMES PEOPLE PLAY

CHAPTER 1

TENNIS, ANYONE?

Growing up, I remember my mother really wanting me to learn how to play the sport. She never asked if it was actually something I wanted to do, and not once did I express even the slightest interest in setting foot on a court. Still, for my twelfth birthday, she handed me a pink envelope with my name, Halston, spelled out in rainbow-glitter glue, and inside was a card announcing that I'd been signed up for a dozen tennis lessons at the local YWCA.

Honestly, I think my mother simply liked the *idea* of having a daughter who played tennis. It conveyed normalcy, as if we were your typical upper-middle-class family living in Westchester, New York. (Spoiler alert: We weren't.)

But that's what most alcoholics do, and that's why my mother used to bury her empty liquor bottles at the bottom of our recycling bins: They try like hell to hide the truth. Or, better yet, they construct their own reality. So whether or not I was having fun playing tennis didn't seem to matter much to my mother. It looked good, like she was being a good parent. Who cared if I enjoyed it? (Spoiler alert: I didn't.)

Still, I never missed a single one of those tennis lessons. I learned how to play, and that of course included learning how to keep score. It's ten years later, I'm twenty-two, and I haven't picked up a racket since then. But I still know how to keep score.

And that's where this story begins.

"Skip, talk to me. How's the volume?" I whisper, testing the level in my earpiece, which is hidden by the blond wig underneath my baseball cap. I'm in Queens at the Billie Jean King National Tennis Center, right next to Citi Field, where the Mets play, so I'm wearing a Mets cap. This whole operation is about blending in.

"Volume's good," I hear back in my ear, "although I'm getting a little static, and you broke up on me there for a sec—"

Skip's voice suddenly cuts out, and I start dropping F-bombs, thinking we're screwed. Skip laughs. He's messing with me. That's what older brothers do. He can hear me crystal clear in his hotel room at the W Hoboken over in New Jersey. The hotel has good Wi-Fi, over 100 Mbps. More important, at least according to Skip, it's got a kick-ass bacon cheeseburger on the room-service menu.

"You logged in?" I ask.

"Yeah," says Skip. "Are they done warming up?"

"Yep. They're just about to start."

It's day two of the US Open tennis tournament, still the first round in a crowded field of over two hundred men and women. That means the most matches are being played on the most courts with the most chair umpires being used, including none other than the man of the hour, Lucas Montgomery.

Lucas is a very tall, lanky Australian in his late fifties who doesn't so much sit in his umpire chair as fold himself into it, contorting his body so his bended knees are nearly as high as his chest. Perched above midcourt, he looks like a human accordion. I absolutely love Lucas. I'd follow him anywhere, and this summer, after graduating college, I literally have. The Mallorca Championships, Wimbledon, the Swiss Open Gstaad. What a great way to see the world, and all of it paid for with wagers placed and won in split seconds.

courtsiding
verb
Transmitting real-time information from a sports event (especially a tennis match) for the purpose of gaining a betting advantage

In other words, if we can place a bet online before the bookmakers adjust their real-time odds, we have the upper hand. Advantage us. All it takes is that certain chair umpire who officially updates the score after each point a teeny bit slower than I update Skip on his laptop at the hotel. Someone like Lucas Montgomery, aka Slow Hand Luke.

Is courtsiding against the law? Technically, no. Just don't try telling that to the guys who run the online betting site offering the highest limits for live, in-match betting. That crew tends to have a slightly different opinion about courtsiding, one that they'd be more than happy to make me painfully aware of—and I do mean *painfully*—should they ever get the chance. Like today, for instance.

Because today I'm going to make a mistake. A big mistake. Huge. The kind that will forever change the rest of my life.

I'm going to get caught.

CHAPTER 2

"FIVE, RED," I whisper just loud enough so Skip can hear me over the cheering crowd.

Five as in *five hundred dollars*. *Red* as in *the Russian*. I never bet during the first few games of a match when the two players are feeling each other out. But once they settle into the first set, I pounce.

Red's opponent is Green, a Brazilian. Flag colors are faster than names.

Lucas, snug in his umpire chair, maneuvers his long arm like a crane and taps his touch screen right as I relay the bet, but I've beat him by a breath. As he announces the score I hear back from Skip. "In," says my brother. He got the bet in before the odds changed.

We've got five hundred bucks on Red, the Russian player, to win the game. He's now ahead, 40–30, but our payoff reflects the longer odds of 30–30. Just like that, we've got a better chance of winning with a bigger payout.

Is it guaranteed? No. Green could win the next point, taking it to deuce, then win two more points in a row after that to take the game. But the chances of that happening are not nearly as good as the chances of Red prevailing. Gambling is about one thing and one thing only: Leverage. You have it or you don't.

We have it. Red wins the game and our account gets credited $1,060 — $500 back for the initial wager, plus $560 profit. And now it's on to the next game and the next bet. That is, until I hear the voice to my right.

"Good match so far," the man says, leaning slightly toward me. "Very entertaining, no?" He's got a thick Eastern European accent. His breath reeks of cigarettes, two packs a day.

I know he wasn't sitting there a minute ago. Now he is. That's what I get for being so focused on placing my bet in time.

"Yeah. It's pretty good tennis," I answer, staring straight ahead. I don't look at him.

"Who are you rooting for?" he asks.

It's a harmless question but I know this guy's anything but harmless. He's not trying to be menacing. He doesn't have to try. It clearly comes naturally. *Keep it together now, Halston. Breathe in, breathe out...*

"I don't know who I'm rooting for," I say. "I guess I don't really care who wins."

I can feel and smell him leaning in even closer. "Yeah, but if you had to bet," he whispers, "who would you bet on?"

For the first time, I turn to him. He's got greasy dark hair combed across his forehead in a guillotine-like slant. He's smiling. He's also big. No, *thick* is a better word. His forearms, folded tight against his chest, look to be the size of ham hocks. I'm guessing they're covered in tattoos, but I can't see them because he's wearing a tragically ugly teal windbreaker. Never mind there's not a cloud in the sky, we're in late August, and it's pushing ninety degrees.

"What do you want?" I ask.

What he wants first is to show me the gun he's got tucked in his waistband underneath the windbreaker. The second thing he wants is my earpiece. He sticks out his palm. "Hand it over," he says. "Along with your phone."

The next game in the match has just gone to deuce on Green's serve. I would've been placing another bet after the following point. *How much of this are you hearing, Skip?*

I glance down again at the gun the guy's got tucked into his waistband and then back up at his eyes. I'm wearing sunglasses; he's not. He wants me to be able to see his eyes. I could play stupid and ask, *What earpiece?* But stupid won't get me anywhere. Coy is a different story, though. Coy buys me a little time.

"We both know you're not about to shoot me in front of all these people, and you're not going to throw me over your shoulder or drag me out of here kicking and screaming," I say. "So what's to stop me from standing up and heading for the first cop I see? There's lots of them around here, in case you haven't noticed."

He laughs. "Such a clever girl, huh? But we also both know you're not going to do that."

"Why not?"

"Because we found you, that's why. Now we'll always be able to find you, Halston." He really enjoys saying my name, showing me that he knows it. "Come with me now and we won't hurt you," he says. "But if you don't come with me now? We'll definitely hurt you."

I think it over for a few seconds, or at least I act as if that's what I'm doing. My mind's been made up since the very second this guy sat down. Meanwhile, Red wins the next point with an overhead slam, the ball careening into the stands. I look up at Lucas, crammed in his umpire chair, as he methodically inputs the score change. Damn; I could've placed ten bets in the time that took.

But my courtsiding days are over for now. I've officially been caught.

I take out my earpiece and hand it and my phone over to my new friend in the ugly teal windbreaker.

"Okay, you win," I say. "Let's go."

CHAPTER 3

HE FOLLOWS ME out of the stands, staying a few steps behind me and talking only when he needs to tell me left, right, or keep going straight. I glance back over my shoulder just once, not at his lumpy face but down at his Gucci-wannabe shoes with inch-high heels that scrape on the pavement, first one, then the other, sounding like a rusted metronome.

"Where do you think you're going?" he asks when I make a sharp turn that he didn't instruct me to take.

"I'm thirsty," I answer.

He looks and sees the water fountain against the wall to our left. What I don't think he sees is the security camera about twenty yards away from it. He of course knows there are cameras everywhere at the tournament but he most likely doesn't realize that this is how the police will know I didn't leave alone. I had company, and it's the guy cooling his cheap one-inch heels behind me while I bend at the waist and take a long sip. No one's ever going to mistake the two of us for boyfriend and girlfriend. I turn around, take another glance at his greasy hair and that god-awful teal windbreaker. *Ugh. At least I hope not.*

He falls in step behind me again, definitely closer now. "Up ahead, just outside the gate," he says. "The Uber lot."

We leave the grounds, passing a couple of cops along the way. I don't look at them, staring instead at the huge black Cadillac Escalade with tinted windows that's idling behind a couple of rows of late-model Nissan Sentras and Toyota Camrys doing pickups and drop-offs. The most unsurprising sentence of the day is when he announces that our destination is the Escalade. As we near it, he walks in front of me, then opens the back passenger door and points inside. The second I get in, I see another huge, hulking guy sitting by the opposite window; he tells me to slide over. He's also got an Eastern European accent, although not quite as thick. I move to the middle seat, and Mr. Ugly Teal Windbreaker climbs in next to me and slams the door shut.

And just like that, I'm the meat in a goon sandwich.

Faster than you can say *rodeo,* my wrists are zip-tied tight together. My wig and sunglasses are yanked off, a black pillowcase is pulled over my head, and I officially can't see where we're going. The driver, who I didn't get a good look at, takes off, but not before turning up the radio in case I decide to scream. Why they didn't gag me too, I don't know. Then again, who says a mob abduction has to be an exercise in airtight logic?

I'm not about to scream. There's no point. Besides, it would only make it hotter underneath this pillowcase, the fabric of which likely possesses the thread count of industrial sandpaper. I remain silent, as do the other three, while Bruce Springsteen belts out "Rosalita." Only when we speed up and merge onto what I'm guessing is Grand Central Parkway does the radio get turned down. Still, no one talks until about twenty minutes later when we veer onto an exit, slowing down. That's when I make an announcement. "I have to pee," I say.

I don't really have to go to the bathroom but it's the quickest way to figure out the pecking order among these guys. Whoever responds to me is a little higher on the organizational chart than the other two. He'll speak up because he knows it's his decision whether or not we stop for me to pee. Already, though, I can rule out the driver. Drivers are always entry-level. My money's on the guy to my left, whose only job thus far has been to sit there and do nothing.

Sure enough: "Hold it in," he tells me. "We're almost there."

No surprise, we're actually not. We're still driving after half an hour. By the time we're done taking all the turns and exits, I don't even know what borough we're in anymore or even if we're still in New York. Finally we come to what I think is another red light, only it isn't. Wherever we are, we've arrived. I listen to the loud, mechanical cranking of a heavy garage door rising. We creep forward only a little farther than the length of the Escalade before the cranking resumes: the same garage door closing. The driver cuts the engine, and the pillowcase gets pulled off my head. Before my eyes can adjust, I'm being manhandled out of the back seat.

A couple of hours ago, I was on the pristine grounds of the US Open making my way through the champagne-sipping, upper-crust crowd gathered to spectate the sport of kings. Now I'm being dragged to a rusted metal folding chair in an empty warehouse that's layered in dust and smells like a dumpster. I spot a second black Escalade, and for a moment, I think my eyes still haven't adjusted and I'm seeing double. I'm not. There're two of them. One was already here, waiting. A man steps out of the shotgun seat of this second Escalade and walks toward me as I get pushed down into the folding chair with my hands still tied. He's wearing black jeans, a black T-shirt, and a look of utter disgust.

Odds are he plans to kill me.

CHAPTER 4

"DO YOU KNOW who I am?" he asks.

I do. He's Blagoy Danchev, aka Blaggy, right-hand man and lead muscle for the Bulgarian mob that usurped all New Jersey–based online sports books due to their crypto prowess. I was courtsiding through their website, GameTime Wagers.

Blaggy repeats the question. *"Do you know who I am?"* Apparently, the higher up on the company ladder you are, the less prominent your Bulgarian accent is. It's barely there.

"No," I finally answer. "I don't know who you are."

"Are you sure?" He scratches his bald head. "Because I once read this story in a newspaper that said over eighty percent of murder victims know the person who kills them."

Blaggy is trying to scare me so I'll tell him everything about my operation, especially any and all partners I have. This is not to say that he won't actually kill me. He might. Blaggy's a cold-blooded murderer who makes people disappear faster than a Vegas magician.

He's capable of putting a bullet through me in a heartbeat. But he won't. Not here. Not now.

Because I'm not dying today.

I look him square in the eye. "Can I ask you a question, Blaggy?"

He squints. "I thought you said you didn't know who I am."

"How did you guys catch me today?" I ask.

"You fucked up," he says, shooting a look at the guys who brought me in. They're surrounding me, but center stage belongs to Blaggy. "Two weeks ago, you gave the same wire instructions for six different accounts on our site to make a withdrawal. Your bank issued a fraud alert, and that's how we figured you out."

"But you didn't freeze the accounts right away, did you?"

"No. We waited until—"

"Until I placed more tennis bets so you'd know which tournament I was at and precisely which match," I say. "It's crazy, right? I might as well have been wearing a neon sign over my head saying 'Come and get me, boys.'"

Blaggy's really squinting now. He hasn't gotten where he is, second in command for the Bulgarian mob, by being slow on the uptake. I was able to angle them for a boatload of money without anyone catching on, so would I really be so sloppy as to give the same wiring instructions for multiple accounts opened under fake names?

Unless...

"You *wanted* to get caught?" he asks.

"What I wanted was this right here, this meeting. It was the only way to get your attention," I say.

"For what?"

"I need your help."

Blaggy laughs in my face. They all do. "My help? You take us for a hundred grand, and now you want my help?"

"It's actually a hundred and fifty grand," I say.

Blaggy stops laughing. The others do too. He reaches for the back of his belt and steps toward me. For the first time in my life, I have the barrel of a gun pressed against my forehead, and I wonder if maybe, just maybe, I pushed the wrong button on the wrong guy at the absolute worst time. *Don't freak out now, Halston. Whatever you do, don't freak out. Hold steady. Hold your ground…*

"Give me one good reason I don't put a hole in your head," Blaggy says, grinding the barrel hard into my skin.

Life is a calculated gamble. Sometimes, so is death. If someone's willing to kill you over money, they'll be just as willing not to kill you if you can deliver even more money. Lots and lots of it.

I swallow hard, pushing down the lump in my throat. It's the only way to get the words out.

"I'll give you better than one reason," I say. "In fact, I'll give you fifty million."

CHAPTER 5

BLAGGY HOLDS OFF on killing me.

I've talked my way into another car ride, this time without the pillowcase over my head. It's okay if I see where the big boss lives. Anton Nikolov, the big boss, hides in plain sight.

My hands are still tied but Blaggy doesn't think I'll do anything crazy. Or at least, not anything crazier than intentionally getting caught stealing from the notorious Anton Nikolov so I can pitch him the art heist of a lifetime.

I'm in the back seat of the other Escalade, the one Blaggy used to get to the warehouse. He's riding shotgun, his own driver behind the wheel. The rest of the guys have been sent on their way, wherever that may be. "See you tomorrow," Blaggy told them, which turns out to be three more words than he says to me during the entire drive to Nikolov's home in Millburn, New Jersey. I'm taking note of everything; there's no detail too small. They originally didn't want me to know the location of the warehouse, but now I know it's in Weequahic Park, near the Newark airport.

Blaggy's silent treatment during the drive is a good thing, a confirmation that I've officially explained enough of my plan to him. He's talking to his boss on the phone, and he's not peppering me with follow-up questions. Does he trust me? Hell no. He doesn't have to, not yet. Maybe not ever. But guys like Blaggy and his boss do plenty of business with people they don't entirely trust. As they say, if you want absolute loyalty, get a dog.

Speaking of which, I can't help noticing from where I'm sitting that the back of Blaggy's bald head looks like the rippled coat of a shar-pei, albeit not in a cute way. Just saying.

Welcome to Millburn. It's the wealthiest town in New Jersey, and Anton Nikolov is one of its wealthiest residents. The feds have tried to link him to organized crime for years, but he pays his team of lawyers extremely well. It helps that he doesn't claim to be in "waste management." A legit shipping-container business has helped Nikolov conceal a host of slightly less legit business endeavors. As for his gaming website, it's fronted by a shell corporation, which is how the gaming license was obtained. Nikolov runs the show but his name isn't on any piece of paper.

We're here, no one says as we arrive at his house. No one has to. The giant gates do all the talking. Blaggy's driver nods at one of the security cameras; the gates part, and we're heading up a long driveway lined by tall trees that eventually opens up to a brick mansion with two humongous bear topiaries flanking the front door. It's all as subtle as the security detail milling about, each guy openly carrying an AR-15. I count a half dozen men and there are probably a few more along the perimeter of the property.

As soon as we stop, Blaggy turns to me and gives me his one and only piece of advice for meeting his boss. What to do and what not to do in the presence of Anton Nikolov.

"You stay shut up until spoken to," says Blaggy.

It's not a question but he stares at me intently, waiting for a response.

"Okay," I say.

"Okay what?" asks Blaggy. My answer clearly didn't cut it.

"I don't speak unless spoken to."

He nods. "Good. Now let's go."

I don't get to walk to the front door between the two humongous bears. Instead, Blaggy takes me around to a back entrance and down a long, narrow hall. All the doors are closed, but if I had to guess, I'd say we're in what was originally the servants' quarters. Still, even the staff would need a bathroom.

"I have to pee," I say.

Blaggy's response is somewhere between a grunt and an exasperated sigh. He's about to tell me no.

"I really, really have to," I say, stopping. "I can't hold it."

"Okay, fine." He starts opening doors around us. The first two are closets; the third is a small bathroom. He looks back at me, and I look down at my hands, which are still tied. Out comes a switchblade from his pocket, because of course he carries one on him. With a quick flick of his wrist, he cuts the zip tie. I'm free to pee.

"Thanks," I say.

He stops me after I take one step. "Wait."

Blaggy frisks me, checking for a weapon. I don't have one, at least not the kind he's looking for. What I do have he's not going to find. I've made sure of that.

Alone inside the bathroom, I remove my right Nike Pegasus running shoe and peel back the insole. They took my phone but I've been walking around—literally—with a second one this entire time.

My text to my brother, Skip, is only two words.

I'm in.

CHAPTER 6

ANTON NIKOLOV KEEPS me waiting in his den for over a half hour. I really do have to pee now.

Also, I'm not sure if this room qualifies as a den. Doesn't a den need to have a television? This room doesn't, although it does have some couches and armchairs. It's too small to be a living room, especially in a mansion like this, and it can't be an office or a library because there's no desk and not a single book in sight. The American dream, it occurs to me, is having more rooms in your house than there are names for.

Blaggy's down the hall. I can hear his voice; he's on his cell. He goes back and forth between English and his native tongue, the latter when he's talking business, it seems. I could be wrong. I took a lot of electives during my four years at Columbia as an art history major, from statistical modeling to abnormal human psychology, but Bulgarian 101 wasn't one of them.

Finally, I hear a different voice in the hall. Everything about it—the tone, the pitch, even the pacing—tells me that it's the boss. The only thing I can't tell is what Anton Nikolov is actually saying to his right-hand man, Blaggy.

Maybe it's that he wants to talk to me alone. Two sets of footsteps get louder and louder, but only one pair of feet comes into the room.

"You're a girl," says Nikolov, taking a seat in the armchair opposite me on the couch. "And you're young."

I'm immediately thinking of Blaggy's one piece of advice, that I should shut up until spoken to, and I'm wondering if this qualifies as being spoken to. Nikolov might simply be talking to himself—not that he's mumbling. It's that same strong, deep, and deliberate voice I heard out in the hall.

I err on the side of caution and remain silent. It's the right call. "Good," he says, nodding. "No smart-ass comeback."

At some point during the day Nikolov might have been wearing a suit, but the jacket's off now, as is the tie; the button-down collar of his blue dress shirt is open, exposing a gold chain with a cross and the outer edge of a large chest tattoo that looks to be the Bulgarian equivalent of Japanese irezumi, given the attention to detail.

It all makes sense in a contradictory sort of way. Nikolov is a rich man with a hard past, one he makes no attempt to conceal and yet doesn't dwell on, if you believe the few interviews he's given over the years. He likes his privacy but is a regular on the charity-gala circuit. He also likes to challenge those in his orbit, whether it's the people on his payroll or those who wish to do business with him. So it's no surprise that he's testing me. Now comes the difficult part: convincing him that my plan is viable and something he wants a piece of.

Nikolov extends his hand toward me, palm open. I've officially been spoken to, and now I have the floor.

You'll only get one shot at this, Halston.

Don't blow it.

CHAPTER 7

"**LAST SUMMER, BEFORE** my senior year of college, I interned at Echelon, which is—"

"The auction house," says Nikolov. "Yes, I know what Echelon is."

Of course he does. Anyone with a lot of money does. Although not every art collector with a lot of money gets to belong. Echelon is the ultra-elite, members-only auction house in Manhattan that out-snobs both Christie's and Sotheby's. Their manufactured exclusivity is a gimmick, but then again, so is everything in the entire art world. In art, there is no reality other than perception, and if you are accepted as a member of Echelon, you are perceived as having scaled the Mount Everest of art high society.

"At the end of my internship," I continue, "I was offered a full-time position in their valuations department after I graduated this year. I asked if I could have the summer off before starting so I could travel around Europe, and because traveling around Europe is a very Echelon thing to do, they said yes. My first day on the job is Friday."

"Three days from now."

"That's right."

"Congratulations." Nikolov crosses his legs and folds his arms. He's smiling but it's more like a Doberman showing his teeth. "Now get to the fucking painting," he says.

"Sorry, yes. The painting. It's a Picasso, but not just any Picasso. No one in the world knew this particular one existed until two years ago. Not even its owner, who was the live-in maid for some French guy who died and left her his villa in Nice. The painting had been wrapped in cheesecloth and stored in the attic of this villa for fifty years."

"Has it been authenticated?" he asks.

This is the first time Anton Nikolov lets on that he's a little more familiar with art than the average tourist walking around in circles at the Guggenheim. A noncollector would never think to ask that question right off the bat.

"Yes, it's been authenticated," I say. "Twice, in fact. Once in Paris and then again last summer by Echelon. It was during my internship. That's how I learned about the painting."

"How was this not in the news? Why haven't I heard about it?"

"Because of a very smart female attorney who's representing the maid. Now ask me how the maid knew to hire her. I'll tell you: She didn't. After the French guy died, the maid went to work for this lawyer, cleaning her house, and no, I don't know why she didn't just sell the villa and retire. Maybe she loves her job. Anyway, a month later, the maid finds the painting in the attic of the old guy's villa, which now belongs to her, and she tells the lawyer about it."

"Let me guess," says Nikolov. "The dead Frenchman has kids."

"Two. A son and a daughter, both in their forties. They were pissed about the villa going to the maid but they were hardly left out of the will. I heard they split the rest of the estate, about two million euros each. But of course, were they to learn about an original Picasso stuffed away in the attic..."

"How much is it valued at?"

"Echelon is expecting it to go for around a hundred million dollars. If it sold for exactly a hundred million, that would make it the—"

"Sixth-highest-selling Picasso ever."

"You know your art," I say. "I'm impressed."

"No, you're not. You did your homework on me, that's all."

"Doesn't mean I can't be impressed."

He picks a piece of lint off the thigh of his pants. "So, a hundred million, huh?"

"The bidding could go even higher, although I'm sure the record for *Les Femmes d'Alger* at a hundred and sixty-nine point four million is more than safe."

"A hundred and seventy-nine point four million," he says.

"Excuse me?"

"*Les Femmes d'Alger,* Version O, actually sold for a hundred and *seventy*-nine point four million."

"Are you sure?" I ask.

"Positive," he says.

It's easy to make a man think he's smarter than you. All you have to do is let him correct you once. That's all it takes.

"So," I say, leaning in, "what can I tell you about the plan?"

"Everything. But first, I want to see the painting," says Nikolov. "I assume you have a picture of it?"

"The auction hasn't been announced yet but I got somebody at Echelon to email me one." I reach into my pocket. Then the other pocket. "Shit."

"What?"

"I don't have my phone. Your guys took it from me."

Nikolov pulls his phone out of his pocket because of course a mob boss never goes anywhere without his cell, even in his own house. "Here, you can use mine," he says. He logs out of his various accounts and hands me the phone. "Go ahead. You just need to sign in."

I now have about thirty seconds to bring up the picture of the Picasso on Nikolov's phone. Any longer than that and he might suspect something. And we absolutely, positively can't have that.

Okay, Skip, it's time to work your magic.

CHAPTER 8

THE SECRET TO convincing anyone of anything comes down to a single moment of clarity.

It might be a sentence, certain words artfully strung together, or maybe a gesture or a demonstration of some sort, something that transcends the limits of language.

I had told Anton Nikolov about my plan and what it would require. I'd shown him a picture of the painting, and he had commented that it was clearly no ordinary Picasso — it was extraordinary.

Still, he wasn't sold. There was one aspect of the plan he had doubts about, serious doubts, and there was nothing more I could say to him to change his mind. Someone else would have to do it for me.

Mr. Nikolov, I'd like you to meet Wolfgang.

I wasn't so much released as furloughed from Nikolov's home to my SoHo apartment. I slept for a few hours, showered, and skedaddled over to the Museum of Modern Art, better known as MoMA, hurrying so I could be there at the appointed time, ten a.m.

For the record, Nikolov did the appointing. "Don't be late," he added after telling Blaggy to give me back my phone, "and don't even think of not showing up."

I had no intention of doing either.

A few minutes before ten I'm standing on the second floor of MoMA's David Geffen Wing with my plus-one, Wolfgang. At ten on the dot, Nikolov arrives with his plus-one, Blaggy.

"Jesus Christ," says Nikolov, looking Wolfgang up and down. "Is anyone over thirty these days?"

I'd already tipped off Wolfgang about the whole shut-up-until-spoken-to thing, including the part about not falling for Nikolov's opening it-doesn't-count-as-being-spoken-to comment. Not only does Wolfgang remain silent—he barely blinks. Wolfgang is super-chill.

"Your biggest concern is the forgery," I say to Nikolov. "So, like I told you last night, it's best that you see for yourself."

"See what, exactly?" asks Nikolov.

"What Wolfgang can do. His talent," I say.

Admittedly, Wolfgang doesn't look like a world-class forger. He's too young and too grunge, although I do think his muttonchop sideburns are pretty cool. Not many guys can pull that off.

"Is that actually your real name?" asks Nikolov. "Wolfgang?"

"That depends," he says. "Is that actually a real Picasso behind you?"

Both Nikolov and Blaggy turn around and stare at the painting ten feet away. "Are you telling me it isn't?" asks Nikolov.

"Go ahead, take a closer look," says Wolfgang.

Everything about the painting says Picasso, from its characteristic cubism to the small brass plaque underneath that literally states that it's a Picasso. Nikolov and Blaggy walk over to the wall. They stare at the painting; they read the plaque; they stare some more. Wolfgang and I join them.

"You'd never know," I say. "In fact, the museum doesn't even know."

Wolfgang points to the plaque. "See how it's on loan from the Rubenstein family, Thaddeus and Camilla? Well, good old Thaddeus sure enjoys the big charitable-contribution tax break he receives for loaning out the painting, but there's one problem. The dude really likes the painting. Loves it, actually. So much so that he was willing to pay me to re-create it so he could keep the original at his home in Malibu, where I'm told he often just sits and gazes at it for hours on end."

Blaggy, who hasn't made a peep up to this point, can't help himself. "Bullshit," he says.

"Yeah, I know, right? It all sort of sounds like bullshit," says Wolfgang. "But do me a favor, big guy, will you? Take a slight step to your left. And Mr. Nikolov, if you could do the same."

"Why?" asks Blaggy.

With one word, Nikolov shows that he didn't get to be the boss by accident. "Cameras," he says.

"That's right. Don't look but there's one up in the corner at three o'clock, and another directly over my right shoulder," says Wolfgang.

I slide over to block the camera behind us. "Got it," I say as Blaggy and Nikolov move to block the one off to the left.

Wolfgang casually glances around. I know what he's doing. He's waiting for the perfect amount of foot traffic behind us, enough bodies in motion to eliminate a clear sight line of what he's about to reveal.

"One of the most notorious modern forgers is a German by the name of Wolfgang Beltracchi," he says, maybe to fill the time. "Beltracchi sold over a hundred fakes; his work was near impeccable. Then he made a mistake and got arrested."

"What was the mistake?" asks Nikolov.

"He sold a piece that was supposedly painted by Heinrich

Campendonk in 1914. The problem was, a specific kind of paint Beltracchi used in his forgery didn't exist until 1920."

"That's a dumb mistake," says Nikolov.

"Very much so. But I've always loved the name," says Wolfgang. "You see, the whole trick to this game is never being known, and yet there exists this overwhelming desire to leave your mark. A psychiatrist might even say that Beltracchi wanted to get caught, you know, subconsciously."

"What about you?" asks Nikolov.

"What about me?" asks Wolfgang.

"Can you leave your mark without getting caught?"

The crowd of passersby grows thick in that instant and Wolfgang reaches into his pocket, pulls out a handheld, filtered shortwave black light, and flashes it over the bottom corner of the canvas. For a split second the image of a howling wolf appears.

"Holy shit," says Blaggy.

"Fuckin' A," says Wolfgang, walking away. "Have a nice day, gentlemen."

CHAPTER 9

THERE'S NOTHING LIKE a mic drop for a moment of clarity. *Nice work, Wolfgang.*

Nikolov watches him walk off, then his eyes snap back to the painting. He's marveling at what it is. Or, more accurately, what it isn't. There's a fake Picasso hanging in MoMA, one of the most famous modern-art museums in the world.

"The kid's got balls," mutters Nikolov, and as soon as he says it I know two things for sure.

One, Nikolov is on board.

Two, the real power play is yet to come.

"Should we talk more elsewhere?" I ask.

"Yeah," says Nikolov. He points at Blaggy. "Go with her to the car. I'll be there in a few minutes. I need to make a call."

Blaggy escorts me downstairs, out of the museum, and into a black stretch limousine parked near the corner of Fifty-Third Street and Sixth Avenue. Less than twenty-four hours earlier, Blaggy had a gun pressed against my head. Now he's opening doors for me.

I'm alone in the back of the limo. The partition's up so I can't see the driver, but I can hear him lower his window and make some small talk with Blaggy, who's waiting out on the sidewalk. I immediately text Skip, and he answers my question before I can even ask it. Yes, he tells me, Nikolov indeed just called someone from inside the museum. With the spyware Skip uploaded, we can now track Nikolov's location through his cell and see phone numbers of incoming and outgoing calls. Skip's already run a trace on the guy Nikolov's chatting with now—it's one of his attorneys. He has several on retainer, mostly for business, legitimate and otherwise, and he also has one personal attorney, a limelight-loving shark named Peter Hammish. It's Hammish whom he's suddenly had the urge to talk to.

Skip texts again minutes later to tell me Nikolov is off the call and heading out.

I stash my phone and wait. The limo door soon opens and in climbs Nikolov, followed by Blaggy. They both sit opposite me. I'm looking only at Nikolov.

"I want it for myself," he announces.

"Excuse me?" I heard him perfectly.

"You want my help to steal a Picasso and replace it with a fake. Then you want to sell the real Picasso on the black market for roughly sixty cents on the dollar. You get ten million, and I keep the rest. That's what you're proposing."

"That's right," I say. "It's your manpower, and you'd have the bigger exposure—you get the lion's share of the money. Figure fifty million, just like I told you."

"And I don't want the money, is what I'm telling you. I want the actual painting."

"But there is no money without selling the painting."

"You're not thinking big enough," he says.

"Okay, then. What do you have in mind?"

"You have to be a member of Echelon to bid on the painting at auction, right? I'm not a member, which is why you initially said we can't control who buys it."

"Exactly," I say.

"But what if we could?" he asks.

"What do you mean?"

"What if we knew exactly who was going to buy the painting?"

"In other words, we'd somehow be working with a member," I say.

"That would open up some other revenue possibilities, wouldn't it?"

"I can think of one."

"I'm pretty sure I'm thinking of the same one," says Nikolov.

"Which is why it's impossible."

"Nothing's impossible."

"This isn't like asking someone for a favor. We're talking about fraud," I say. "Why would any Echelon member take the risk?"

"Normally they wouldn't."

"So why are you smiling like that?"

"You're right, this isn't like asking someone for a favor," he says. "But what if I was the one who was owed the favor?"

"You have someone in mind, don't you?"

"I do. There's a member of Echelon who owes me."

"Are you talking a dollar amount?" I ask. "Someone who owes you money?"

"Not exactly. Let's just say he's in my debt."

"You really think he would do it?"

"I do. But he'll need some convincing. We'll need to work him a little bit."

"The auction's in three weeks. We don't have a lot of time."

"Then we better not waste any," he says. "What size dress do you wear?"

"What size?"

"Yes. You need a dress."

"What makes you think I don't own a dress?"

"I'm sure you do. You just don't own the kind you're going to need Saturday night."

"What's happening Saturday night?" I ask.

"You're going to a party."

"Because the guy who owes you a favor—"

"Will be there, yes," says Nikolov.

"How do you know?"

"Because it's his fucking party."

"So you're invited?"

"No, actually, I'm not. So we're both not. But with the right dress, you won't need an invitation. Do you know what I mean?"

"Unfortunately, yes," I say. "I do."

"And do you already own a dress like that?"

"No. Not exactly."

"Докато умните умуват, лудите лудуват," he says.

"I don't speak Bulgarian."

Blaggy translates. " 'While the supposed smart ones are thinking, the crazy ones are doing.' "

Nikolov leans forward, rests his forearms on his knees. His stare burns right through me. "What it really means is this," he says. "The next time I ask you a goddamn question, Halston, just goddamn answer it."

"Four," I say. "My dress size is four."

CHAPTER 10

NOW THE REAL work begins.

How an auction house gets the super-wealthy to massively overpay for paintings and the occasional sculpture is an art form in and of itself, a delicate balancing act. The firm must radiate wealth and privilege while its staffers assure the clientele, the ones raising those pretentious little paddles, that they are the ones who enjoy the real wealth and privilege. The House of Echelon manages the game to perfection. *Sucking up with a stiff upper lip,* as Jacinda describes it.

Jacinda Jefferson is head of human resources for Echelon, and there's very little, if anything, that happens under its gilded roof that she doesn't know about. If the secret of thriving is surviving, few have done it more impressively. Jacinda spent two years of her childhood homeless, living with her mother and father in their Subaru Outback on the outskirts of Atlantic City. She had every excuse to fail but didn't; she graduated from Rutgers, started at Echelon as a receptionist, and ultimately rose up to be the head of HR with a salary of over $600,000 a year. That doesn't happen by accident. That's also not a guess on how much she makes. It's a fact, one she shared with me over lunch early on during my internship last summer for one simple reason: I asked. "The cojones on you," she said, smiling. Then she answered my question. I knew she would because Jacinda Jefferson has lived what I've always been taught: If you don't ask, you usually don't get.

And that is exactly why I'm sitting in her office at nine o'clock sharp on a Friday morning, my first day as a paid employee of Echelon: Because I asked her to hire me. Moreover, I asked her to hire me for a job that no new graduate is ever hired for—an appraiser in Echelon's valuations department. Neophytes should have no say in determining what a van Gogh, Matisse, Rothko, or Rembrandt is valued at before coming to auction. That goes for Picassos too. In fact, they shouldn't even be involved in the research required to value a piece of art, no matter how pedantic or tedious that research might be.

Of course, that's not my opinion. No, this is all according to Terrance Willinghoff, the guy who oversees the entire valuations department at Echelon. In other words, my new boss.

"He's going to be an asshole to you," says Jacinda from behind her large glass-topped desk as she gathers the various forms I need to sign on my first day. "But don't take it too personally. Terrance is an asshole to almost everyone."

"He really put up a fight on me, didn't he?" I ask.

"No one likes being told what to do or, in this case, whom to hire, especially around here. Let's just say that in the end, Terrance saw the wisdom of going along with my recommendation. But, yeah, don't expect him to welcome you with open arms."

"I won't, and thank you again for going to bat for me."

"Bullshit," says Jacinda.

"What do you mean?"

"You graduated second in your class from Columbia, so playing clueless isn't really your thing. I'm using you, Halston, and we both know it. You're now my eyes and ears in the one department here that I don't always know everything about."

You're right, Jacinda. We do both know it. You're absolutely using me.

Terrance Willinghoff and the rest of the stuffy staff that make up the valuations department do indeed play things close to their tweed vests. How they work, the methods they use, are akin to a secret family recipe, not to be shared with those outside the bloodline. Such mystique pays dividends for Echelon's exclusive reputation among art collectors worldwide, but in-house, such cliquishness can mess with company morale, which happens to be Jacinda's domain. The valuations department can't have their own sandbox. They need to share it with the auctioneers, the finance team, the PR people, and so on—and they all have to play nice.

"Regardless," I say, "thank you for helping me. I really appreciate this opportunity."

Jacinda stops shuffling her papers and stares at me. "What I just said doesn't bother you?" she asks.

"Which part? That I owe you for this job and therefore you *own* me?" I say. "Do you mean that part?"

There it is. Jacinda's stare is gone, replaced by the same approving smile she gave me that day last summer when I asked what her salary was. Cojones, yes. Clueless, no.

I'm Jacinda's mole, and I'm okay with it.

"Here," she says, handing me a half a dozen documents to sign, including a nondisclosure agreement. She points to the NDA. "You're going to see and hear some things that you're not ever going to be able to talk about outside these walls. And within these walls, as part of the valuations department, you're going to have access to certain areas that not everyone else has. Echelon requires your utmost discretion at all times, no exceptions. Understood?"

"Completely."

"That's good enough for me but apparently lawyers still aren't cool with verbal commitments," she deadpans, handing me a pen, "so start signing."

I sign the NDA, turn my attention to the next document, then stop and oh so casually ask the all-important question: "When do I get my security card?"

"As soon as we complete your background check," says Jacinda.

That's not the answer I was expecting. "I thought that was done before my internship."

"It was, but we've since had to update the parameters, as it were."

"What does that mean?" I ask.

"It means last fall we hired an auctioneer whose sister, it turns out, was being investigated for financial fraud. Suffice it to say, that didn't go over too well internally. So now we take a peek at family members."

"A peek?"

"Nothing that isn't out there in public records. Still, your signature on this page here," she says, sliding another piece of paper in front of me, "acknowledges that you're aware we're doing it and have no objections."

Shit.

"Oh," I say. But it's the way I say it. Uncomfortably. It's pure reflex; I can't help it. For the first time, I've gone off script.

"You don't have a problem with that, do you?" asks Jacinda.

CHAPTER 11

"WELCOME, HALSTON!"

With just two words, Terrance Willinghoff immediately has me off balance. This is not the Terrance I know. This is someone else. This guy is effervescent, exuberant, buoyant—adjectives that I can safely say have never been used in reference to Terrance Willinghoff once in all the years since he was born, which was most likely in some cold, dank hospital on the outskirts of London. The word to describe me now is *suspicious*.

This nice-and-welcoming Terrance is far worse than asshole Terrance. People acting like you expect them to is rarely unsettling. It's only when people play against type that the alarm bells sound. Has he truly bought into Jacinda's mandate that the valuations department needs some young blood, a person who isn't eligible for AARP membership? It's possible. It's also possible that he's merely playing mind games, that this is a ruse designed to do exactly what it's doing, which is make me wonder what the hell is happening. If that's the case, well...what an asshole.

"Thank you so much," I say. "I'm really excited to be working here, Mr. Willinghoff."

"Please, call me Terrance. We're all on a first-name basis here. We're like a family."

Maybe it's the British accent combined with the Cheshire-cat smile, but never have the words *We're like a family* sounded more ominous. My only angle at this point is to play along. Better yet, play it up.

"Thanks so much, Terrance. You know, that's exactly how Jacinda described this department," I say. "A real tight-knit unit, like a family."

"Brilliant," he says, giving nothing away. There's not even a hint of a flinch at my mentioning Jacinda. "So let me introduce you to some of your, shall we say, siblings?"

He laughs. I laugh. And the Oscar for Best Duo Faking It goes to Terrance Willinghoff and yours truly.

We leave Terrance's office and he ushers me down the hall and through the subterranean space of Echelon's valuations department. It's technically the basement but to call it that would be like calling the ceiling of the Sistine Chapel "a decorative mural." The House of Echelon was, once upon a time, the home of John D. Rockefeller—one of many, I'm sure—and his "basement," all that remains of the original structure, was perhaps the very first man cave, an epic lounge-meets-speakeasy space with a Tiffany glass bar and an actual vault where Rockefeller supposedly stored everything from fine wines to gold bullion.

Nowadays that same vault is where Echelon locks up its art prior to auction, which explains the valuations department's proximity to it. They need access to the vault more than other departments do. Simple as that.

As for how it's accessed, that's more complicated. Only certain employees can set foot in the vault, and only after swiping their security cards and having their thumbprints scanned. Throw in an iris scan and some voice-recognition software, and we'd be on the set of the next movie in the Mission: Impossible franchise.

Suffice it to say, I'll probably never be given access to the vault.

So I'll just have to take it.

CHAPTER 12

TERRANCE WALKS BRISKLY. It's hard for me to keep up. "And finally, let me introduce you to Pierre. He hopefully should be in by now," he says before lifting his hand to the side of his mouth to whisper, mock conspiratorially, "You know the French, always setting their own pace."

We've made the rounds of my new so-called family. If they're my siblings, then I'm clearly the "whoops" child, the one Mommy and Daddy weren't expecting. I'm the youngest, not by a few years but by decades.

"Actually, I met Pierre last summer during my internship," I say.

Terrance grins. "Of course you did." This is a less than subtle reference to Pierre Dejarnette's other stereotypical French attribute: He is a lover of wine and women (and it's only the wine that he likes aged). He is handsome and charming, can quote Victor Hugo and Charles Baudelaire, and is equally comfortable discussing the impact of realism in art during the Age of Enlightenment and his beloved Paris Saint-Germain football club.

"That's soccer to you Americans," he said to me at Echelon's rooftop Fourth of July cocktail party last summer not long after introducing himself. He also said he wanted to take me to dinner. Never mind that I was less than half his age.

We compromised and had lunch. Pierre flirted and I acted flattered. I also made a point of telling him how in love I was with my boyfriend, although I didn't actually have one. That didn't entirely stop Pierre from flirting, but he graciously accepted that he was never going to sleep with me and never made me feel pressured or uncomfortable, which probably explains why Echelon tolerates his behavior, even when he's hitting on the home-team roster, so to speak. Pierre is a lot of things but he's also a gentleman. He never crosses the line.

In return, as second in command under Terrance Willinghoff in the valuations department, Pierre provides Echelon with something well beyond his keen appraising skills. He gives Echelon access to the highest of high-end collectors as well as the latest gossip from Paris to Nice and all points in between. In short, he's Echelon's French Connection.

Which is how, the story goes, he was the first to learn of a certain never-before-seen Picasso that had been tucked away in a Frenchman's attic for over fifty years. And any minute now, Pierre is going to be texting Terrance to tell him that he won't be coming into the office until later today because he's currently waiting on someone from ConEd to come and check his brownstone penthouse apartment for a gas leak. Pierre woke up this morning, and the smell was unmistakable, he'll say. How my brother dragged that propane tank and hose up to the roof vent without being seen, I'll never know. More important, no one else will ever know either.

"Hmm. He's not in yet," says Terrance when we arrive at Pierre's empty office. Instinctively Terrance takes out his cell, checks his messages. Sure enough, there's the text. He even mutters the words out loud: "Gas leak?"

"Excuse me?" I ask.

"Nothing," he says. "Well, actually, it's something. Pierre's going to be out for the morning, an issue at home..."

Terrance's voice trails off. He's distracted, wondering if and how this affects him. Perfect.

"You look like you need to call him," I say. The power of suggestion.

"I do," he says. "He's supposed to have lunch with a potential client visiting from Avignon." He hesitates. "But I still have to show you your desk and get you situated."

"Of course. Tell you what—while you go make the call, I'll use the bathroom. I think I saw it earlier. Down the hall?"

"Yes, at the end of the hall on your left. Swing by my office afterward, okay?"

We both head down the corridor in separate directions, and Terrance never looks back. Why would he? If he did, though, he'd see me returning to Pierre's office.

I've got about two minutes, tops, to find what I need. It's a small key.

A key that unlocks everything.

CHAPTER 13

"DON'T DROP ME off in front," I tell the driver. "Go past the house about a hundred yards."

Make that two hundred yards. That's how big Enzio Bergamo's East Hampton estate is. It's like that joke: By the time you're finally done mowing the lawn, it's time to mow the lawn again. The mansion, the oceanfront property it sits on—everything about this place is over the top. Just like the man himself.

Enzio Bergamo is known for two things. The first, in case you've been living under a rock for the past decade, is his fashion empire, Bergamo Fashion and Design, BFD for short. It became a household name around the world on the heels of its Bergy bag, a square-shaped purse that is now a must-have for the insecure wealthy who feel the need to announce publicly that they have fifty thousand dollars to spend on some sewn-together pieces of leather with a shoulder strap. After the Bergy bag came other BFD designs, including shoes, clothing, and accessories. It's been an amazing American success story for the first-generation Italian, and Enzio Bergamo has embraced every penny of it. Or, rather, spent every penny of it.

Which brings us to the second thing Bergamo is known for: his lavish and outlandish parties. They're epic, and they attract every boldface name from actors to athletes, rock stars to rocket scientists, a true cross section of the entire fame spectrum. Bergamo welcomes them all and basks in their limelight, ever the charming and charismatic host, with his wife, Deborah (pronounced "De-*bore*-ah"), alongside him.

Is there an actual guest list for this party? Maybe, although it's not as if anyone's walking around with a clipboard. But supposedly, someone *is* walking around. If you believe the tabloids, Enzio Bergamo employs a spotter, a man whose sole job is to roam the party and make sure every woman is wearing at least one thing with a BFD label. If she's not, she's asked to leave or, worse, brought before Bergamo for a public shaming.

Odds are I could crash this party by simply walking through the front door, but since I'm not wearing a stitch of BFD clothing, I need to make sure I'm not intercepted by the spotter—if there truly is such a thing—before I get close to Bergamo. Better safe than sorry, according to Anton Nikolov. I believe his exact words were "Don't get your ass kicked out before you even get in."

So, wearing my new black Bottega Veneta dress, courtesy of a Bulgarian mob boss, I walk around some tall hedges to the backyard, which faces the beach, and wait for the perfect moment to step out of the shadows and blend in as if I've been at the party for hours.

Once I've done that, I wait for the next perfect moment—when the ever-schmoozing Bergamo is between conversations and finally alone for a split second.

"So, is it true?" I step up behind him and ask.

He turns around. "Excuse me?"

"That you actually pay someone here at the party to make sure all the women are wearing at least one of your designs?"

Enzio Bergamo smiles. "Now, where would you ever get a silly idea like that?"

"I read it somewhere."

"And do you believe everything you read?" he asks.

"Only the gossip pages," I say.

"That's funny," he says. "You're funny." He looks me up and down. "You're also quite beautiful."

Actually, there's a third thing Enzio Bergamo is known for: philandering.

"That's a nice compliment," I say. "Thank you."

"No, I really mean it. You're beautiful." Bergamo sounds as if he's had a little too much to drink. It's to be expected. It's baked into the plan. Men are capable of making plenty of bad decisions while they're sober, but nothing greases the wheels of indiscretion quite like alcohol. "What's your name?" he asks.

"Halston," I say.

"She's beautiful *and* named after one of my favorite designers."

"What are the odds, right?"

"Which makes this even harder for me," he says, straightening his shoulders. "I'm afraid you need to leave."

"Wait—*what*?"

"You heard me."

"But why?" I ask.

"You know exactly why."

"You're serious? Just because I'm not wearing one of your designs?"

"How did you get by my spotter? He's definitely fired," he says.

Bergamo holds my stare. Then he starts laughing. We both do.

"You big jerk," I say.

"I totally had you."

"You totally did."

He gives me another head-to-toe. "Bottega Veneta, right?"

"That's right."

"It's very nice. Still, I can't help thinking you'd look even better in something of mine," he says.

"Is that a sales pitch? If it is, you can forget it. I couldn't even afford this dress; it was a gift. Which means I definitely couldn't afford a BFD."

"Well, I happen to know the head of the company quite well. He and I are very close. Extremely so, in fact."

"So you have an in, huh?"

"You could say that. Would you like to try one on?"

"Where?" I ask.

Bergamo nods over his shoulder at his quaint twenty-thousand-square-foot home. "Inside, of course. Rumor has it the handsome devil keeps an entire showroom here."

"Is that like the rumor about his having a spotter?"

"No, this rumor's actually true," he says. "Come, I'll show you."

CHAPTER 14

BERGAMO LEADS THE way, although not in a manner that overtly suggests we're heading inside the house together. He meanders, even shaking a few hands and giving air-kisses to some guests. His life is fashion, after all. Appearances are everything.

I follow right along but keep a safe distance, even once we're both inside. Servers from the catering company come and go. We aren't completely alone until he turns a corner off the foyer and into a living room.

"Wow," I say, looking at the massive S-shaped sofa. "Is that a Vladimir Kagan?"

"The girl knows her furniture." He doesn't break his stride. "Come, it's this way."

We walk through a den and into his office, then go through a sliding door.

"Wow again," I say, doing a quick pirouette. Welcome to the greatest woman's closet of all time.

"Do you see anything you like?" he asks.

"Absolutely."

"Yeah. Me too." Only he's not looking at the racks and racks of BFD dresses, gowns, and coats. He's looking at me. "Did I tell you how beautiful you are?"

"Yes," I say. "A few times, in fact."

"Once more couldn't hurt, then, right? Because you really are stunning," he says. "Are you attracted to me?"

I don't answer, but I do smile. He smiles back, stepping toward me.

"What about your wife?" I ask.

"What about her?"

"You're married."

"A minor inconvenience at the moment."

"I'm serious."

"I am too. You're irresistible," he says. "I can't help it. You're like the Ferrari in the showroom window—I just have to have you."

"Okay, but not here," I say.

"Where, then?"

"Maybe somewhere with a bed?"

"Yes, of course. A guest room. I've got lots of those."

We're face to face. I lean in, whisper in his ear, "Do I look like a *guest-room* kinda girl?"

I can almost hear Bergamo's engine revving. "Are you saying what I think you're saying?" he asks.

"Yes, but I want you to say it. Tell me."

"That turns you on, doesn't it?"

"Yes, tell me what you're going to do to me," I say.

"How bad do you want to hear it?"

"Really bad."

"Good. Because I'm about to fuck you in the master bedroom, Halston."

"Now you're talking," I say. "Let's go."

To watch Enzio Bergamo sneaking through his own house is a sight to behold, but he's awfully good at it. so I'm the only one who gets to see. Bobbing and weaving, stopping and starting at the sight of servers and a stray guest or two, he leads me through the living room, out to the foyer, and up the spiral staircase to the second floor, which is perfectly quiet.

"That was the hardest part," he says. "We're alone now."

Not for long.

We go down a wide hallway to a double door straight ahead. Bergamo pushes through it and stops dead in his tracks.

"Hi there, Enzi. Long time, no see."

CHAPTER 15

"**SON OF A** bitch," says Bergamo.

"Funny," says Anton Nikolov, leaning against the front of the giant four-poster bed. He points at me. "Because she happens to be young enough to be your daughter."

Bergamo looks truly stunned. It's perfect. "What the hell do you think you're doing?" he asks.

"The very same question your lovely wife would be asking were she here," says Nikolov. "How is Deborah, by the way? I assume she's downstairs somewhere at the party?"

Bergamo glares at Nikolov. "So this . . . what? This whole thing was a setup? If you wanted to talk to me, Anton, you could've just picked up the damn phone."

"Not exactly," says Nikolov. "Nice work, by the way, Halston. Very nice. Although, not to take anything away from you, but most men will follow their dicks just about anywhere. No offense."

"None taken," I say.

Bergamo's now glaring at the two of us, his head on a swivel. "You? Him? You're... working together or something?"

"Something like that," says Nikolov. "Now that you mention it, we're actually looking for another partner. That's why I'm here."

"No. That's why you're leaving," says Bergamo. "You and I have no business to discuss. We're square. Even. I owe you absolutely nothing."

"That's where you're wrong, and you know it," says Nikolov. "You owe me everything."

"You mean everything except the only thing that actually matters: money. Have I not thanked you enough? You gave me a loan years ago, and I paid you back, with hefty interest. What more do you want from me?"

That's my cue. I explain the whole plan to Bergamo, tell him exactly what we need him to do for us, go through every last detail. When I'm done, he has only one question for me.

"Are you fucking crazy?" he asks. "That's not a favor, that's a felony."

"Only if you get caught, which you won't," says Nikolov. "And I never used the word *favor*."

"Call it whatever you want but I'm not doing it," says Bergamo. "I won't."

"Yes, you will," says Nikolov.

"Or what? Are you threatening me? Are you going to sic your goons on me now?"

Nikolov laughs. "Do people still say *goon*? No, Enzi. No one's laying a finger on you. Like with all fools, the greatest threat to you will always be you."

Again, that's my cue.

When Nikolov took me shopping, he had three requirements for the dress. One, it had to be drop-dead sexy. Two, it couldn't be one of Bergamo's. And three, it had to go with a purse I owned that had an outside pocket.

Actually, that third one wasn't really a requirement. "If you don't have a purse like that, I'll buy one for you," he said.

No need, I told him.

Now I reach into the outside pocket of my black Saint Laurent handbag that perfectly matches my new Bottega Veneta dress and remove my iPhone. If Bergamo had looked closely, he would've seen it sticking out just a smidge, enough so the microphone was exposed. But Bergamo was looking at nothing but me the whole time. That's the power of a woman in the right dress.

He knows what's coming even before I press play, but I press play anyway because making a married man listen to himself telling a woman who isn't his wife that he plans to have sex with her in the exact spot where he and his wife sleep every night guarantees that he will undergo a major realignment of his thinking.

"Okay," says Bergamo with a defeated sigh. "When's the damn auction?"

CHAPTER 16

MICHELLE STARES AT me across our table the next day in the Empire Diner, her head tilted slightly as if she's trying to make up her mind. The way she's been picking at her bacon and cheese omelet, I can tell something is bothering her.

She's nine years old.

"Halston, is it okay if I... you know, like, ask you something?"

"Of course," I say. "And you never have to get my permission, Michelle. You can always ask me whatever you want. It's okay."

With her fork, she pushes a small piece of bacon around her plate. "Why do you do this?" she asks finally.

"Do what?"

"This. You know, spend time with me and everything."

"That's easy," I say. "It's because I like to spend time with you, Michelle. That's why."

"Janet says it's because a judge makes you do it."

"A judge?"

"Yeah, Janet says you probably got arrested and this is your punishment, having to hang out with me."

"Who's Janet, by the way?" I ask.

"She's someone new at the house. She's weird. The other girls call her 'Janet from Another Planet.'"

"I hope you don't call her that."

"I don't," she says. "But is she right? Does a judge make you do this?"

"No, of course not," I say. "No one makes me do this. I spend time with you because I want to. I'm your friend. You know that, right?"

"Yeah, I guess." But Michelle's not looking at me. Her eyes are down, fixed on that small piece of bacon doing another lap around her plate.

The Sisterhood Project doesn't have a handbook for new volunteers but the mantra I heard over and over in the interviewing process is "We are all worthy." Most of the girls they help are in difficult family situations and are living either in the Sisterhood Foster Home or with a relative who can't realistically be a strong female role model—in other words, a man.

Michelle was a baby when her father left her mother. She's never met him. Her mother's a drug addict, currently trying to get clean. Her rehab is split between three months in an upstate facility followed by another three months in a halfway house in Queens. Naturally, Michelle feels abandoned. I don't have a magic wand that can make those feelings disappear but I do have every Saturday at noon. That's when we meet for lunch, followed by an "educational, entertaining, and/or empowering activity."

It's been a total of four Saturdays now. I thought this moment might come.

I'd love to be able to tell Michelle that it's all going to be okay, that her mother's going to quit the drugs and get better, and that they'll be back living together soon. But I can't do that. I can't lie.

I don't know if everything's going to be okay. Her mother might not get better. Michelle might never get to live with her again. Filling a young girl with false hope is simply cruel, and Michelle's already had far too much cruelty in her life already.

"Michelle, look at me," I say. Slowly, she does. "I know you're missing your mom and I know how much it must hurt that she had to leave. But she left because she loves you, not because she doesn't. You're the reason she wants to get better."

"But what if she doesn't?"

"It won't be because of anything you did. You're the one giving her the strength to try, and no matter what, that makes you special."

"I don't feel special," she says.

"But you are." I watch Michelle, hoping that I'm getting through to her. Judging from her expression, though, I may have gotten through a little too much. "What is it?" I ask.

She puts her fork down slowly. "I feel bad," she says finally.

I don't ask why. I know why. I remember all those nights I spent alone crying in my room after my mother killed herself. "You mean you feel guilty," I say. "Because you're so mad at her."

Michelle looks up; her eyes lock on mine. She's on the verge of tears. "Yeah," she says.

"It's okay that you're angry at your mom," I tell her.

"I'm angry at both of them. They both left me."

"I know how it feels—"

"No, you don't," says Michelle. "You can't."

"Actually, I can. In fact, I wish my mother were here so I could yell at her and let her know how mad I am. But she's not alive anymore. Your mother's very much alive and fighting hard to come back to you."

Now we're both on the verge of tears. Michelle reaches across the table and puts her little hand on mine. "I'm sorry," she says. "Did your dad also die?"

"No. He's still alive. But he left me too. At least, that's how I felt at first," I say. "Just like you."

"Where'd he go?" she asks.

CHAPTER 17

WAKE UP, HALSTON.

My alarm goes off Sunday morning and the routine begins. I shower, put my hair in a ponytail, dress in baggy clothes, and apply absolutely zero makeup. I grab a coffee and a buttered roll from the Peruvian deli on the corner, then walk the four blocks west to the Budget car rental despite the fact that I have a perfectly good, albeit old, Jeep Cherokee in a nearby parking garage. More often than not, I'm offered a complimentary upgrade to a full-size rental but I always stick with the midsize that I reserved. I'm never picky about the model either, and any color will do. Well, except white. White cars are boring.

Not that there's anything exciting about this weekly trip. I mean, I look forward to it, and when I'm traveling or unable to make it there for some reason, I miss it. But the trip itself—the drive upstate, passing the same signs, getting off at the same exit—is always this strange combination of solace and sadness. It's completely my choice, something I want to do. And yet I absolutely hate why I'm doing it.

"Your pockets...empty your pockets...make sure everything's out of your pockets," says the guard in a robotic monotone, striding up and down the long line of visitors waiting to walk through the metal detector. He's talking to everyone but makes eye contact with no one.

My driver's license and my rental-car key. That's all I bring inside. When it's my turn, I place both in the chipped plastic bowl, and even though I've taken the next five steps countless times, when I pass through that machine I feel like I'm entering another world. Maybe that's because I am.

First comes the smell. It hits me after I turn the corner beyond the check-in desk. Whatever bleach cleanser they're using, it's not coming out of a spray nozzle; more like a fire hose. I breathe it in, this antiseptic stench, and it stings my nostrils, then my throat, then settles into my lungs like a cactus. Nasty.

Next comes the sound. It's actually a lot of sounds but I hear it as one noise. The clanking of sliding metal doors, the drumming of heels against the poured-concrete floors, the murmur of voices, the hushed conversations—all of it combines into a singular pounding against my ears. It took me about six months to learn how to block it out. I know the noise is still there but now I can barely hear it.

Fred, however, comes in crystal clear. He's the one guard who talks to me beyond simply telling me where to walk or stand or when I need to leave. That's how much I get from the other guards. But Fred's different. He's been here since I first started coming, which is why he calls me kid. Fred looks a bit like Kenan Thompson from *Saturday Night Live* (well, if Kenan were a former offensive lineman for Fordham University), and he talks with this deep, halting baritone that seems to have its own echo.

"Any change?" I ask before entering the visitation room.

"None that I can see," says Fred.

"For real?"

"See for yourself. But..." His voice trails off.

"But what?"

"I was only going to say—" He stops, thinking of the right words. "He missed you over the summer. This helps, your being back. It makes a difference. You probably know that already, but just in case you don't."

"Thank you, and I do know...and I really appreciate your saying that."

"I wouldn't say it if it weren't true." Fred points toward the back of the room. "Go ahead, kid. Third from the end."

I take my seat in front of the far wall at a small table that's bolted to the floor. Prisoners enter one at a time through a door, each flanked by two guards. Finally the one I come to see each week sits down in front of me.

"Hi, Daddy."

ACT II

MOVERS AND SHAKERS
AND ALL THE WORLD'S TAKERS

CHAPTER 18

THE OLD GENTLEMAN behind the wheel of the white Rolls-Royce Phantom parked down the street from Osteria Contorni watched the beads of water trickle down the windshield. The heavy rain that had blown through the city at sunset was now barely a drizzle.

"This too shall pass," he muttered.

The young man sitting shotgun turned to him. He'd been killing time by looking at the fake driver's license in his wallet. It truly was a spot-on replica of a real one. "What was that?" the young man asked. "What'd you say?"

"A lot of people think that line is from the Bible," said Amir, adjusting the rearview mirror. "It's not. It's actually an old Persian expression. *This too shall pass.*"

There were two things Amir never talked about. One was how much money he had. The other was what his life had been like before he had any.

Amir and his wife, newlyweds at the time, had escaped Iran on

Valentine's Day 1979, three days after the end of the revolution that saw the overthrow of Mohammad Reza Pahlavi, better known as the last shah of Iran. After living in abject poverty in Pakistan for a year, the couple immigrated to the United States, where they settled in New Jersey.

"Are you okay?" asked the young man.

"I'm fine," answered Amir. "What about you?"

"I'm okay."

"Are you nervous?"

"No. Not really."

"You should be," said Amir.

"If this is your idea of a pep talk, it needs a little work."

"When's the last time you took a punch?"

"For real?" asked the young man.

"Yeah, a real punch. Something hard. A teeth-rattler."

The young man, Malcolm, smiled. "It was in the fourth grade. During recess. Joey Mendelbaum, next to a jungle gym."

"I'm serious," said Amir.

"So am I."

"The last time you were in a fight was *the fourth grade*?"

"That's not what you asked. I've had plenty of fights since then. But only Joey Mendelbaum landed a solid one," said Malcolm. "The little bastard was left-handed."

Amir laughed. He believed every word of what Malcolm had just told him. There was a reason the kid was sitting next to him in his Rolls-Royce, and it wasn't his sense of humor. Malcolm was six foot two, two hundred and twenty pounds, and shredded. Most important, he was smart. Really smart. He had the best education money could buy combined with the kind of education money can't buy — the kind you get on the battlefield.

Still, this was new territory for the kid.

Amir glanced at the rearview mirror again. "Okay, they're here," he said. "They're just walking in now."

Malcolm turned, looked over his shoulder. "I see 'em."

"We'll wait a few more minutes, then you go in."

The two fell silent, both considering what lay ahead. "So you really think someone's going to take a swing at me in there?" asked Malcolm. "Like it's some initiation type of thing?"

"Not exactly."

"Then what?"

Amir turned to the kid. There was a big age gap between them. Amir had had forty-plus more years of living.

And learning.

"They'll check you for a wire, then they'll check you for a weapon," he said. "You have neither, and you'll act ticked off that they suspect otherwise. You know it's not personal, they have to do it to anyone new, but you don't give a shit because you're not just anyone, and they need to know that. You have to show them and in no uncertain terms."

"How?"

"The only way you can. By being the biggest badass in the room," said Amir. He pulled back the cuff of his dress shirt, glanced at his gold Rolex. It had been more than a few minutes. "You ready?"

Malcolm nodded. "Ready," he said.

Malcolm stepped out of the car and was about to close the door behind him when Amir told him to wait a second. Malcolm watched as Amir got out from his side and joined him on the sidewalk in the slight drizzle.

"The ring," said Amir, pointing at Malcolm's right hand.

"What about it?" It was a black opal ring that Malcolm had picked up at the Pul-e Khishti bazaar in Kabul during his second tour in Afghanistan. He almost never took it off.

"Let me see it for a second," said Amir.

Malcolm removed the ring and handed it to Amir, who immediately put it on the middle finger of his left hand, front and center.

"What are you doing?" asked Malcolm.

He never saw the answer coming. Amir, a southpaw, wound up and punched Malcolm as hard as a seventy-year-old man could. The edge of the ring caught Malcolm's cheek, immediately drawing blood, and he staggered on his feet.

"Now you're ready," said Amir.

CHAPTER 19

THERE'S BETTER ITALIAN food to be had on the Lower East Side of Manhattan than the heavy red-sauce-and-garlic fare offered up at Osteria Contorni. But for authentic old-school Italian ambience, nothing else comes close. The fact that the restaurant still uses vintage Chianti wine bottles, the kind with straw wrapped around the base, as candleholders says it all. Time moves a little slower here.

So do the staff. There's not a single out-of-work actor playing the role of waiter at Osteria Contorni. Nor are there any females. These guys are lifers; each one seems to be older than the next, and all of them have a slight hunch to their backs from leaning forward to take orders all these years. They joke, they bicker, they bust balls, but they always look out for one another. No one ever pockets a cash tip for himself.

No wonder it's Dominick Lugieri's favorite restaurant.

Over here, mouthed one of his crew to Malcolm when he walked in, motioning with a fat finger. The guy was standing by a red door next to the nearly empty coat-check room. August in New York City is the definition of *sticky*. Not a lot of layers being shed.

The closer Malcolm got to him, the more the guy squinted. He was looking at the open cut across Malcolm's cheek, the streak of blood.

"You should see the other four guys," said Malcolm.

It was a waste of a good line. Dominick Lugieri's front man hadn't been chosen for his sense of humor. He didn't even crack a smile. He just pointed with that same fat finger at the red door. He wanted Malcolm on the other side of it.

That's where the full pat-down happened. It was a narrow hall with another red door on the far end. Malcolm spread his arms and got treated to all ten fat fingers, head to toe. Satisfied—no weapon, no wire—the guy pressed a small buzzer on the wall and motioned for Malcolm to keep walking. The second red door opened, and that's when Malcolm saw him. The man himself, Dominick Lugieri. Eating a bowl of pasta e fagioli.

Of course a man like Lugieri never eats at a restaurant alone, even in his own private dining room at his favorite establishment. There were, count 'em, one, two, three henchmen hovering near his table.

Lugieri angled his spoon on the side of his bowl and eyed Malcolm up and down, then up and down again. He could clearly see the cut and blood on Malcolm's cheek but when he spoke, he didn't ask about it.

"We have a mutual friend," he said, leaning back in his chair. Lugieri had a bit of a belly but was otherwise in decent shape for a fifty-year-old guy who had survived two attempts on his life. Two attempts that made the papers, at least. "Our friend tells me that you're good, but all my guys are good. So do you know why you're here?"

"Our friend wouldn't tell me," said Malcolm.

"You're here because you don't look like all my guys."

That got a snicker out of the one with a short ponytail of jet-black hair who was standing off to the side of his boss. His teeth were crooked, his nose was crooked, and his pockmarked skin suggested the surface of the moon. Plus, his ears were huge.

"You'll have to forgive Carmine here," said Lugieri, pointing. "He doesn't like outsiders. And he really doesn't like pretty boys."

Malcolm turned and looked square at Carmine. "I wouldn't either with a face like that," he said.

The acoustics in the room were such that the laughter erupting from Lugieri's other men sounded even louder than it was. One was cackling like a hyena.

"Fuck did you say?" asked Carmine, taking a step forward.

Malcolm didn't flinch. There was a fine line between crazy and brave. "You heard me, Dumbo," he said.

The men howled again with laughter, only now it was joined by disbelief. *Did the kid really just say that?*

The cut beneath Malcolm's eye dripped a drop of blood as Carmine came at him. Again, he didn't flinch. Not even as Carmine balled his right fist, raised it high, and landed it square against Malcolm's jaw, knocking him down.

But only for two seconds.

There was something about the way the new kid rose to his feet — the whole room saw it. The pain didn't show on him. There was no stagger, no wobble. Just a smile.

"That one was free," said Malcolm. "Any more, you gotta pay."

The warning was lost on Carmine, his rage rendering him deaf and blind. He wound up again, his fist a blur, but Malcolm was more than ready for it; he ducked beneath Carmine's second swing and immediately rose up with two quick jabs and a roundhouse punch that landed so hard against Carmine's chin, you could hear his teeth crack. The next sound was Carmine hitting the floor with a thud.

Now the room was silent. That should've been the end of it, and they all knew it. All of them except for Carmine. Slowly, he pushed himself to his knees. He spit out blood. He spit out half a tooth. He reached for the sheath strapped against his ankle and removed the blade.

"That's enough, Carmine," said Lugieri.

The boss had spoken. But humiliation can wreak havoc on a man's hearing. Carmine lunged with the knife. He was fast but Malcolm was faster, grabbing Carmine's wrist and sweeping his legs in one motion. In the blink of an eye, Carmine was flat on his back, the tip of the knife now an inch from his own throat. Carmine was a dead man if Malcolm wanted that.

But he didn't. Malcolm straightened up and turned to Lugieri, who was out of his chair. Lugieri walked around the table and hovered over Carmine. When he spoke, he was looking down at Carmine but clearly talking to the other men.

"I told you that was enough," said Lugieri. "Never make me say it twice."

"I'm... sorry," said Carmine, his voice trembling.

But it was too little, too late for his boss. *Pffft. Pffft.* Lugieri fired two shots through the Banish 45 suppressor attached to his Glock 19, right between the eyes of Carmine's ugly face.

Lugieri turned to Malcolm. "Looks like we have an opening," he said.

CHAPTER 20

I'M NOW ONE week into the job. Terrance Willinghoff, head of the valuations department, is still being nice to me. And his second in command, Pierre Dejarnette, is still hitting on me.

"When are you going to break up with that boyfriend of yours and run off with me?" he asks, sipping his French-press coffee in his office. He assumes my stopping by that morning to say hello is an open invitation to flirt. Not that Pierre ever needs an invitation, open or otherwise.

"That depends," I say. "When are you going to give me a tour of the vault?"

He smiles. "It is pretty sexy, isn't it? The vault."

"I was thinking more along the lines of *educational,* but sure, *sexy* works too."

"Did you ever hear the story about Bruce and Mindy?" he asks.

"Who were they?"

"Two people who worked here about ten years ago."

"Here, as in—"

"Yes, valuations."

"Why do I feel like I know where this is going?"

"Because you have a dirty mind, Halston Graham."

"No, that's only you, Pierre," I say. "But, really? In the vault? They must have known there were cameras."

"They did. But they also knew the blind spots."

"Blind spots?"

"Actually, there's really only one, an area toward the back with this high shelf that the cameras can't see."

"And that's where they—"

"*Avoir des relations sexuelles.* Had sex, yes. It was after hours when they were 'working late,'" he says, putting air quotes around the words. "They thought they were in the clear, so to speak, and they probably would've been."

"What happened?"

"Terrance! That's what happened. The boss. He had forgotten something here in the office that he needed and he came back late that night. Apparently, Mindy was quite the moaner."

"Pierre!"

"What? That's what Terrance said, although you didn't hear that from me, okay? The funny thing was, Terrance had only just been named head of the department a week earlier. So his first big executive decision was firing them. And that's the story of Bruce and Mindy."

"I take it back," I say.

"What's that?"

"Maybe I don't want you to give me a tour of the vault after all."

Pierre laughs. "Are you sure? The blind spot is still there."

"Really? They never fixed that?"

"Well, after Bruce and Mindy, it was safe to assume no one else was going to use the vault as their motel room."

I've spent so much time doing the necessary research, gathering all the intel I need. You can never rely on luck when it comes to what I'm doing. But that doesn't mean you still can't get lucky.

I'm smiling. Pierre thinks it's because of the story of Bruce and Mindy, and it is. But not for the reason he thinks. It's barely ten o'clock in the morning and it's already been a good day.

"Anyway," says Pierre, "I couldn't give you that tour. You haven't received your security clearance yet."

The timing's unbelievable. Only a few seconds later, Jacinda Jefferson is standing at the door to his office.

"There you are, Halston," she says. "I tried calling your extension a few times."

The fact that she couldn't wait, that she had to come all the way down from HR to find me, says plenty. None of it good. But, lest there be any doubt...

"Is everything okay?" I ask.

Jacinda glances at Pierre, then hesitates slightly before she looks back at me. "Why don't we head to my office," she says.

And that's when I know for sure.

Halston, we have a problem.

CHAPTER 21

WE NEVER MAKE it to Jacinda's office. As soon as we reach the women's bathroom on the way to the elevator bank, she turns on a dime, pushes through the door. "In here," she says.

Like high school or a cop show or whatever scene in a movie that has someone ducking down to make sure no one's in any of the bathroom stalls, Jacinda checks. There's no one there. We're alone, just the two of us.

"What's wrong?" I ask.

Jacinda leans up against the sink counter, folding her arms. "You know exactly what's wrong."

"I don't know what you're—"

She cuts me off, palm raised. "The lying stops right now," she says. "*What's wrong?* Let's start with your last name."

"What about it?"

"Halston Graham."

"That's right," I say.

"What did I just tell you? No more bullshit. Your last name isn't Graham. It's Greer. As in Conrad Greer, your father. Last summer you told me your father was dead. Turns out he's very much alive."

"I wouldn't go *that* far."

"Okay, he's very much in jail," she says. "Is that better?"

"Not for him. Or me."

"Not for me either. And sure as hell not for Echelon. For Christ's sake, what were you thinking?"

"Which part?" I ask.

"All of it. Lying about your name, your father being in jail. Most of all, about *the reason* he's in jail."

"You asked me what I was thinking? *That's* what I was thinking. Right there, your reaction. Because if you'd known the truth, I wouldn't be working here."

"You're right, you wouldn't be," she says. "And you won't be, now that I know the truth."

"But you don't. You only think you do," I say. "My name *is* Halston Graham. It once was Greer but I changed it. Legally. I never lied about that."

Jacinda's not impressed. "Oh, congratulations," she says, dripping sarcasm. "You get to keep your monogrammed towels. In fact, that's probably why you chose the name Graham."

"You keep proving my point."

"Which is what?"

"The reason I had to lie to you is the same reason I had to change my name," I say. "Who would hire me?"

"Plenty of people would hire you. But you had to go and choose a job in the art world, didn't you."

"It's what I know. It's what I love."

"You were raised by a father who was convicted of a multimillion-dollar art scam. What's not to love, right? And God knows the things you learned along the way," she says. "Do you have any idea how bad this looks for Echelon?"

"What you really mean is how bad it looks for you."

"Same difference."

"This is just your job, Jacinda. You and Echelon couldn't be any more different," I say. "You know, most people would think that being homeless for a couple of years as a kid would make for a terrible childhood, and they'd be right. But I'm almost jealous of you. You lost your home but you never lost your family. My father was arrested on my thirteenth birthday. The news stories don't mention the birthday part, but you can read all about that art scam. I'm guessing, though, that you stopped with my dad and didn't search for anything about my mother. Because if you had, you'd know that two weeks shy of my sixteenth birthday she committed suicide. One dead mother, whose body I found, and a father serving fourteen years upstate. You want to switch childhoods? You want to ask me more about why I changed my last name?"

There's a moment when you know you've gotten to someone. It starts with the body language—a hesitation, a pause. It's as if you can see your words sinking in, a new perspective being formed. It's almost always followed by some utterance along the lines of...

"Jesus Christ," says Jacinda. "That's horrible."

That's when you have to pounce. "What if I told you my father wasn't guilty?" I ask.

Of course, Jacinda's no sucker. She plants a hand firmly on her hip. "He was convicted, Halston."

"He was set up."

"I'm sure you want to believe that."

"I can prove it."

"If you actually could, he wouldn't be in jail, would he?"

"He won't be," I say.

"What's that supposed to mean?"

"Give me maybe a month. If he's not out of jail by then, you won't have to fire me — I'll quit."

"What, are you planning some big prison break at midnight?"

"No, what I'm telling you is that he'll be released. He'll walk out the front door in broad daylight, a free man."

"Do you know how crazy you sound right now?" she asks.

"A month, Jacinda," I say. "Just give me a month."

CHAPTER 22

WOLFGANG DOESN'T LIKE surprises. What forger would? As he told me when I hired him, "My world is expectation and duplication. Lather, rinse, repeat."

Those words quickly come back to me the second he opens his door and angrily points a paintbrush at Enzio Bergamo. "Who the hell is this?" he asks.

Bergamo's more amused than insulted. "Really, kid? You don't know who I am?" He peeks into Wolfgang's windowless basement studio. "You really need to get out more."

I make the formal introductions and apologize to Wolfgang for not giving him a heads-up. Then I roll my eyes at Bergamo as I walk into the studio. "Not everyone reads *Vogue* and Page Six of the *Post*," I say.

This gets a chuckle from both Blaggy and Anton Nikolov, who are bringing up the rear of our cozy foursome on this field trip to inspect our fake Picasso. It's just another Wednesday night in Manhattan.

Me, a Bulgarian crime boss, his right-hand man, and a famous fashion designer, albeit one who's not quite as famous as he thinks he is.

But it's not Bergamo's humility we need. It's his commitment. And I can tell that Nikolov has his doubts.

Yes, we have the recording of Bergamo making a pass at me at his party. It should be more than enough to keep him in check, especially since Bergamo has no prenup with his wife, Deborah. Excuse me, De-*bore*-ah. When the two of them married, Bergamo's fledgling fashion company was a household name in only one house — his own.

Still, Nikolov knows Bergamo. Although he's the one who roped him in, he's still wary. Nothing's a done deal until it's a done deal.

"Okay, so where is this masterpiece?" asks Bergamo.

So much for any small talk. Wolfgang walks us back to the far wall of his studio. The place is a mess. I don't know if Wolfgang truly needs to get out more but he for damn sure needs a maid.

"Here it is," he says, pointing with his paintbrush.

"What's with the glass box?" asks Bergamo.

"Or maybe 'Wow, that looks incredible, and I could never tell the difference between this one and the real one,'" I say. "Maybe start with that?"

"'Wow, that looks incredible, and I could never tell the difference between this one and the real one,'" Bergamo parrots back. "Now, what's with the glass box?"

"It's actually Lucite," says Wolfgang. "And the box is an oxidizing accelerator."

Bergamo knows about fine art, but he's a novice in the world of fakes and forgeries. The same goes for Nikolov. My only request of Wolfgang prior to the meeting was that he educate them a bit. But not that much. "Talk over their heads for the most part," I told him. "They'll nod along."

Wolfgang steps next to the painting in the Lucite case, which is sealed except for two hose attachments in the back that are connected to a device the size of a microwave oven.

"We're not re-creating some Dutch master from the seventeenth century, so we don't have to be concerned with carbon dating or even white-lead dating for verification purposes," says Wolfgang. "And while Picasso was known to paint over his own paintings, there are plenty of works that he did using a fresh canvas. Thankfully, the piece discovered in that old Frenchman's attic was one of them, so no one will bother x-raying the fake. Still, the attic presents a challenge."

I'm waiting for Nikolov to engage. He finally does. "How so?" he asks. "What's the challenge?"

"Craquelure," says Wolfgang.

"In English," says Nikolov.

"As a painting ages, it develops random, unique formations known as craquelure. In other words, cracks in the paint. Using computer mapping, these cracks can be measured to establish a digital fingerprint, if you will, of the original artwork. A Picasso, or any painting from only the past century, wouldn't normally experience significant craquelure, but this particular painting is a little different. Sitting in that attic for so many years, it experienced massive fluctuations in temperature between hot and cold."

Nikolov nods. "It got old a lot faster, is what you're saying."

"Exactly," says Wolfgang. "So this oxidizing accelerator is an attempt to mimic the craquelure."

Bergamo steps forward, takes a closer look at the painting. "An *attempt*?" he asks.

"Like I said, the pattern is random and unique. There's no way to duplicate it exactly," says Wolfgang.

"And it's the authenticator who does the scan?" asks Bergamo.

"Actually, no. It would be the insurance company on behalf of the buyer," says Wolfgang. "They would send a representative to Echelon after the auction to do it before the painting left the premises."

Bergamo spins on his heel and fixes his worried stare on me. "That's going to be a problem, isn't it?"

"No, it's not," I answer. "It'll be fine."

He's hardly convinced. "How is it not going to be a problem?"

"Just trust me."

"*Trust you?* I have T-shirts older than you."

"That didn't stop you from wanting to fuck her," says Nikolov. "And if you don't want to trust her, trust me. It's not going to be a problem. If I thought it was, I wouldn't be putting up the money."

"Yeah, but I'm the one putting up the paddle," says Bergamo. "It's my neck out there. My name. My reputation." He's pacing, working himself into a frenzy. "You know what? Fuck it, play that little recording for my wife, I don't care. I'd rather her take me to the cleaners than end up in jail. I'm out."

"You're not going to jail," says Nikolov. "And you're not out. You're very much in."

"The hell I am," says Bergamo.

"The hell you are," says Blaggy, stepping forward. He's pointing something, but it's not a paintbrush. It's a gun. He's picked a fine time to join the conversation.

"Whoa!" says Wolfgang. He drops his brush and puts both hands up, full surrender. The gun isn't even pointed at him.

"Please lower that," I tell Blaggy. "There's no reason for—"

"Keep it right where it is," says Nikolov, cutting me off with a look that says *Shut the hell up*. He shoots that same look at Bergamo. "This is the first and last time we're having this conversation. We told you the plan, and you agreed. There's no changing the plan, and there's no changing your mind. Do you understand?"

Bergamo's eyes dart back and forth from Nikolov to the barrel of

Blaggy's gun. Wolfgang keeps inching farther away, surely thinking this wasn't part of the bargain. I stand, frozen, waiting for Bergamo to make up his mind.

He's a proud man. He's a stubborn man. Question is, is he a stupid man?

No. He's definitely not. Bergamo fakes a tension-defusing laugh. "This goddamn plan better work," he says.

CHAPTER 23

THE ARCHITECTS OF the Echelon auction floor knew exactly what they were doing. Their inspiration? The Roman Colosseum.

Let the superrich battle each other to the death with their massive bank accounts or at least until everyone except the winner screams for mercy by lowering their paddle swords in shame. The room is round and offers tiered seating above the auction floor for special invited guests. A veritable cheering section.

Although tonight there are no guests. It's a strictly private affair due to the "delicate circumstances" surrounding a Picasso never before sold, let alone seen by the public—not until a few weeks ago, when Echelon discreetly announced the painting's existence to its members. Of course, nothing creates a buzz quite like a hush-hush announcement.

"This is some turnout," I say. "Is there anything I can do to help?"

Terrance Willinghoff, in his three-piece navy suit and pink bow tie, looks at me as if he'd forgotten I was here. I'm not surprised. He's preoccupied, surely thinking—hoping, praying—that Echelon scores a huge sale tonight with the Picasso. Meanwhile, I'm simply doing what the new girl is supposed to do in this situation: help wherever needed.

I'm not needed. "Huh? Oh, no. You're fine, just fine," says Terrance. "Our work's done."

Meaning that the valuations department has little to do with running the auction. That's a whole other department, the auction team.

"Yes," says Pierre, stepping into the conversation with his open collar and ascot. "Valuations is behind the scenes; we don't make the scene."

Which explains why we're in the back of the room looking on as the members begin to settle into their seats after enjoying a cocktail hour featuring caviar and Cristal. Champagne loosens up the shoulder muscles, or so the old auction joke goes. More paddles get raised.

Terrance uses Pierre joining us to escape, mumbling about needing to go check on something.

"So," says Pierre once we're alone, "welcome to your first auction night. What do you think?"

"It's a spectacle," I say.

"That's a very good word for it. The same in English as in French. *Le spectacle.*"

"How many of these have you been to over the years?"

"More than I can remember," he answers, "although this one's right up there on the panache scale—another good word. All the usual suspects are here, of course, but there are a few boldface names we don't always see. Real characters."

"Like who?"

Pierre motions. "Second row, on the aisle. Letitia Collingsworth. Widow of Bradford Collingsworth. Do you know who he was?"

"I don't," I say.

"It's okay, most people don't. He was the largest grower of oranges in the United States. Do you see the empty seat next to her?"

"Yeah."

"Look again."

I stare across the room, squinting. "Wait, what is that?" There's something on the seat. "Is that a lunch box?"

"It is. And do you know what's inside?"

"A peanut butter and jelly sandwich?"

"Her husband's ashes."

"C'mon."

"I'm serious. She takes him everywhere with her. She—" Pierre suddenly freezes. "Holy shit. What's he doing here?"

"Who?" I ask, although I know exactly who he's talking about.

"Enzio Bergamo," says Pierre. "He just walked in."

I turn to look. "He's not a member?"

"Oh, he's a member, all right. Mr. Fashion himself. Loves Chinese vases, huge collector. Obsessive, really. But I can't remember the last time he showed up to bid on a painting. Then again, it's not your average painting, is it?"

"I wouldn't know," I say.

"What do you mean?"

"I haven't seen it. Like, up close. Someone was supposed to give me a tour of the vault but never did. Hint, hint."

"You were supposed to have drinks with me first, as I recall."

"You have it backward. First the vault, then the drink."

"*Drinks,* plural."

"That depends on how good the tour is," I say.

I'm now officially flirting with Pierre. He's fluent in French and English but this is the only language he truly understands.

"I assure you," he says, "no woman has ever complained."

"Are we still talking about your tour?"

"I don't know—are we?"

I keep up the banter with Pierre, I'm looking at him and smiling, but my attention's elsewhere. The moment's coming. Any second now. *Just keep smiling and wait for it, Halston.*

Then I see him out of the corner of my eye. Terrance Willinghoff is heading back to us, but he's looking only at Pierre. He's walking as fast as he can without drawing attention to himself. His pink bow tie is crooked.

Terrance whispers when he arrives, "We have a situation."

CHAPTER 24

PIERRE HEADS OFF with Terrance, leaving me alone. I'm now invisible.

I slip through the back exit, quietly go up the stairs, and find a spot next to a pillar where I can view the auction floor. If anyone turns around and looks up, I'm just the new girl watching and learning. But no one's turning and looking. The works of art, the objects of their desire, hold their attention like superglue. All the action's in front of them. That's what they think.

From the moment Anton Nikolov told me in his limo parked outside MoMA that he wanted the dead man's Picasso for himself, the calculus changed. Instead of trying to jack up the price, we're now trying to limit it. We want to suppress the action, do whatever it takes to prevent a bidding war.

"Skip, can you hear me?"

My brother doesn't respond. I casually reach up under my hair as if I'm scratching the back of my neck, but I'm actually tapping my earpiece for more volume. "Skip?" I whisper more loudly. Still nothing.

Panic sets in. The only thing I can hear is my heart pounding faster and faster, about to explode through my chest. "Skip, are you there? *Skip?*"

"Gotcha," he says finally.

I'm too relieved to curse him out. "Seriously?"

"It never gets old."

"And if it ever gets funny, I'll let you know," I say. Okay, it's a little funny, but I'm not about to admit it. "How's my level?"

"You're good, coming in clean," he says. "How's the room?"

"Over two hundred billion in net worth."

"Big turnout, huh?"

"Huge," I say.

"Any surprises?" he asks.

"Only the one you just gave them."

I can see Terrance and Pierre off to the side of the stage talking intensely to Charles Waxman, CEO of Echelon. What rhymes with *charm*? *Smarm*. That's Charles Waxman. His slicked-back hair says it all. Technically I work for him but he has no idea who I am. That will change soon.

In the meantime, with the clock ticking, Waxman's trying to figure out how the hell Echelon's encrypted VPN phone lines just went down. Surely there's a little sweat building at the base of that slicked-back hair.

Like falling dominoes, Waxman grabs Terrance, and Terrance grabs Pierre, because while Echelon's clients stretch worldwide, it's the heavy hitters from France who will be out in droves for this auction—or, rather, sitting in droves in their giant châteaus and bidding on the phone. French billionaires have a very proprietary view of all things Picasso. Never mind that the artist was Spanish-born; he *created* in France, and this newly discovered masterpiece landing in foreign hands would be *un désastre*.

That's why I needed that small key in Pierre Dejarnette's office.

Pierre's old-school ways don't end with wine and women. Although he reluctantly accepted the technological age, he has never fully embraced it. The cloud? Letting his golden list of clients and secret sources just float around in the ether for anyone to steal as if it were some nude selfie of a celebrity? Not a chance. Pierre backs up everything with pen and paper, an actual handwritten directory that he keeps locked in a desk safe. I saw him open it once when he invited me for a tour of the valuations department during my internship. What I didn't see was where he kept the key. As it turns out, it's the bottom drawer on the left, tucked underneath a ceramic ashtray with the logo of his beloved Paris Saint-Germain football club.

Score.

"How much longer?" I ask Skip.

"I can't see the overlay patch in real time but I'm guessing another minute or so."

Step 1: Create a problem that Echelon's IT department can solve but only in a MacGyver kind of way, the digital equivalent of a paper clip and chewing gum. For example, rerouting their VPN phone lines through a single-source entry point via a temporary overlay patch. In layman's terms, allowing overseas Echelon clients to call in on their personal phones without any encryption.

Step 2: Make the IT department think they've saved the day—or night—by having that paper clip and chewing gum hold up through the early part of the auction. Until...

Step 3: All hell breaks loose during the Picasso sale.

CHAPTER 25

OF COURSE THE IT guy sports a ponytail.

"Here he comes now," I whisper.

"How does he look?" asks Skip.

"You mean besides his Men's Wearhouse suit that's two sizes too big for him? I can't tell yet."

I watch as the IT guy weaves his way through the last of the Echelon members entering the room to take their seats. He's heading for the very anxious trio of Terrance, Pierre, and Waxman, although it's Waxman who's hiding it best, which is a bit counterintuitive, given that as CEO of the auction house, he has the most to lose with this sudden crisis. It's near impossible to fetch a hundred million dollars for a Picasso if most of Europe and Asia aren't in the game.

I glance over at Bergamo, who's seated with his wife. They're chatting with another couple. Bergamo's doing most of the talking. He looks calm.

"What about now?" asks Skip.

I look back at the mini-conference of Waxman and company. The IT guy is still talking. Terrance and Pierre are nodding. Waxman is still putting on his best fake smile: *Nothing to see here, folks. Nothing at all.*

"You'd think they'd have the sense to step out of the room," I say.

Skip chuckles. "It's too late for that. The optics are worse if Waxman suddenly disappears. The auction's supposed to have started by now."

"Any chance the IT guy didn't figure out the solution?"

"He'd have to be the most incompetent nerd in the world. I all but teed it up for him," says Skip. "No, right now he's explaining the fix, and Waxman is contemplating the risk."

"It's taking too long," I say.

"It's a big risk."

"We may have misjudged him."

"Waxman? His last marker at the Bellagio was for three million. Give him another minute."

I feel my heart begin to race again. *C'mon, c'mon, c'mon. Look around the room, dude. Everybody's waiting, excited. You can't shut this down, right? You're the CEO, make the call.*

He makes it. With one quick nod of approval, Waxman takes the bait.

"We're on," I tell Skip. "Do your thing."

CHAPTER 26

CHAT WITH ANY real horse-racing fans and they'll tell you about some race at Churchill Downs on the same day as the Kentucky Derby that was better than the derby. Ditto with true boxing fans. There were certain bouts on the undercard before a Mike Tyson or Floyd Mayweather prizefight that were, punch for punch, more entertaining than the main event. But that's horse racing and boxing.

This is art.

Sure, as I watch from the cheap seats in the back, a Degas sculpture, the third item up for bid, goes for a cool twenty million. And with the champagne flowing, the adrenaline pumping, and the anticipation building, a Rothko self-portrait from his early realist years sells for twenty-four million, six million above its reserve price. It's a good night so far for the House of Echelon.

Still, there's no doubt in the room that the best is yet to come. Major art auctions are always like Fourth of July fireworks: There are plenty of oohs and aahs throughout, but nothing compares to the finale.

"The last item up for bid this evening is a first-sale untitled Picasso believed to have been painted at the tail end of what's commonly known as his cubism years," declares the Echelon auctioneer, sounding as monotonal as humanly possible. The man is a pro, and he knows exactly what he's doing as the painting is carried out to the stage and placed on an easel by two members of the auction team wearing white gloves. The auctioneer knows that no one in the audience is looking at him. Barely anyone is even listening to him. They're well aware of what's being brought out. His job is to set the mood and play to the moment, and nothing titillates the ultra-wealthy more than an understated approach. Less does mean more in this case. More drama. And ultimately more money.

Damn, he's good. It's an auctioneer's master class. He's doing our plan to limit the price absolutely no favors. *You're killing me, buddy.*

He's killing me even more when he starts the bidding higher than what Pierre told me the proposed opening would be. Instead of fifty million dollars, it's fifty-five. He's reading the room, the hunger. He can see it in their eyes.

I can't see any eyes except for those of the Echelon staffers manning the phones along the side. I'm looking at everyone's back, and as fast as you can say *Do I hear sixty million?*, I'm looking at the backs of a sea of raised paddles.

Skip, who's not even in the room, is expecting this. "Don't worry. They're just posers," he whispers.

"They can't all be," I say. "What about the phones? Anything yet?"

"Too early."

Of course. I knew that, and yet I still asked. My nerves are kicking in. Phone bidders, the ones who hunt major works, always linger on the sidelines at the start. They want a sense of the action before becoming part of it. For the same reason, Enzio Bergamo is sitting quietly, his paddle resting in his lap.

"Do I hear sixty-five?" asks the auctioneer, zooming past sixty million in a flash.

Whoosh! The same sea of paddles goes up.

"Okay, here we go," says Skip. "First phone bid."

"From where?"

"You have to ask?" In other words, Paris.

Skip's tapped into the makeshift patch serving as the hub for all the phone bidders. The patch is unsecured. Skip can't see names, but he knows locations, can tell where every call comes from, be it a landline or a cell tower. More important, he knows what's being said; his backdoor software gives him real-time, voice-to-text playback of the conversations. In short, he can see everyone's cards.

"What's the bid?" I ask.

"It's a brake pumper. Instructions to come in at seventy-five and a half."

That's someone who wants to get in on the action and force the increments down to a half million. Sometimes it works, sometimes it doesn't.

"Seventy million, do I hear seventy-one?" asks the auctioneer. He points at a paddle. He has lots to choose from. "Now seventy-two. Front left, now seventy-three."

"Hello, Tokyo," says Skip in my ear. "Seventy-four with a ninety ceiling."

As soon as I hear it, I see it. A woman on the far end of the phone desk wearing her royal-blue Echelon blazer raises paddle number 36 to bid seventy-four million on behalf of someone in Tokyo.

The dam breaks. The posers in the room give way to a flood of phone bids, one after another. They're coming so fast, Skip can't even read them. He doesn't have to. I'm watching it all unfold before me.

The auctioneer blows through the guy from Paris trying to pump the brakes, the increments remaining at a million.

"Seventy-seven," he says. Then seventy-eight, followed by seventy-nine million.

Eighty million comes and goes in the blink of an eye. Then eighty-five. There's still a handful of paddles going up in the room but the phone bids have them outnumbered. I grab my cell and text Bergamo. His paddle hasn't budged from his lap, but that's about to change. Two words: **Get ready.**

I watch his head tilt to read the message. The next message I send will be the last.

"Tokyo's bumped his ceiling to ninety-five. Three bidders now from Paris, one from Nice," says Skip. "A half dozen more from all over. One of them from Monaco."

"Shit," I say.

"Yeah," says Skip.

Guys from Monaco really don't like to lose. Another reason for Skip to do what he's about to do.

"When?" I ask. "When do you think?"

"At a hundred," he says.

"Are you sure?"

"What, you think that's too high?"

"No, I mean are you sure it's going to work?" I ask.

Skip's laugh does nothing to settle my nerves. "It's a little late for you to be asking me that, sis."

CHAPTER 27

"DO I HEAR ninety-six? Ninety-six million?"

My eyes dart from the seats to the phones and back as I try to get a count. We were hoping to be down to a half a dozen bidders by now, but it's looking close to twice that. Maybe even a baker's dozen.

"Yes, thank you, ninety-six," says the auctioneer, pointing at the front row. "Now asking ninety-seven. Ninety-seven million."

"We've lost Tokyo," says Skip. It's the first good sign, and it's quickly followed by the second. "Paris number three is out too."

It's not enough. There're still four active paddles in the room. Not that they're all bidding at the same time, but I can tell from their postures, even from behind them. The way they're sitting, the straight shoulders. And their heads are still. At these stakes, there's no neck swiveling, no checking out the competition.

"Bid ninety-seven...yes, on the aisle there, thank you. We continue, asking ninety-eight...ninety-eight million."

Only three paddles now. The fourth slumps his shoulders, shakes his head. He's out. The price is climbing too high. Altitude sickness kicks in.

C'mon, one more. We need one more in the room to drop...

"Ninety-eight, accepted. We have ninety-eight million," declares the auctioneer, pointing to the end of the phone table.

"Ninety-eight. That's Mr. Monaco," says Skip. "Ha. He's probably French."

"And he's probably just getting warmed up," I say. "It's time."

"You're right," says Skip. "Give me the signal."

"Texting him now."

I get back on my cell and type two letters to Bergamo. My thumb hovers over the send button, my eyes and ears locking in on the auctioneer, who's pausing after ninety-eight million. He's milking the moment with a sip of water. To hell with ninety-nine million. The second he puts the glass down, he lets it rip. No more monotone. Big round numbers always get the hype.

"Ladies and gentlemen, do I hear one hundred million?"

Bang goes my thumb: **GO!**

Bergamo looks down at his cell, and his paddle immediately shoots up. Current bid plus ten—those were his instructions, and he nails the delivery as he breaks decorum, calling out his bid in a booming voice and raising the stakes high enough to kill the action.

"One hundred and ten million!" Bergamo announces.

Audible gasps fill the room. "Now!" I tell Skip.

I watch the phone table, see a wave of confused looks. Their lines have all gone dead, only they don't know it. No one does. No one's even looking in their direction; they're too busy gawking at Bergamo, who overbid by ten million. Is he a fool? A genius? They can't figure it out, but when the dust settles, the headline will write itself. Sometimes you've got to spend a small fortune to save an even bigger one.

But the dust is still swirling. The crowd's murmuring. Still, no one notices the staff at the phone table frantically motioning for their CEO. Waxman makes a beeline toward them while the auctioneer does exactly what he's supposed to do in this situation: He takes back control. He's a pro.

"We welcome a new bidder and a new bid," he smoothly announces. "One hundred and ten million. Do I hear—"

He stops mid-sentence as he finally notices Waxman huddled with his staff at the phone table. The room follows suit, everyone turning to see what's holding up the auction. It's the moment of truth. Or, in Waxman's case, the moment he tries to conceal the truth. The paper-clip-and-chewing-gum fix of the phones has given way; the hub is down. There'll be no more phone bids. An hour ago, it could have been chalked up to mechanical difficulties. Now it's on Echelon. He owns it. There's no way Waxman's stopping the auction. Not now. Not this far.

With a quick, discreet twirl of his index finger, he instructs his auctioneer to carry on.

Bergamo seizes the moment, calling out from his seat, "Let's go! One hundred and ten million," he says. "That's the bid."

"Indeed it is," the auctioneer says, and as soon as the words leave his mouth, I know those three remaining paddles aren't going in the air again. It's not that they don't have the money. It's that they don't want to look like idiots. Bergamo just did something crazy, and only crazy can beat crazy. The auctioneer knows it too. "One hundred and ten million going once..."

"What's happening?" asks Skip.

"We're almost home," I say.

The auctioneer raises his hammer. "One hundred and ten million going twice..."

"One hundred *and eleven*," comes a voice from the back of the room.

CHAPTER 28

DAMN.

That's the PG version of what I'm thinking and then saying to my brother over and over. Skip's cursing too. We're a chorus. We were so close to getting it done. The phones are dead, but suddenly the room is very much alive.

Everyone's looking to see who made the bid. They heard it, and now they're all thinking: *A woman?*

All I can see is the back of her long, blond hair and the straight shoulders of her eggshell-and-pink-striped Chanel jacket. And her paddle. Number 5. It figures. Out of nowhere comes Chanel No. 5.

Jesus, Enzio. Don't you stare at her too. Turn around, you've still got a painting to buy. Not that I can blame him. It was a wrap. A done deal. Bergamo had one-upped everyone in the room, and then—boom. Make that *almost* everyone.

Now there were two. Not to mention the threat of more bidders joining back in, which would spell disaster. Although that threat disappears as fast as—

"One hundred and twelve million," says Bergamo, raising his paddle.

"One thirteen," says Chanel. She has a French accent.

Bergamo wastes no time. "One fourteen."

Neither does she. "One fifteen."

"One sixteen."

"One seventeen."

"One eighteen."

"One nineteen."

Shit, shit, shit. Who the hell is she?

We can stomach paying the money—to a certain point—but not losing. And whoever she is, she seems hell-bent on winning. Of course, so does Bergamo. "One twenty," he says.

"One twenty-one," she counters.

They're not even raising their paddles. Echelon members are literally cheering. It's a free-for-all, a million bucks at a time. A record-breaking sale is happening right before their eyes. The auctioneer, the seasoned pro, has been relegated to the sidelines. But not for long.

"Lady and gentleman, please," he interrupts the two bidders loudly. *"Please."* The bidding stops; the room hushes. All eyes shift back to the auctioneer. "We very much appreciate the enthusiasm, and we all love a horse race."

"Then take back the reins!" someone yells. Heckling—surely this is a first in the history of Echelon.

The auctioneer, momentarily stunned, gathers himself and glances over at Waxman, who's still at the phone table, probably working through his conflicting CEO emotions. He never should've let this auction take place without the encrypted phone lines, and yet now he's presiding over what will be Echelon's single largest sale ever.

The auctioneer clears his throat. "The bid is a hundred and twenty-one million dollars. Do I hear one twenty-two?"

He doesn't hear anything. Bergamo raises his paddle without saying a word. The only sound now is the deafening silence of anticipation.

"Is she with anyone?" asks Skip in my ear. His hushed voice sounds like a scream. That's how quiet the room is.

"I don't think so. Not that I can tell," I whisper back. "But she seems really set on taking home this painting."

The bidding hits one hundred thirty million. Then one thirty-five... one forty... one forty-five. If Anton Nikolov were in the room, he'd call the whole thing off. But he's not. For the first time I see what looks like a crack in Bergamo's facade. He turns around in his seat but not to look at Chanel. He's looking for me. He's looking for guidance. *How high can we go? What now?* Our eyes lock, and I do something I don't even realize I'm doing until after I do it. I shrug. I honestly don't know the answer.

Bergamo turns back around. The bid is now one hundred forty-eight million.

"One hundred and forty-eight million going once," says the auctioneer. Bergamo doesn't budge. "Going twice..." Everyone's looking at Bergamo. The buzz is getting louder and louder. The room can't help itself.

And neither can Bergamo. He raises his paddle.

This isn't an auction. It's a tennis match. All eyes swing back to Chanel as the auctioneer takes another sip of water. Another big fat number is coming.

"One hundred and forty-nine million," he announces. "The bid is now one hundred and forty-nine."

Going once. Going twice.

Her paddle doesn't go up. But she does. Chanel stands and walks out of the room. Everyone gasps. For the first time I see her face, and all I can think is *Did we just get played?*

CHAPTER 29

I TELL SKIP what happened, that Chanel just up and walked out, and he knows exactly what I'm doing now. And what I'm *not* doing.

"Stop staring at her. You're wasting time," he tells me. "You've still got a job to do. Get moving, metalhead."

The only thing I hate more than my big brother being right is him calling me that. Metalhead. And, no, it has nothing to do with my taste in music. It's because I had to wear one of those ridiculous headgear contraptions when I was eleven years old to fix my overbite. He never let me forget it. He still hasn't.

Point taken, though. Enzio Bergamo just bought a Picasso for a hundred and forty-nine million dollars. Well, technically, Anton Nikolov bought it, but what no one in the room knows won't hurt them. Right now everyone's treating Bergamo like he's more than a fashion icon. Tonight, he's a certified rock star. They can't get enough of him; an entire fawning mob of the filthy rich are all rushing from their cushioned seats to be the first to say congratulations.

"Introduce me," I say to Pierre.

He didn't hear me slink up behind his left shoulder. I made it from the upstairs seating to the auction floor in twenty seconds flat.

Pierre turns and looks at me, chuckles. "Introduce you to Bergamo? No way," he says.

"Why not?"

"Because he's a womanizer."

"You're a womanizer," I say.

"Trust me, he's in a different league," says Pierre. "Enzio Bergamo makes me look like a eunuch."

"First of all, eww. Second of all, his wife is with him." I look over at Bergamo and the throng around him. "Well, she was a second ago."

I'm really making Pierre laugh tonight. "Bergamo being with his wife is hardly a deterrent for him," he says. "As for her whereabouts, I'll bet you a hundred and forty-nine million dollars she's off getting another drink."

That's fine by me. I've been listening to Pierre but my eyes are scanning the room. I don't want to see anyone who was at the Bergamo party I crashed. Or, more important, I don't want any of them seeing me. This level of wealth isn't exactly the party-in-the-Hamptons crowd, but better safe than sorry. That's why I opted for a sedate pantsuit and minimal makeup tonight.

"Pierre Dejarnette, are you worried that I might think Enzio Bergamo is more witty, charming, and handsome than you are?" I ask.

"Of course not," he says, playing along.

I nudge his rib cage. "Then prove it."

"Fine. I'll introduce you," he says.

The crowd finally begins to thin around the man of the moment, not that it matters. Bergamo knows I'm coming. He knows what to do.

"Pierre!" Bergamo exclaims as he sees us walking toward him. "Can I borrow some money?"

The joke gets a laugh from the few people still within earshot. Pierre and Bergamo shake hands, and Pierre wastes no time offering his congratulations. After some brief chitchat about the excitement of the auction, Bergamo notices the young woman standing next to Pierre, otherwise known as me.

"And who's this?" asks Bergamo.

"This," answers Pierre, "is someone who would like to meet you."

"Hi," I say, extending my hand. "I'm Halston Graham."

"Nice to meet you, Halston. Very nice indeed." He turns to Pierre. "Where have you been hiding her?"

Pierre shoots me a quick, knowing glance: *I told you. World-class womanizer.* "In the basement. That's where we've been hiding her," he tells Bergamo. "She works with me in valuations."

"I just started," I say. "Tonight's my first auction."

"And what a night for it to be your first," says Bergamo. "For a while there, I wasn't sure who would prevail."

"Me neither," I say, matching his poker face. "Congratulations."

"I have to tell you, Enzio, I was surprised to see you here," says Pierre. "You normally don't—"

"Do paintings? You're right." Bergamo points up at the auction block. "But that's not your normal painting, now, is it?"

"No, you're quite right about that. It's very special," says Pierre. "And now it's yours."

"I definitely like the sound of that," says Bergamo.

"As you should. Are you ready to make it official?"

"Ah, yes. The requisite paperwork." Bergamo points again up at the auction block. "Let me go take one more look before you put it away for the night."

"Actually," says Pierre, "we're not vaulting the painting just yet. There's something new we're doing, a new security measure."

"There is?" asks Bergamo. There goes his poker face. I can see him trying to think quick. I'm doing the same.

"Yes," says Pierre. He motions to the doors. "You know Terrance Willinghoff, right? The head of valuations? He's waiting for us downstairs. Don't worry, it won't take long."

And just like that, in an instant, we're screwed.

CHAPTER 30

MY JOB WAS misdirection. Make Echelon and everyone else zig while I'm busy zagging.

I needed to place myself at the scene of the crime without later being seen as an accessory to the crime. That meant making sure everyone at Echelon thought I had no connection to Enzio Bergamo. How could I? I only just met him the night of the auction—right, Pierre?

Now, out of the blue, I have another job. I have to figure out what the hell is happening with this supposed new security measure that, for sure, no one mentioned to the low girl on the totem pole.

But I can't figure it out. At least not on my own. I need Bergamo's help. *C'mon, Enzio. Come up with something. Anything.*

Suddenly I see a spark in his eye. It's followed by an easy laugh. "Well, Pierre, whatever this new security measure is, it must be a pretty big secret," he says.

"What do you mean?" asks Pierre.

"I'm looking at your newest hire, and she has no clue what it is. Isn't that right, Halsey?"

"It's actually Halston," I say.

"My apologies," says Bergamo. "Wrong about the name but right about that look on your face. You clearly haven't been instructed about this new security measure, and beauty should never be kept in the dark." He loops his arm through mine. "Shall we go learn it together, Halston?"

Pierre thinks Bergamo's just being Bergamo, laying it on thick and hitting on me. He suspects nothing else. *Well done, Enzio.* Score one for the quick-thinking doyen of fashion.

Not so fast.

"I hate to be a spoilsport," says Pierre, "but I'm afraid Halston won't be able to join us."

"Why not? Why can't she join us?" asks Bergamo. "Let me guess— you're going to say it has something to do with added precautions, and it's for my protection."

"That's right," says Pierre.

Bergamo's laugh echoes through the now-empty auction room. "Do I look like I need protecting from Halston here?"

"I don't think that's—"

"Do you know what I think? I'll tell you," says Bergamo, cutting Pierre off. "I think I just bought that Picasso for a hundred and forty-nine million dollars, and on top of that, I'm going to pay Echelon a buyer's premium of over twenty million dollars. Do you know what that entitles me to, Pierre? *Anything I fucking want.*"

"And what is it that you want, sweetheart?" a woman says.

I don't have to look to know who it is. And Bergamo *definitely* doesn't need to look. He's married to her.

As fast as you can say *prenup*, Bergamo unloops his arm from mine, turns, and smiles lovingly at his wife, Deborah, a former runway model who's now strutting up to us. She has clearly enjoyed the champagne this evening and is somewhere between tipsy and tanked.

"I want for nothing, darling," says Bergamo, kissing her cheek. She rolls her eyes.

"When can we go home?" she asks. "I'm bored."

The fact that De-*bore*-ah couldn't care less about announcing her boredom in front of Pierre and me is pretty much all you need to know about her. It's as if we don't exist in her eyes. Until suddenly we do. Or at least, I do.

"Wait," she says, turning in my direction. She puts a hand on her hip. "Weren't you at our last party?"

Thankfully she's looking at me and not her husband because I've never seen a man's jaw tighten so hard so fast.

I feign an acute case of deafness. "Excuse me?" I ask.

She squints. "Yes, that was you, wasn't it? In the black Bottega Veneta," she says. "I never forget a dress, especially one that isn't my husband's."

"I think you might have her confused with someone else, darling," says Bergamo.

"No, she's the one. You were flirting with her," she says. "Or she was flirting with you. Same difference."

It's amazing how fast sweat can appear on a man's forehead. I can feel a few beads forming myself.

"I wish it were me," I say. "Not the flirting part. The dress. If I were the one at your party in that dress, that would mean I could actually afford a Bottega Veneta."

I turn to Pierre with a look that says *Help me — I'm in the crosshairs of a drunk Deborah Bergamo.*

"Well, I'm afraid I can vouch for her not being able to afford it," says Pierre with a soft touch on my arm. "Given what Echelon pays its entry-level employees—"

"Oh, never mind," says Deborah, turning back to Bergamo. "Now I'm even more bored."

"I have the cure for that," says Pierre. "Why don't you join your husband and me downstairs in our vault while he signs a few papers? I promise you won't regret it."

Deborah manages a slight shrug of approval and takes her husband's hand while Pierre shoots me a stealth wink. He thinks he's done me a favor. Forcing a smile, I watch everyone march off to the vault without me, no closer to knowing the answer to the one-hundred-forty-nine-million-dollar question:

What the hell is this new security measure?

CHAPTER 31

ONE THING I know: Never make a Bulgarian mob boss angry.

Skip can see it coming. He sounds the alarm, talking so loudly in my earpiece, I have to turn down the volume while walking out of the Echelon building. He's telling me I should be meeting Anton Nikolov in a public place. Imploring me.

But we both know I can't do that. I can't risk being seen with Nikolov at this point.

"Then I'm coming along as backup," says Skip.

Again, we both know I can't bring him. I had to take a car ride out to Jersey with a pillowcase yanked over my head, followed by a gun pointed directly *at* my head, before I got the chance to see Nikolov. This is no time to introduce any new faces.

Don't get me wrong, I appreciate Skip's concern. But when my big brother goes into his little-sis-protector mode, all logic goes flying out the window.

"I'll be fine," I assure him.

"You better be, metalhead. Call me back right after the meeting."

In the Uber over to Tribeca, I'm thinking about how Skip and I weren't allowed to watch R-rated movies while we were growing up—or at least up until our father was sentenced. It was his rule, and there was only one exception. Or two, technically: *The Godfather* and *The Godfather Part II*. Those we were allowed to watch, and the reason was simple: Our father, an art dealer, believed those two movies were masterpieces.

My guess is that Anton Nikolov is also a big fan, and if there's a scene that speaks to him more than others, it's when Tom Hagen, played by Robert Duvall, gets told by the big-shot Hollywood producer that Vito Corleone's godson will never be in his movie. Says Hagen on his way out: "Mr. Corleone is a man who insists on hearing bad news immediately."

At least Nikolov isn't making me go all the way out to his home in New Jersey. Instead, he's waiting for me in a penthouse apartment in Tribeca. I assume it's his, although I'm not about to ask. Also not asking any questions is the doorman, who gives me a slight nod as I walk right by him. Clearly, I'm expected.

Now for the unexpected.

"You've got to be fucking kidding me," Nikolov says, his thunderous voice echoing throughout his huge, sparsely furnished living room. His dress shirt is half unbuttoned, the chest tattoos of his brutal youth exposed, and as he speaks, one hand slashes through the air while the other cradles a scotch on the rocks. *"How much did it go for?"*

When I repeat the purchase price, even Blaggy, over in the corner, shakes his head. Nikolov is quickly running the math, but I try to be quicker.

"With an ARPL you can cover the entire buyer's premium on top of the hundred forty-nine million, but, yeah," I say, "the two percent rake for the insurance policy means—"

"That this bitch bidding against us just cost me an extra million."

"Give or take."

"No. It's definitely take," says Nikolov. He throws back the last of his scotch and nearly shatters the glass when he slams it down on an end table. "Who the hell is she?"

"I don't know," I say.

"How do you not know? You goddamn work there."

"I told you, there's no printed-up list of members. And whatever list is sitting in some database, it's not as if the file is labeled *Membership*. That's on purpose. Only a few people at Echelon know all the clientele, and even then, you have to account for special proxies. They're granted on a case-by-case basis."

"Then at least find that out, if she's a proxy or not."

"I can definitely try, but how's that going to change anything? The good news is she bowed out."

"Oh, yeah, great news. I'm always happy about coughing up an extra mil for an ARPL."

"You're the one who wants to keep the painting. The insurance angle was your idea," I remind him.

I watch as Nikolov processes everything. He's trying his best to focus on the big picture but he's forgotten to tell his fists. They're balled so tight, his knuckles look whiter than a J. Crew catalog.

Meanwhile, Blaggy's trying to catch up. "What's an ARPL?" he asks.

"It's an all-risk-of-physical-loss policy," I say.

"How much longer?" asks Nikolov.

"Until the policy is signed? I told you, it's probably two days, maybe—"

"No," says Nikolov, folding his arms. His eyes narrow until they're as keen as a knife's edge. If looks could kill... "How much longer before you finally tell me what you haven't told me yet?"

CHAPTER 32

SOMETIMES IT'S BEST to play dumb. This ain't one of those times.

"How'd you know?" I ask.

"Your right ear," he says. "You tuck your hair behind it when you're hiding something."

"Bullshit."

"You did it when we first met. Of course, a tell isn't a tell until you do it more than once. You've done it three times in the past five minutes."

Note to self: Never play poker with Anton Nikolov. "I'm not so much hiding something as stalling," I say. "We're waiting on a phone call."

"From whom?" he asks.

"Bergamo. We had a bit of a curveball thrown at us after the auction. It's a new security measure Echelon's implemented."

"What kind of security measure?"

"That's the problem. I don't know what it is yet."

"Once again, *you work there*. How do you not know?"

"Because I don't run the place," I say. "But it's not going to be a problem."

"How do you know that if you don't know what it is?"

I take out my phone. "Because Bergamo is about to call and tell us. And then, whatever it is, we'll deal with it."

"Or maybe I just don't transfer the money for the painting. Maybe I bow out," says Nikolov. "How about that, huh? And why the hell are we waiting on Bergamo? I'll call him myself."

"You can't."

"Of course I can."

"No. I mean he won't pick up, not if he's still in the Echelon building," I say. "Plus, he might still be with his wife."

"The way that woman drinks, she won't remember a damn thing in the morning."

"Okay, that one I'll give you."

Nikolov scoops up his glass, heads for a credenza doubling as a bar, and pours himself some more scotch, all but emptying a bottle of Macallan. As soon as he takes a sip, my phone rings.

"Put it on speaker," says Nikolov.

I walk over to him, place the phone on the credenza, and accept the call. "You're on speaker," I tell Bergamo.

Nikolov wastes no time. "What are we dealing with?" he asks.

"A number," says Bergamo.

"What do you mean?"

"A serial number," he says. "It's handwritten with a black charcoal pencil on the back of the frame."

"How do you know it's a charcoal pencil?" I ask.

"Because they told me," says Bergamo.

"So what's the number?" asks Nikolov.

"That's not the question," I say.

"What do you mean? How can it not be? Of course it is," says Nikolov.

"It's not just the numbers we need, it's the handwriting. The style." I take a deep breath, then exhale. I edge closer to my phone and almost whisper to Bergamo, "Please tell me you took a picture."

CHAPTER 33

WOLFGANG WORKS FAST, as he always does.

Within hours he creates an acetate stencil from the picture Bergamo snapped and replicates the serial number to perfection on the back of his forgery. When he shoots me a photo of his handiwork, I could swear it's what we originally sent him.

Satisfied, Nikolov wires the money to an account in the Cayman Islands already set up by Skip; the entire sum is then transferred through an Irish shell corporation Bergamo uses to avoid taxes and ultimately lands in one of Bergamo's legit bank accounts here in the States. From it, Bergamo draws a certified check to cover the price of the real Picasso plus Echelon's buyer's premium.

Meanwhile, the painting gets the sign-off from Bergamo's insurance company. It's a formality, especially since Bergamo "lets slip" that he intends to keep it in a freeport facility until further notice.

freeport

noun

A government-designated area within a country, most often near a shipping port or airport, where its normal tax and tariff rules don't apply as long as an otherwise taxable item remains within the area.

Companies that insure fine art absolutely adore these tax havens. A freeport warehouse offers nuclear-bunker-type construction, boasts Fort Knox–level around-the-clock security, and delivers the ultimate in climate-control technology—what's not to love?

Of course, no one knows that the painting will never arrive there. It won't even make it out of Manhattan.

"One more time," I say. "Let's go over it one more time."

I'm back in Nikolov's Tribeca apartment a few nights later for dinner and a final run-through. Nikolov's providing the dinner (Chinese takeout) and I'm making sure everyone is on the same page. My schematic of the streets and the city's CCTV cameras around the Echelon building doesn't have a title but if it did it would be "How to Steal a One-Hundred-Forty-Nine-Million-Dollar Painting and Make It Look Like It Gets Smashed to Smithereens a Few Minutes Later." Catchy, isn't it?

"The guys know what to do," says Nikolov. "They've got it down cold."

"I'm sure you're right, but let's run it one more time anyway," I say, looking around the table.

These are Nikolov's best men, or so he tells me, and they've had the plan and the schematic for over a week now. That hardly reassures me. They're not brain surgeons; they're criminals. Then again, if I had to choose between brain surgeons and criminals for this job, I'd go with the wiseguys every time. Show them an angle in life, and they'll never have to think twice about running with it.

In this instance, literally.

I reposition all my props on the table, putting everything back to square one on the schematic. The Chinese takeout has definitely come in handy: Fortune cookies represent the men on Nikolov's crew; the real and fake paintings are soy sauce packets; and the cement mixer is a leftover egg roll.

The real Picasso, packed by Echelon in a nondescript protective case easily duplicated by Wolfgang, will be brought out of the Echelon building. The first fortune cookie will sprint up and snatch it before Bergamo hands it over to the courier hired to drive it down to the Delaware freeport facility. Later, the courier company will be among the first targets of the police, the thinking being that the culprit was somehow connected with the company if not actually employed there. Either way, it'll shape up as an inside job. For that same reason—having explicit knowledge of where the painting was going to be and at what time—the next target of the police investigation will be Echelon.

But I'm getting ahead of myself.

I slide the first fortune cookie up to the one-forty-nine-million-dollar soy sauce packet and move them both southbound down the block. "And off we go," I say.

Immediately, Nikolov blocks the path, his hand coming down like a gate. "Tell me again," he says. "Why won't the cop draw his gun? What'd you say his name was—Eddie?"

He's talking about Echelon's security guard. "First of all, Eddie's an *ex*-cop and has been for thirty years," I say. "Second of all, Eddie hasn't missed a meal since the day he retired."

"So he's fat and old. But he's still carrying," says Nikolov.

I know where he's going with this, and I don't like it. Not at all. "No one's shooting anyone, and Eddie's *definitely* not shooting anyone."

"Once again, how can you be sure?" asks Nikolov.

"Remember that chair umpire I told you about, the one I court-sided on through your betting site from one tournament to the next? Slow Hand Luke, I called him."

"Yeah, I remember. What about him?"

"Eddie would make Slow Hand Luke look like the fastest draw in the West," I say. I slide the fortune cookie and soy sauce packet around Nikolov's hand until they're all the way down the block and around the corner. "By the time Eddie even thinks of reaching for his gun, he won't even know in what direction to aim."

"Okay, keep going," says Nikolov. But from the way he nods when he says it, I know I haven't quite convinced him. He's still thinking about what he might and might not do about Eddie being armed.

As if I didn't have enough things to worry about with this heist, now I have one more.

CHAPTER 34

FUNNY THING ABOUT a piece of art that sells for a hundred and forty-nine million dollars: No one wants to touch it unless they absolutely, positively have to.

Another funny thing about that same piece of art: Although no one wants to touch it, everyone wants it out the door as soon as possible. The buyer, the seller, the auction house—they all have something to gain. Or lose.

"Ladies and gentlemen, may I present the man of the hour, Mr. Enzio Bergamo!"

Charles Waxman is in full smarm mode, standing in the center of Echelon's lobby, a two-story foyer of polished marble boasting a massive spiral staircase. He has his arms spread wide and turns in a circle on the heels of his wingtips, milking the applause. He's not a CEO; he's P. T. Barnum.

As is tradition after a major sale, the entire Echelon staff has gathered on the ground floor, up the stairs, and all along the balconies to welcome and congratulate the high bidder. And as major sales go, this one takes the cake.

Which explains the actual cake that Bergamo has the honor of cutting. But first, he says a few words of thanks to "the distinguished men and women of Echelon" and jokes that he'll need to sell a lot more dresses now to pay for his new Picasso.

The joke was his but the use of the word *distinguished* came from me. "Whatever you do, don't reference their expertise or professionalism or say anything that implies competence," I told him. Bergamo didn't have to ask why.

"Not having any cake, are you?"

I jump at the sound of Terrance Willinghoff's voice behind me. How long has he been standing there? Could he see what I was texting? Could he see *who* I was texting?

"You scared me," I say, casually lowering my phone. I take a quick glance around; people are gathered in small groups, talking and enjoying slices of Black Forest gâteau. "Oh…no. I mean yes, I'm passing on the cake."

Terrance, sporting a double Windsor knot in his tie twice the size of the Hope Diamond, looks suspicious, as if we're not actually talking about cake. "I know what you're up to," he says.

Gulp. "You mean you know I'm watching my girlish figure?"

"No, but perhaps somebody else is. And perhaps you're more than okay with that. Courting it, even."

"Excuse me?" I don't have to pretend to act incredulous. If Jacinda had heard him say that, she would've dragged him by his ear into the human resources office.

But Terrance is undeterred, on a mission. "Your hearing is just fine, Halston."

He's my boss. I work for him. But still. "Are you accusing me of something?" I ask.

"Of course not," he says.

Liar. I'll rephrase. "Did I do something wrong?"

"Pierre told me he introduced you to Mr. Bergamo at the auction."

"That's right, yes. I asked him to."

"Pierre told me that as well. Then he mentioned that Mr. Bergamo seemingly took quite a shine to you."

Do people really still use that expression? I stare at him blankly. "A shine?"

"Mr. Bergamo is under the impression that you are being deprived of your growth potential here. I believe it has something to do with the new security measure that you're not privy to."

"I wouldn't expect to be privy to it at my level," I say, trying to get ahead of the story.

"Well, good, because we're not letting clients dictate how we handle things in-house."

"Of course not. And it's not as if—"

"Not as if you discussed any of this with Mr. Bergamo? Yes, I understand that. But nonetheless, he is still a valued client, so in the interest of appearances, I'd like you to be present as we escort the painting into his possession after the party here."

"That's really not necessary."

"No, it isn't," he says. "But it's going to happen, and Mr. Fashion Designer is going to see that it's happening because, again, he seems a bit taken with you."

"I'm sorry," I say. Not sorry.

"May I give you a piece of advice, Halston? There are no shortcuts here at Echelon, and we trade only on our talent and professionalism. Anything other than that is, in a word, unprofessional. Is that understood?"

I nod at Terrance Willinghoff, resisting the overwhelming temptation bubbling up inside me to rip that smug, self-satisfied smile off his face and kick him in the balls.

But that's the beauty of guys like him. They go through life thinking that women get ahead in the workplace only by sleeping their way to the top. Terrance Willinghoff is a fool, a simp, a misogynist.

But he's also the one thing I need him to be today.

A mark.

CHAPTER 35

"IS THAT HER?" asked Agent Tau, scanning the area with his Steiner M80 binoculars. "Main entrance, two o'clock?"

He started to hand over the binoculars but got waved off by his partner, Agent Sigma. He remained staring at his phone, reading a *Bleacher Report* post about a possible trade between the Knicks and the Chicago Bulls. "Seriously," said Sigma without looking up from his phone, "are you going to ask about every brunette in her twenties?"

Agent Tau peered through the binoculars again, slightly adjusting the diopter. "It sure looks like her."

"That's a horrible trade," said Sigma, thumb-scrolling. "The Knicks should just trade their owner."

"Or maybe I could trade my partner," Tau muttered under his breath.

"I heard that," said Sigma, eyes still down.

"Oh, now you're listening." Tau lowered the binoculars. "I said, it sure looks like her."

"It's not." Sigma hadn't even bothered to look over the ledge of the roof.

"How do you know?"

"Is she alone?" asked Sigma.

"Yeah."

"Is it the side entrance?"

"No," said Tau.

"That's how I know," said Sigma. "When she comes out, it will be the side entrance, and she won't be alone."

"What kind of a hoity-toity name is Halston anyway?" asked Tau.

"I don't know," said Sigma. "What kind of guy actually goes around saying *hoity-toity*?"

"You're just pissed because you choked that putt on the eighteenth yesterday."

"I didn't choke. I just misread the break."

"Either way, you still owe me a hundred."

"Put it on the Underhill tab."

"Funny," said Tau, back to the binoculars again.

Sigma was done reading about the possible Knicks trade. He was done with this whole damn assignment. There was something about it he didn't like, something that didn't sit right, although he couldn't put his finger on what. Just a gut feeling.

For sure he didn't like baking in the hot sun on the rooftop across from the Echelon building. He hated stakeouts. The waiting. And waiting...and waiting...

Working with his longtime partner made it bearable, but he'd much rather be losing to him on the golf course than doing this.

Sigma cleared his throat and spoke, his voice dropping an octave so he sounded like a late-night-TV infomercial host. "Are you looking for excitement? Do you crave a life on the cutting edge? If so, look no further than the FBI. All the glitz, all the glamour, and all while carrying a Glock. That's right, the FBI: Fun Beyond Imagination. Sign up today!"

Tau always laughed no matter how many times he heard Sigma do his FBI-promotional-brochure routine. That's what partners did. The expected. The great partners, at least. The ones who always had each other's backs.

But Tau didn't laugh this time because he was still looking through his binoculars, and at that very moment, he saw her. He was sure of it. She was coming out the side entrance and she wasn't alone.

"Hey, it's her. It's definitely her," he said, tapping Sigma on the shoulder. "Get ready to shoot."

CHAPTER 36

AGENT SIGMA WASN'T sure how he ended up being the designated photographer, although of the "Two Greeks," as everyone in the New York field office called them—though neither one was actually Greek—Sigma was viewed as the more tech-savvy. He knew it wasn't necessarily true, but his partner, Tau, still used a flip phone, so there was no convincing anyone otherwise.

Whatever.

Sigma picked up the Sony Cyber-Shot RX10 resting on the camera case by his feet and raised it to his right eye. "Yeah. That's her, all right," he said. "Hellooooo, Halston." *Click, click, click.*

Tau spoke the names of the people with Halston as if taking attendance, his eyes going back and forth from the binoculars to the cheat sheet of headshots arranged on the inside of a manila folder like a family tree. "The Frenchman, Dejarnette," he said. "Walking next to her."

"Got him," said Sigma. *Click, click, click.*

"Waxman, behind them. The CEO."

"Yep." *Click, click, click.* "Man, that's some slick-looking hair."

"What's he got on there, shoe polish?" asked Tau.

"More like Valvoline."

Tau jerked his head, shifted the binoculars. "Next to Waxman. You see him, right? Bergamo?"

"Hard to miss." *Click, click, click.* "Jesus, buddy, don't trip."

Sigma zoomed in tighter on the padded case Bergamo was gripping with both hands and snapped a few more shots. He barely had to move his long-range lens to include Echelon's security guard, who was practically joined at the hip with Bergamo.

"Anyone missing?" asked Tau.

"Just the thief himself," said Sigma, pulling back from the camera for a moment to wipe the sweat from his forehead. "Olly, olly, oxen free, motherfucker."

Tau panned left, right, up, and down, and his hands suddenly locked. "Six o'clock, black T-shirt, heading right for them," he said.

There was no headshot, no cheat sheet for the thief. There was only the intel that said he'd be coming, and coming fast, on his own. Solo. The bigger the heist, the smaller the footprint.

Sigma put his eye back against the camera and aimed south down the block. "Got 'im," he said. "Damn, he's flying. Here we go."

"Stay on him," said Tau.

"Trying to. Switching to vid. What about the girl?"

Tau shifted back up the block to view Halston. "She just saw him. Quick peek."

"Anybody else see him?" asked Sigma.

"No. No one's looking that way. They're all — oh, shit!"

"What?"

"We've got company," said Tau.

"Who?"

"Don't know, but he shouldn't be there."

Sigma hastily zoomed out. "Where is he?"

"Nine o'clock, across the street. Leaning against the building."

"In the raincoat?" asked Sigma.

"That's him."

"There's not a cloud in the sky."

"Exactly," said Tau. "Right knee. Is that..."

Sigma zoomed back in, filling his frame with the guy in the raincoat. There it was—the tip of an AK-47 sticking out by his knee. "Shit! It is."

Tau threw down the binoculars and scooped up his Delta 5 Pro long-range rifle. "What the hell's the ROE on this?" he asked.

"I don't know," said Sigma.

It wasn't supposed to go down like this. Rules of engagement had never been discussed. Not in the briefing, not ever.

"No matter what, stay with the painting," said Tau, resting the bipod of the rifle on the edge of the rooftop.

"You got the shot?" asked Sigma.

"Not yet."

"Hurry."

"I am."

"Hurry faster."

"I am, damn it," said Tau, adjusting his scope. It sounded a lot like Sigma's camera—*click, click, click.*

"Any day now, partner," said Sigma.

"I'm close."

"Horseshoes and hand grenades."

"You're not helping," said Tau. *Click, click.* "And don't say it."

Too late. "That's right, the FBI," cracked Sigma. "Fun Beyond Imagination."

Click.

"Got it!" said Tau. "I've got the shot."

CHAPTER 37

IT'S ALL UNFOLDING in front of me, and I can't slow it down.

I glance to my left and spot Nikolov's guy, the first fortune cookie, breaking into a sprint down the block. Bergamo doesn't see him; he's not supposed to. He keeps talking to Waxman while carrying the painting, completely unaware of what's about to happen—or so he'll tell the police. But Bergamo hears my signal, a quick cough, and he knows he's got only about ten seconds to hit his mark. *C'mon, Enzio. Pick up the pace!*

He walks a little faster, making a beeline to the back of the van. I begin counting down in my head. *Ten...nine...eight...*

Pierre's by my side as I look over my shoulder and spot Eddie and the holstered gun that he hasn't touched in years. You can almost see the cobwebs on the grip.

Seven...six...

Bergamo arrives at the back of the van, the doors already open courtesy of his driver, who's standing off to the side. No one can actually see what Bergamo's doing but no one has to. He's obviously loading the painting, securing the case. What else could he be doing?

Five...four...

Suddenly, out of the corner of my eye, I see him across the street. Someone who doesn't belong, who shouldn't be here.

I know the face. I recognize him from Nikolov's apartment last night. He wasn't seated at the dinner table but he was there, lurking in the background, just as he is now. There's no rain in the forecast, nothing but blue sky overhead, and yet he's wearing a raincoat. Like a sucker punch, the panic hits me as I spot the reason for the raincoat.

It's all unfolding in front of me, and I can't slow it down.

In a blur, the case gets snatched from the rear of the van. Bergamo turned his back on it for only a few seconds, right on cue, to shake hands with and say goodbye to Waxman.

Waxman doesn't see the thief because he's blocked by Bergamo, but Pierre gets a good look at the man in the mask sprinting away with the painting. Pierre frantically points. He yells, screams. And that's when everyone turns to look. Everyone but me.

I'm fixed on Eddie, waiting, hoping he doesn't make a move for his holster. If he does, he's a dead man, as sure as that guy across the street has a semiautomatic tucked inside his raincoat.

But no. There's no time to wait and hope on Eddie. I can't risk it. *Nothing can happen to him or anyone else.* As soon as Eddie takes a few steps forward, I turn and start running. I'm chasing after the bad guy with the painting. Later I know I'll be asked why I did it, and I'll say I don't know, that I just did it. It was instinct. They'll never figure out it was the plan from the get-go, and they'll never question why I bumped into Eddie, given all the commotion. *It was like I had blinders on and all I could see was the thief getting away,* I'll say. Something like that.

I slam into Eddie and he falls hard to the ground, arms flailing.

He'll have a scrape on his elbow, and his wrist will be sore for a few days, but he'll have the rest of his life to recover. He doesn't go for his gun, he can't, and as I continue running, I glimpse the man across the street, his raincoat thankfully still closed.

And off I go. To catch a thief.

CHAPTER 38

I'M OUT OF breath within a block. I'm out of shape for an art heist.

I keep running because I have to, because I need to see this through, and because all the street cameras are watching. There's one on top of a traffic light ahead, one in the entrance of the bank I just passed, several of them all along the route. They're seeing everything. Then, after the thief makes a quick turn and I follow, they're seeing nothing.

The thief cuts hard right down an alley where no one's watching. No cameras. It's only the two of us running.

And one person waiting. Fortune cookie number 2.

Blaggy doesn't say a word, doesn't move—his body, his bald head; everything is perfectly still.

At the last second he holds out a case that's identical to the thief's, this one with Wolfgang's fake inside it. They exchange cases, and the handoff is seamless; no one breaks stride, and we both come out the other end of the alley in view of another security camera.

I'm gaining on the guy and he knows it, and that's what the footage will show. He's looking over his shoulder again and again, and as we approach the intersection, as another camera will show, the cement mixer approaches, an accident waiting to happen.

It happens.

The cement-mixer driver—fortune cookie number 3—hits his horn; the sound startles the thief, who trips, falls, and goes sprawling, sending the case directly underneath the truck's right front tire, which smashes to smithereens the supposedly priceless Picasso that no one but a handful of players in this game and the few fortune cookies working for them will ever know was a forgery, especially after the police forensics unit pieces together just enough of the remains to see the Echelon serial number, the newly added security measure that the new girl in the valuations department has no idea about.

If you're having a hard time keeping track of all that, good. Because that's the beauty of organized chaos.

You're only supposed to see the chaos.

CHAPTER 39

IT'S NOT A crime scene. It's a crime zip code.

The cops don't know where to begin their report. Where the painting was stolen? Where the painting was destroyed?

When I make it back to the Echelon building, the first squad car is just arriving. There's a large crowd gathered, mostly Echelon employees who have spilled out onto the sidewalk and some lookie-loos who were just passing by. All of them are fixed on the flashing lights and an apoplectic Enzio Bergamo. No one notices me.

Two officers step out of their car. Both have mustaches, but otherwise they're polar opposites, short and lumpy walking next to tall and lean. Waxman and Bergamo come forward and begin to tell them what happened. I can't hear every word from the back of the crowd but I can hear enough. A Picasso's been stolen.

"It's worse than that," I announce.

Everyone turns. *Now* they notice me. I'm disheveled and dripping with sweat, and my face is beet red.

Word about what I did has already spread; no one from Echelon can believe I tried to chase down the thief. But that's nothing compared to the news I give them.

"*Destroyed?*"

I'm not sure who echoes the word first; it's a chorus, but Bergamo absolutely says it the loudest. He borderline screams it and then goes full-tilt crazy before I can give the details—which is exactly how you'd expect Enzio Bergamo to react in this situation.

Waxman tries to calm him down while the cops, like two Moseses, part the crowd and approach me. As everyone steps back, they all see it, and the gasps come one after another in a chain reaction.

I have the Picasso with me. What's left of it, anyway.

Lying at my feet is the crushed case. Parts of the torn canvas are sticking out of the sides with pieces of the shattered frame dangling. Bergamo, on cue, runs to the remains of his one-hundred-forty-nine-million-dollar investment and drops to his knees like Willem Dafoe at the end of *Platoon*.

With all eyes on Bergamo, I quickly look across the street to see if Anton Nikolov's paranoid addition to the party is still lingering. He's not. Raincoat man is gone.

Waxman finally gets Bergamo to his feet, literally pulling him up and dragging him away so the cops can talk to me directly. They have questions. Everyone has questions. And I have answers.

The first rule of getting away with anything?

Control the narrative.

CHAPTER 40

THREE NIGHTS LATER, I'm back in the living room of Anton Nikolov's Tribeca apartment nursing a lime-flavored LaCroix and checking the time on my phone for, like, the tenth time in the past two minutes.

"Remind me again," I say. "Why exactly are we doing this?"

"Because he asked," says Nikolov without looking at me. He's over at his bar, laser-focused on making the second bourbon old-fashioned he's had since I arrived. Blaggy's not looking at either of us; he's on the leather couch opposite me watching the Yankees game on mute, the flat-screen as big as the wall.

I make no attempt to hide my frustration. *"Because he asked?"*

"Yeah," says Nikolov, dropping a sugar cube in his glass. "We're doing this because Bergamo asked me to. Any other questions?"

"Yeah," I say. "Since when did you become such a softy?"

There was a time only a few short weeks ago when I wouldn't have dared crack a joke like that at Nikolov's expense. I remember Blaggy jamming his finger in my face, warning me not to even speak to his boss unless spoken to. But that was then. This is now. Now Nikolov's the proud owner of one of the world's most valuable Picassos, and he got it for a steal. Pun intended. What's more, he knows he couldn't have done it without me, which explains why all he does is smile at my joke about his being a softy.

"That's funny," he says, meticulously adding a few drops of bitters and a splash of water to the sugar cube. He reaches for a muddler. "*Zabaven,* as we say in Bulgarian. That means 'funny.'"

According to Nikolov, Bergamo wanted the chance to take one last look at the real Picasso. He'd formed some kind of bond with the painting while bidding on it, or so he said, even though he knew all along that he'd never own it. He'd done a favor for Nikolov, albeit not by choice, and to Nikolov's credit, that fact wasn't lost on him.

"Okay, I get it," I say. "I understand why you're letting him come here. But why do I have to be here?"

"I told you. He asked." Nikolov reaches for a few ice cubes and finally glances at me. He squints. "Why do you look so concerned, Halston?"

"Because this wasn't part of the plan," I say.

"You're right, but the plan's over. It worked. Relax." He eyes my LaCroix as he pours the bourbon. "Maybe even have a real drink."

I pass on the drink but take him up on the relaxing. He's right. The plan worked. And yes, Bergamo had played his part, and played it well. The way he ripped smarmy Waxman a new one, threatening to sue Echelon over its lack of adequate security, did wonders for speeding up the insurance review. Even better were the city's security cameras that supported every word of what I told the police, right up to the painting being squashed like a bug underneath the wheel of the cement mixer.

The police are still looking for the thief. *Good luck with that, guys.* He was on the first flight back to Bulgaria.

As for the cement-mixer driver, cameras showed him getting out of the truck, looking thoroughly confused, then listening to me explain what had happened. He gave me his cell number and helped me gather the remains of the painting in its crushed case. The next day, the police called him to set up a time for an official statement. We coached him to act scared and ask a lot of dumb questions, like "Am I going to have to pay for the painting?" Not for a minute did the police think this rocks-for-brains guy was an accomplice.

The investigation will continue. Detectives will focus on the idea that it was an inside job, that someone with either Echelon or the courier company hired by Bergamo to transport the painting was involved. How else did the thief know exactly where to be at exactly the right time?

For sure, no one will be above scrutiny. But if there were one person they wouldn't suspect, it might be the young woman working for Echelon who actually chased the thief for ten blocks.

Just saying.

CHAPTER 41

THE DOORMAN RINGS up to the apartment as Nikolov stirs his drink. For the record, you never shake an old-fashioned. You always stir it.

Bergamo walks in, all smiles. This is the first time we've all been together since the day of the heist. I told Nikolov that was one time too many. Yes, the insurance got paid, but the police investigation is ongoing. This is not the moment to get sloppy.

Speaking of sloppy.

I can smell Bergamo from across the room. He's been drinking. A lot. Everything about him is loose—his shirt, his tie, and, especially, his tongue. He's slurring his words.

"Do you know where I'm supposed to be right now? Back uptown at a Dior party surrounded by supermodels—I mean dozens of gorgeous girls, some of the most beautiful women in the world, each one flirting with me more than the next so they can be the face of my next ad campaign. But instead I'm here. I'm fucking here, all right?" he says, turning on his heel and almost losing his balance. "Where is it?"

Nikolov casually points at the far wall, behind the couch where Blaggy's sitting. "Over there," he says.

Bergamo does this combination walk/strut across the living room and stops as soon as he gets past the couch and sees the painting leaning against the wall. He was smiling when he came in, but now he's positively beaming.

"It really is beautiful," he says. "So beautiful."

He stares at it in silence, barely blinking, and Nikolov shoots me a quick, knowing smile. Bergamo truly wanted to have one last look at it, just like he said.

"Enzi, can I fix you a drink?" asks Nikolov.

The question snaps Bergamo out of his trance. "Huh? Oh, no. No, thanks."

"Are you sure?"

"Yeah, I'm good," he says. Bergamo literally waves goodbye to the painting and walks toward Nikolov at the bar. "But speaking of good..."

Nikolov nods. "I know what you're about to say."

"I don't even know what I'm about to say." Bergamo laughs, raising his finger in the air. "But I know what I'm thinking, so just hear me out, okay?"

"Okay," says Nikolov. "I'm listening."

"What I want to say...what I need to know is that we're square. I owe you nothing, Anton, no more favors. No anything. That's what I need," he says. He balls his fists and says, à la Al Pacino, "'Just when I thought I was out, they pull me back in!'"

Nikolov is thoroughly entertained and more than willing to play along, assuring Bergamo that they are indeed square. "You're out for good, Enzi. You have my word."

They shake hands and Bergamo spins around and points at me, again almost losing his balance. "And you," he says. "You and I aren't done yet."

"Actually, I'm pretty sure we are," I tell him.

"No. Not until I see you do it," says Bergamo, coming toward me.

"Do what?" I ask.

"Do what? Do what?" He's mimicking me. Nikolov's eating it up. Even Blaggy's chuckling. "You set me up. Seduced me, recorded me, blackmailed me—now it's time to erase me," says Bergamo.

"So that's why you wanted me here," I say.

"I want you to take out your phone and get rid of that recording of us. Delete it. *Poof.* Straight into the trash can."

I glance over at Nikolov, who's mixing his third old-fashioned, and he gives me a nod. I've got his blessing. I imagine he's given that same nod countless times over the years to people who work for him, and that was always the end of the story.

But I don't work for Anton Nikolov.

"No," I say.

Bergamo blinks in disbelief. *"No?* Did you just say no?"

"Did you just suddenly go deaf?" I ask.

Nikolov's no longer mixing his third old-fashioned. Blaggy's no longer watching the Yankees beat up on Boston's middle relief pitcher. They're both looking at me. Staring. Wondering, *What the hell are you doing, Halston?*

Bergamo lunges for my phone on the end table next to me but I beat him to it, sweep it up in my hands.

"Fucking bitch," he says, undeterred. He grabs my arms and tries to pry the phone from me. We're like a couple of children fighting in the back seat of the minivan. This is really happening.

Then, with one swift kick, it isn't.

I land one right between Bergamo's legs, and just like that, the only thing he's grabbing is his crotch.

Nikolov's seen enough. He puts down his drink, walks over to Blaggy. "Give me your gun," he says.

Blaggy hands him his Glock, and two seconds later it's pressed against my forehead—just like when Nikolov and I first met. We've come full circle.

"Erase the goddamn recording," says Nikolov.

"Maybe you can trust him, but I can't," I say.

"Erase. The goddamn. Recording," he repeats.

Nikolov's not kidding around. This isn't *zabaven* anymore. It's not funny, and this is my last warning. He will not be asking again. There'll be no counting down from three.

"Okay, okay," I say. I swipe left on my phone to show him and Bergamo the recording. I play a second of it so they know for sure that's it. Then, with one press of a button, I erase it. *Poof.* Gone.

Just like me.

The second Nikolov lowers his gun I make a beeline for the door and walk out of his apartment without looking back. "Screw you guys," I say over my shoulder.

And that's that.

Until an hour later, when Bergamo shows up at my apartment.

CHAPTER 42

I OPEN THE door and stare at him. He stares back. He smiles.

"Well done, partner," he says.

"Right back atcha, partner," I say.

Bergamo hands me a chilled bottle of champagne and walks in, a spring in every step. He still smells like a whiskey house but he's as sober as a judge. He never wasn't. Eau de Johnnie Walker. A few dabs here, a gargle there, and — *voilà* — the scent of inebriation.

He turns around in my foyer and says, half joking, "Although you didn't have to kick me *that* hard, did you?"

"No pain, no gain," I say. "Besides, it was your idea."

It truly was. Bergamo wanted to make sure we were thoroughly convincing in our finale with Nikolov, and nothing says *convincing* quite like a kick in the balls.

"Glasses?" he asks, pointing at the champagne.

"Coming right up."

He follows me into the kitchen. "I don't know how you kept it together when Anton put the gun to your head."

"Let's just say it wasn't the first time I've had that done to me."

"Still."

"I know," I say. "I wasn't expecting that."

"You knew everything else that would happen, though. That I'd be the first name he'd think of at Echelon, that I could be blackmailed..."

"Well, you do have a certain reputation with women."

Bergamo laughs. "I never thought that would work in my favor."

"You know, if this whole fashion-empire thing of yours ever gets old, there's always acting."

"You as well," he says. "The party at my beach house? You were very believable trying to seduce me."

"And you were very believable falling for it." I grab two champagne glasses from a cabinet. "Here," I say, handing him back the bottle. "You do the honors."

He unwraps the foil on the Krug Clos d'Ambonnay. I know it's expensive but I don't know how expensive, so I ask.

"Three grand a pop," he answers. "But as someone once told me, when celebrating success, you should never skimp on the champagne. In fact, you know the guy who said it."

"Who is he?"

"Your father."

"I should've known."

Bergamo begins untwisting the wire muselet holding down the cork. "But you let me know if I overpaid," he says with a wink. "Hey, speaking of which, no word on that mystery woman, the one bidding against me?"

"No, but I'm still trying," I say.

"Sort of moot now, right?"

"Yeah, sort of."

He pops the cork, pours two glasses. The bubbles look like tiny pearls racing to the top.

"We should toast in front of it," he says.

"Absolutely."

I lead him over to the case and unhook the latches. Bergamo can hardly contain himself. The original Picasso, the *real* real one, waits inside.

Why make just one fake when you can make two?

Everyone saw Bergamo take the original to the back of the van. What they didn't see—what they *couldn't* see—was where he put it. We had a hidden compartment built just for the occasion. It functioned like a trapdoor, and on top of the door was Wolfgang's second masterpiece waiting to be snatched by the thief. The thief grabbed the case, took off, and did the exchange with Blaggy. Everything went according to plan, which included making Anton Nikolov believe that he was the proud owner of the original. Which he does believe. Fell for it hook, line, and sinker. And he will always believe it, especially because it's got Echelon's stamp of approval on it. The serial number. Wolfgang duplicated it not once but twice.

Bergamo raises his glass. I raise mine.

"To the art of deception," he says.

And it's only just beginning...

ACT III

SLEIGHT OF HAND, TWIST OF FATE

CHAPTER 43

DOMINICK LUGIERI'S CREW looked like a pack of wolves, Malcolm thought. Their hair slicked back, prowling in unison, eyes darting — they were hungry for a fight.

Malcolm stayed a few steps behind them as they crossed Moore Street in the Bushwick section of Brooklyn, a neighborhood that featured more street-art murals, facial hair, and organic-juice brands per square foot than any other part of the country. It was hipster heaven or it was hell, depending on who you asked.

Malcolm hung back because he was the new guy. New guys followed; they didn't lead.

New guys also weren't fully trusted. Malcolm wanted to keep an eye on these wolves, and he knew the feeling was mutual.

Today was a test. He clearly had impressed Lugieri when they'd met in his private dining room at Osteria Contorni, but now the boss wanted to see how Malcolm handled himself in the field. Could he mesh with his crew? Lugieri's men — one of them, at least — would surely be reporting back to him about the new guy, giving him the lowdown. That was the way it worked.

Malcolm knew he was being groomed for something big. That was the whole reason for the Lugieri introduction. Until he was fully trusted, Malcolm would be tasked with smaller things. Kid stuff. In this case, literally.

Bushwick was hardly Lugieri turf, but the "kids" they were paying a visit to were definitely under his rule. The kids—that's what Lugieri liked to call them. A group of about a dozen recent grads from NYU who were pursuing "alternative career paths" in the post-COVID economy. Forget grad school or even Wall Street—these kids were opting for sales and marketing in a particularly high-demand area of medicine: designer weed.

Business was booming for the Grass-Fed Pandas, as they labeled themselves, in part because these kids had had the foresight to partner with a one-stop shop for protection against gangs, the police, and even state legislators.

In return, Lugieri received a cut of 40 percent. But he had the sneaking suspicion that the Grass-Fed Pandas were cooking the books, pocketing more of the profits than they were reporting.

Had they never seen the pilot episode of *Ozark*?

Still, Lugieri was first and foremost a businessman. He could mete out brutal punishment with the best of them, but cartel justice in this situation would amount to cutting off one of his prime sources of cash flow. He didn't want to kill the Pandas. He just wanted to teach them a lesson. Take them back to school. Give them a little refresher course in the fundamentals of proper accounting.

The blood and broken bones would be viewed as extra credit.

As Lugieri's crew approached the three-story brownstone that functioned as the combined home and headquarters for the Pandas, Malcolm had a quick flashback to his time in the Panjshir Valley of Afghanistan. Anything with a wall or a door in that desert hellhole was treated as if the devil himself were waiting behind it. Flank formation, a finger on every trigger—every possible precaution was taken. And when they came upon the sketchiest of buildings, the "Pandora's boxes," they wouldn't enter without first sending in one of the remote-controlled bots for a look-see.

But Bushwick wasn't the Panjshir Valley, and the Pandas weren't the Taliban. Nor were they the Crips or the Bloods or any other street gang. These kids carried 4.0 GPAs, not guns. And half of them were probably asleep now after sampling their own product, which they did on a daily basis.

So there was no flanking or fanning out around the brownstone. No fingers on triggers. Lugieri's men kept their Glocks, Walthers, and SIG Sauers tucked in their belts. They even rang the doorbell.

Still, for all that was different, for all the miles and missions that separated Malcolm from that time in Afghanistan, he got the same bad feeling in the pit of his stomach that he used to get before certain raids.

It was the sense that something was about to go sideways.

CHAPTER 44

MALCOLM HADN'T LEARNED all the wolves' names yet. Not that he really needed to call anyone by name. Almost everything they wanted to communicate could be accomplished with a simple nod or a finger point.

Including which Panda would get the first beating. That was easy.

The first kid dumb enough to deny the wolves' accusation.

"Whoa, I think there's been some kind of mistake," said the tall, lanky one wearing flip-flops and a purple NYU T-shirt. With his palms raised, he stepped forward near the staircase on the first floor of the brownstone, doing his best to sound calm and convincing despite clearly being scared as shit.

Malcolm watched from the back of the pack as one of Lugieri's men nodded to another; he immediately stepped forward and punched the kid in the gut so hard that he puked even before he keeled over, his just-eaten SpaghettiOs shooting out of him like a firehose. Red sauce splattered everywhere, including on the shoes of one of Lugieri's other men. He didn't wait for any nod or finger point before he compressed his anger into a balled fist and delivered a vicious uppercut to the puking Panda and then to a kid who had come to his aid. Both of them were now on the floor, blood gushing from their noses.

Did anyone else want to deny they were skimming money?

The question hung in the air for barely a second before a scream came out of nowhere and a kid appeared, the knife in his hand held high. None of Lugieri's men had time to react.

Malcolm didn't either, and yet his legs still moved, his arm still swung, the instincts kicking in like a mule, courtesy of living every day in a war zone halfway across the planet where death was always lurking over your shoulder.

Before any of the crew could reach for a gun, Malcolm had sprung forward and grabbed the kid's wrist; the tip of the knife was only inches away from ensuring that everything was truly, horribly, irrevocably about to go sideways. With a twist and a pull, all in a blur, Malcolm knocked the knife to the ground, put the kid in a headlock, and jammed the barrel of his Beretta against the kid's temple, ready to blow his brains out.

"I'm only going to ask this once, and you've got three seconds to answer," said Malcolm calmly. "Yes or no: Are you boys skimming?"

Maybe it was the shock, or maybe it was fear of the unknown. If they confessed, came clean, would they all be killed? Malcolm could see it in their faces. The anguish. The torment. Not a single kid understood that this stranger in their house, the guy who didn't look at all like the other men, was doing them the biggest favor of their lives.

Malcolm had reacted when no one else could. In the blink of an eye, he'd moved from the back of the pack to front and center. He was no longer the new guy. Among Lugieri's men, right here and now, he was the wolf in charge.

"One," said Malcolm.

The kids shifted back and forth on their feet, a wave of panic crashing over them. They were desperately looking at one another, asking with their wide eyes what to do.

"Two," said Malcolm. *For Christ's sake,* he thought. *Someone better speak the hell up. I can't help you if no one speaks up.*

Malcolm had no intention of killing the kid or anyone else. But if he got to three and didn't shoot, he'd no longer be in charge. If he didn't pull the trigger, one of Lugieri's men surely would.

There was only one more thing he could do before getting to three. A version of "two and a half." Malcolm cocked the hammer on his Beretta; the loud, metallic click pierced the silence.

"Yes!" came a voice. One of the kids stepped forward. "Yes!"

"Yes what?" asked Malcolm.

"Yes, we've been skimming," he said.

"How much?" Malcolm watched as the kid hesitated. "And don't make me ask twice."

"About half a million."

"Is it here?"

"Most of it."

"Where?" asked Malcolm.

"A safe in the basement," said the kid. "You can have it all."

"No shit, Sherlock." Malcolm lowered the hammer on his Beretta. "On top of that, for the next six months, every penny you take in flows directly to Mr. Lugieri. Is that understood?"

"Yes," the kid said.

"All of you say it."

"Yes," they all echoed.

Malcolm nodded at two of Lugieri's men to go to the basement with the kid to get whatever money was in the safe. The two men nodded back, not thinking twice about taking orders from the new guy. Malcolm was the leader of the pack now.

He was a big bad wolf.

CHAPTER 45

"**SO DO YOU** like it?" I ask.

Michelle leans her head forward, staring at the gigantic canvas in front of her while rocking on the toes and heels of her pink Reeboks. The sneakers, scuffed up and old, are clearly hand-me-downs, once belonging to another little girl, if not several. The head of the foster home made a point of telling me that I shouldn't be buying clothes for Michelle. *No shopping sprees, please. It breeds jealousy and resentment among the other girls.*

"Um...I don't know," says Michelle, still with her head tilted. "I can't tell."

"You can't tell if you like the painting?"

"Yeah...I mean no, I'm not sure. Am I supposed to like it?"

I motion to the wall where Jackson Pollock's gigantic *Autumn Rhythm* doesn't so much hang as float. "Stare at it a little longer," I say.

"Okay."

I don't know what the right age is for a child to take her first trip to an art museum. You see parents lugging around toddlers and preschoolers all the time, clearly thinking they're giving their kids some amazing leg up on their education, a head start on their applications to Harvard and Yale. Inevitably, these kids, barely out of their strollers, look bored out of their gourds or, worse, angry to the point of throwing a tantrum.

My father took me to the Metropolitan Museum of Art for the first time when I was seven. That seems like the right age, if only because I can remember that day vividly, as if it happened yesterday. And I'll never forget what he told me.

I point to Michelle's eyes, then to her head. "Art isn't just what you see or what you think," I say. I point to her heart. "It's how it makes you feel."

"Feel?" she asks.

"Sure. Like, does it make you happy inside, or sad, or maybe something else?"

I watch as Michelle stares again at the Jackson Pollock, narrowing her eyes to a squint. She's really trying. Finally, she says, "Confused?"

"That's so interesting," I say.

"It is?"

"Absolutely. In fact, I think you're onto something. All those squiggly lines and drips of paint, the splatters and the splotches. It is confusing, isn't it?" I take her hand, and we walk closer to it. Real close. Our noses are only a couple of feet from the canvas. "Now look at the colors. There's really only black and white on top of a few shades of brown, but the black paint and the white paint are everywhere. It's a mess, right?"

"Like the artist spilled a lot of it," she says.

"That's right. You'd think Mr. Pollock was really clumsy with his paint cans or something. Totally confusing."

"So I'm right?"

"Yes, but that's because you can't be wrong. The right answer is how the painting makes *you* feel, Michelle. You and only you," I say. "That's what's so beautiful about art. Everyone gets to have their own feelings about it."

"So you agree with me? You think it's confusing too?" she asks.

"Well, that depends on how you look at it."

"What do you mean?"

"I'll show you," I say. "Follow me." I lead her across the room, a good twenty yards from the painting. "Now tell me what you think."

Michelle turns and immediately bobs and angles her head to get a clear view. But she can't. There are too many people walking or standing in front of her.

"I can't really see it," she says.

"Give it a minute — just keep looking. Wait for it."

"Wait for what?"

"You'll see," I say.

The moment comes, as it always does. A seemingly random point when everything shifts just so and gives you that perfectly clear view. Only it's not random. It's meant to be. And it's—

"Beautiful," whispers Michelle. "It's not confusing at all. It's beautiful."

"I think you're right."

"It's everything around it that's confusing. All these people moving..."

The whole world.

"So how does it make you feel?" I ask.

Michelle answers quickly, *beautifully*. "Like someone just told me a wonderful secret and I'm the only other person who knows," she says.

CHAPTER 46

DEENA MAXWELL GREETS us with a huge smile as we walk through the door of the Sisterhood Foster Home. "Hi there, Michelle! Did you have fun with Halston today?" she asks.

Deena's official title is facility director, although everyone calls her "Miss D." The woman's a saint. In the chaotic lives of these girls, Miss D is the definition of *calmness*. Their port in the storm.

"I had such a great time," says Michelle, beaming. "I went to my first museum today. It was really neat."

"I can't wait to hear all about it," says Miss D. "Tell you what, why don't you go wash up for dinner. I'm just going to talk to Halston for a minute, okay?"

From day one Michelle has always been polite with her good-byes to me, always saying thank you. Today, for the first time, she hugs me.

"I can't wait for next weekend," she says.

"Me neither," I tell her.

"And guess what? A few weekends after that, you get to meet my mom!"

I'm about to say how much I'm looking forward to that when I catch Miss D's eye. It's just for a second, but that's all it takes—something's up. Miss D intervenes.

"Okay, sweetheart," she says, cupping the back of Michelle's head. "You don't want to be late for dinner. Go wash up, okay? It's pizza night, you know."

"Yum!" says Michelle, racing up the stairs.

Miss D waits until Michelle's out of earshot. "I've got a horrible poker face," she says to me. "You saw that, huh?"

"Is there a problem with her mother?" I ask. "Has she—"

"Relapsed? No, that's not it. In fact, from what I've been told, she's doing very well in the halfway house."

"So what's the problem?"

"It's what happens next," says Miss D. "Michelle keeps looking at the calendar, counting down from six months because that's how long the rehab program is. Her mother hasn't had the heart to tell her that it's going to take longer. The two were living well below the poverty line beforehand. The state will help with at least a minimum-wage job and, eventually, housing, but not until they're convinced that Michelle's mother can hold down a job while staying clean."

"How long will that take?"

"It depends. There'll be a caseworker assigned, and it will ultimately be based on his or her recommendation. The goal is for Michelle's mother to be able to deal with the daily pressures of life without succumbing to the temptation of her addiction."

"But on average?" I ask.

"Figure another four to six months."

"You're kidding me."

"I wish I were."

"That will absolutely crush Michelle."

"It will, yes, at first," she says. "But in the end—"

"I don't know if Michelle will make it to the end."

"You'd be surprised how resilient these girls can be. Trust me, I've seen it."

Trust me, I've lived it. "What keeps Michelle going isn't spending Saturday afternoons with me or pizza nights," I say. "It's only one thing—hope. And it's the only thing she has left. Take that away from her, and she's lost."

"We all want the same thing for this little girl, Halston. We want Michelle to be reunited with her mother. But without changing what caused the problem in the first place, the circumstances, there truly isn't any hope. They can't live in a homeless shelter. There needs to be an income, stability."

"So it's about money."

"It's about more than money, but, yes," she says, sighing, "it's about money. The biggest gateway drug in the world is poverty."

Miss D is the way she is for a reason, and I know she's not wrong.

"When's Michelle going to be told?" I ask. "And who's telling her?"

"It can only come from her mother. That's why I stepped in when Michelle mentioned your meeting her."

"I understand. I get it."

"I know you do," says Miss D.

"But, again, it's not me I'm worried about."

"I know that too."

"What if there was another way?" I ask.

"For Michelle to hear the news?"

"No. What if Michelle didn't have to hear the news at all?"

"I don't follow," she says. "What are you suggesting?"

"I'm not sure yet."

Miss D smiles. I don't blame her for thinking I'm a bit naive. I'd be thinking the same thing. I'm a lot closer to Michelle's age than hers.

She says, maybe only to placate me, "When might you be sure?"

"That depends," I say. "When's her mother coming to visit?"

CHAPTER 47

"HI, DADDY."

"Hi, sweetheart."

Technically, I'm not supposed to hug my father in the visiting room, but technically, I stopped giving a crap about that prison rule a few years ago. About six months after that, the guards finally gave up and stopped scolding me.

"How do you feel?" I ask as we sit down. My father creaks louder than our old metal foldout chairs. He's only fifty-eight.

"Pretty good," he says, looking away for a moment.

When I was little, maybe six or seven, my father began teaching me about tells, the things people told you without saying a word. Body language speaks volumes, he often said, you just have to pay attention. For example, people who have a hard time maintaining eye contact are probably not leveling with you.

My father isn't feeling "pretty good." I'd know that even if he hadn't looked away when he answered. Still, I don't call him on it.

He doesn't want to talk about how he's feeling or how he needs better care than what he's getting from the poor excuse for a medical staff here. His heart attack was six months ago; he needs angioplasty and a stent and possibly a bypass, but the attending cardiologist is content to "monitor" the blockage in his right coronary artery and put him on blood thinners. Meanwhile, my father is getting weaker and weaker. What the prison is really monitoring is their bottom line. Heart procedures are expensive, and a cost-benefit analysis never favors the prisoner.

I've adapted to my father being here. The prison part, I mean. I've gotten used to the long drive north from the city and the stench of this place, to waiting in line for the metal detectors, then waiting in more lines to see him. The regimen has become habit, and the habit has become numbing, so much so that I almost don't feel the crushing sense of loneliness and regret that fills every corner here.

But what I've never made peace with is how a place designed to let nothing and no one escape permeates every aspect of my own life. Who I was, who I was embarrassed to be—it all changed as fast and loud as the crack of a judge's gavel. I was the daughter of none other than Conrad Greer, the man convicted of perpetrating a massive art scam, among various other crimes. Money laundering, wire fraud. And the hits just kept on coming.

"Greedy Greer!" read the headline in the *Post* when he was arrested. Then, when he was convicted: "Guilty Greer!"

Was he in fact guilty? Yes.

And no.

It wasn't his scam, and he was taken advantage of by someone whom he had trusted. There came a point, however, when my father figured out what was happening and had the opportunity to put a stop to it. He would've been destroyed as an art dealer, his reputation ruined, but he almost assuredly would've suffered the consequences as a free man. In what should have been a moment of clarity for him, when he had the chance to clear his conscience, he allowed his fear and pride to trample his sense of right and wrong. Instead of taking action, he froze. Then he rationalized, thinking if he just went along with the scam and saw it through to its end, he could live with the guilt.

Instead, he now lives in a federal correctional institution.

The prosecution portrayed him as the living example of the rich just trying to get richer with no regard for the rules. If I were them, I'd have made the same claim. But in reality, my father was a man who desperately didn't want to be an embarrassment to his family. It was his worst fear, a nightmare in his mind, and the irony is inescapable. In his efforts to protect us, my father made the nightmare come true.

And when my mother couldn't handle the Greer family's epic fall from grace, she added pills to her drinking regimen. Then, one night, she mixed a deadly concoction of both and managed to make the nightmare even worse than any of us could've imagined. She went to sleep and never woke up.

I still remember shaking her that morning, waiting and waiting for her eyes to open. Her skin felt so cold.

Maybe that's the reason for what I'm doing: to get this nightmare to end once and for all.

The hour passes. Even when I'm with him, I miss him. "I'll see you next week, Daddy."

I hug my father goodbye and leave the prison, walking through the same corridor and out the same door as I always do. Only this time, when I get in my car, I do something I haven't done for years.

I cry.

CHAPTER 48

I WAKE UP the next morning to a text from Skip. He wishes me luck and attaches a screenshot from the New York State Department of Labor website. It's a form to file for unemployment benefits.

Funny guy, my brother.

I get out of bed, shower, and go to my closet to pick out just the right outfit. I stand in front of my entire wardrobe with my arms crossed and wonder what says *I'm outta here* the best.

I opt for a simple black skirt and white blouse as if to make clear that there's no gray area in what I'm doing. I'm giving Echelon my two weeks' notice.

Ha. By quitting, I won't even be eligible for unemployment.

"Good morning, Jacinda," I say, standing at the door of her corner office in the HR department. "How was your weekend?"

I don't really listen to her answer. At least, not to the words. This is simply about gauging the moment. I need her to be somewhat distracted, a bit preoccupied, perhaps, with the start of a new week and what's on her plate.

Jacinda says, "It was fine," or something to that effect. What she doesn't do is elaborate. There are no details or anecdotes, and she does not ask how my weekend was. She barely even gives me a glance. Her head's buried in a file on her desk.

The timing is perfect.

"I know you must be super-busy, but do you have a moment?" I ask, then quickly add the two words that will guarantee she won't say no. "It's important."

Telling people something's important almost always gets their attention. But in the wake of the Picasso theft, with the entire House of Echelon on edge, saying it to the head of HR is a showstopper. Jacinda closes the file, motions to the chair in front of her desk. She asks me to close the door.

"Before you say a word," she says the second I sit down, "does this have anything to do with your statement to the police? Because if it does, I've been instructed by in-house counsel to refer that to them."

She sounds like she's reading off a cue card.

The police took statements from every person who was on the scene when the painting was stolen or who had advance knowledge of the day and time the painting was leaving the building. Add them all up and you get about fifty Echelon employees. In other words, it wasn't exactly a closely guarded secret.

"No. This isn't about anything I said to the police," I say. "But it does have to do with what happened."

Jacinda blinks as if I've just short-circuited her brain. She has no cue cards for this scenario. Should she stop me or should she let me keep talking?

"Maybe you should run this by the lawyers first," she says.

"No," I tell her.

"*No?*"

"You're the one I need to talk to." I cross my legs, settling into the chair. "Over the weekend, I got approached by a reporter from the *Post*."

"*Approached* as in the reporter called you?"

"*Approached* as in he stalked me. He literally came up to me in a Starbucks."

"Shit," says Jacinda. "What'd you tell him?"

"Nothing. But he knew I was the one who ran after the thief."

"How?"

"I asked but he wouldn't tell me. Probably because I wasn't giving him anything in return. I wouldn't even confirm that I worked here."

"Good."

"For now, maybe," I say. "Which is why we're having this conversation."

"Listen, if you're worried for your safety, then—"

"No, that's not what I'm worried about…"

I watch as it clicks for Jacinda. She suddenly connects the dots the same way that imaginary reporter might.

"Oh," she says with a sigh. "I get it."

It might have been no secret within Echelon as to when Bergamo was picking up his Picasso, but once it was stolen and destroyed, this place, as I knew it would, switched into a communications lockdown. Smarmy Waxman gathered every Echelon employee on the auction floor and laid down the law: No talking to the press. No talking to your family. No talking, period. Well, except to the police. If you were asked, you answered their questions. Other than that, it should be as if the Picasso had never existed.

"The House of Echelon lives or dies based on how we conduct ourselves from this moment forward," Waxman declared.

The line was overly dramatic, perhaps, but it got the job done. Collective amnesia set in. Especially when Waxman tacked on "Anyone caught betraying my trust will be terminated immediately."

"As you said yourself, Jacinda, it would be a bad look for Echelon if it was known that you hired the daughter of Conrad Greer. When you confronted me about it, I didn't think anyone would ever find out. But things have obviously changed. Echelon's now under a microscope. You don't disagree, do you?"

She can't. She doesn't. "I don't," she says.

Mission accomplished. Sayonara, House of Echelon.

It's a clean break; I'm leaving without a whiff of suspicion. If anything, I'm taking one for the team. All that's left for me to do is say the words out loud and make it official. It couldn't be any easier.

"Knock, knock!" someone says, barging in. Even before I turn my head, I know there's only one person at Echelon who can open a closed door anytime he wants. "Am I interrupting?"

"No," a startled Jacinda tells her boss. "Halston was just—"

"Halston, indeed," says Waxman, only there's no smarm this time. There's no anything. His face is expressionless. He points at me. "You and I need to talk."

CHAPTER 49

CALL IT A CEO power move. Or just Waxman being Waxman.

Instead of heading back with me to his office, he hijacks Jacinda's. "Can you give us a few minutes?" he asks, although it's definitely not a question.

The look on Jacinda's face when she realizes she's being kicked out of her own office is priceless. "Oh, um, yes, of course," she says.

Waxman strolls in and immediately takes a seat on the couch against the wall behind me. "Oh, and Jacinda?"

"Yes?"

"Close the door on the way out, will you?"

Normally I'd be enjoying the hell out of this moment, but now all I can think about is what's going to happen after that door closes. Does Waxman know something? My mind's scrambling, trying to figure out what it could be. Did I overlook a detail? Have I somehow left a loose thread dangling over me like a noose?

"Halston, let's talk over here. Have a seat," he says, nodding at the chair opposite him.

I do as he says. Everyone at Echelon does as Waxman says.

We're face to face. I still can't get a read on him. There's only a glass coffee table between us, but it might as well be the Grand Canyon. "Is everything okay?" I ask.

"That's an interesting question," he says.

"How so?"

"You know. With everything that's happened."

"Right," I say. "Of course."

"So what were you and Jacinda talking about?" he asks.

I hesitate on purpose. I need to appear uncomfortable answering. It's only natural. "I was resigning," I say finally.

"*Resigning?* Why would you do that? You just started. You don't like it here?"

"I do—"

"Good." He cuts me off. "Then it's settled. Congratulations, Halston."

"On what?"

"Your promotion," he says. "I'm making you vice president of member relations."

"*Vice president?*"

"I know, right? Getting that title while still so young—it's really going to piss off a lot of people around here. But that's a good thing."

"It is?"

"Absolutely. They all need to see what I truly value, and that's commitment," he says. "In the heat of the moment, when everyone else, including me, froze, you took action." He leans forward and whispers, "You chased the thief."

"I just wish I could've caught him," I say.

"It doesn't matter." Waxman stops and smiles. "Well, I suppose it matters to Enzio Bergamo, but that's what insurance is for, right? He'll be just fine."

"I suppose."

"I don't mean to be flip about the guy but..." His voice trails off.

"What?"

"I shouldn't tell you this," he says. Which is what everyone says before they end up telling you. Waxman leans in again. "Do you know what that prick had the nerve to tell me the next day? Bergamo said he wished you hadn't tried to run down the thief. Can you imagine?"

"To be honest, I had a similar thought. Or, actually, I was worried others might think it. You know, because—"

"Because the painting got destroyed? Nonsense." He gets up from the couch and sits on the edge of the coffee table directly in front of me. "That's how the sheep think, and you're no sheep, Halston. That's why you're moving upstairs to the top floor. That's where the shepherds are. You are a shepherd, aren't you?"

He stares at me and I realize it's not a rhetorical question. *Okay, sure, I'll play along.* "I'm definitely not a sheep," I say.

"That's right, you're not. Even I didn't run after the thief, and I'm supposed to be the king shepherd around here." He places a hand on my knee. Above my knee, actually. He's almost in thigh territory. "So how 'bout it, Halston? Will you help keep me in line?"

Just like that, I go from being promoted to being hit on, and in the office of the head of human resources, no less. I'm not sure exactly what's happening, but I do know one thing.

Smarmy Waxman has just made it impossible for me to leave Echelon.

CHAPTER 50

I TELL BERGAMO to pick me up that night in the cheapest car he owns, something inconspicuous. He and his driver show up in a four-door Porsche Cayenne Turbo GT.

"Really?" I say, climbing into the back seat. "The cheapest car you own is a Porsche Turbo?"

At least he got the time and location right — midnight and nowhere near my apartment. The address I gave him is a parking lot on the Lower East Side near the Houston Street entrance to FDR Drive.

Bergamo thinks I'm being silly with the cloak-and-dagger arrangements. There's a fine line between prudent and paranoid, he tells me, and paranoid never looks good on a woman.

He ain't seen nothing yet.

"No driver," I say.

"What? What do you mean?"

"You heard me," I say. "This trip can only be the two of us."

"Halston, you haven't even told me where we're going," he says.

"You'll see." I lean forward and tap his driver on the shoulder. "No hard feelings, okay? There's a diner across the street. We won't be more than an hour."

Bergamo's driver doesn't work for me. He waits on his boss to tell him what to do, his eyes fixed on the rearview mirror.

"Apologies, Nico," says Bergamo. "Grab some coffee. We'll be back."

Nico steps out and I go around and take his place behind the wheel. Bergamo doesn't budge from the back seat. It figures.

I might be driving, but I'm not about to be his driver. "Get in the front, Enzio," I say.

"Christ, you're bossy." He takes his time walking around the car and plops himself in the shotgun seat with a sigh. "You do have your driver's license, don't you?"

I answer by gunning the gas and peeling away from the lot. I think Bergamo curses my name but the screeching tires drown him out.

Porsche. There is no substitute.

After a few blocks I still haven't told Bergamo where we're heading, but it doesn't take a rocket scientist to figure it out.

"Chinatown," he says. "We're going to Chinatown?"

"Yes."

"Are we eating?"

"No," I say. "Gambling."

Minutes later, I turn onto Mott Street, then go down an alley that gets only garbage and delivery trucks for traffic. When the sun's up, at least.

Bergamo chuckles as he looks ahead. "Seriously? Valet parking?"

There are two young guys, Chinese and in their twenties, standing by a small podium near an unmarked door in the alley. One of them holds a clipboard. "Yeah. Valet parking," I say. "If you're on the list."

"And are we?"

I pull to a stop, roll down the window. "Guests of Shen Wan," I announce.

The guy doesn't even have to check his clipboard. He nods, opens my door for me. As he leans forward, I spot the holstered gun beneath his jacket.

"Shen Wan? Is he the one?" asks Bergamo as we enter a small, narrow hallway with red velvet drapes lining the walls. "Is he the guy? Shen Wan?"

I ignore the question and tell him to take out his cell. "And anything else that's metal."

There are two more guys in front of us, twice the size of their counterparts outside. One's waving a mag wand — a handheld magnetometer — and the other holds out a couple of Yondr pouches.

Bergamo's never seen a Yondr before. "What are those for?" he asks.

"You can't use your phone inside."

"Forget it. I'm not handing over my phone to anyone."

"You don't have to. The pouches lock up the phone. You get to hold on to the pouch."

I watch as Bergamo's fashion mind kicks in; he's obviously thinking about how he could make designer Yondr pouches. The man who got rich with the Bergy bag strikes again.

We get ushered in.

"Is this one of those underground casinos you see in the movies?" whispers Bergamo.

Not exactly.

There are no craps or roulette tables and definitely no slots. There's only baccarat, a dozen tables or so with a thousand-dollar minimum, and a bar and lounge area. We walk by them all and go into a back room. That's where the real action is.

Mah-jongg. Only not the way your bubbe plays it. This is ridiculously high stakes, and only men. One of them being Shen Wan.

He's known me since I was seven. "Lucky Seven" he dubbed me when my father introduced us. As soon as Shen sees me now, he nods.

Bergamo and I stand in the corner, waiting for his game to end, the room silent save for the continuous clacking of mah-jongg tiles. No one gives us a second look. If you've made it into the casino, let alone into this room, there's a reason. It so happens Shen Wan owns the casino.

"What's funny?" I ask. Bergamo's chuckling to himself.

"No one in this room knows who I am," he says. "I mean, maybe they know the name but certainly not the face."

"They better not."

It dawns on him. "Yeah, you're right."

I know I'm right. No one can know what we're about to do. No one except for the one man who will make it happen.

Shen Wan walks over and gives me the kind of embrace that says what no words can. I'm like a daughter to him.

He's maybe an inch or two over five feet, but he carries himself like a giant, and for good reason: In the kingdom of the connected Chinese, Shen Wan is royalty.

After I introduce him to Bergamo, Shen asks if we'd like something to drink. We both decline.

"In that case," he says, "come with me."

CHAPTER 51

AND I THOUGHT Echelon had a cool basement.

We follow Shen through a door that leads to a room with a pristine marble floor made up of black and white squares, like a chessboard. The room is about the size of a two-car garage but it's completely unfurnished, empty. Also, there's no other way in or out. I spin around, taking it all in, the weird nothingness. Bergamo's doing the same; the two of us are standing in the middle of the room like a couple of tourists.

"Over here," says Shen off in a corner. We take a few steps toward him. He motions with his hand. "Closer."

I assume he wants to tell us something, but he simply looks at our feet, waiting. For what, I don't know. Then I do.

We needed to cross the invisible line.

Shen presses a button on a small fob that I didn't realize he was holding. Suddenly, our section of the floor begins to move. We're going down. Like an elevator, only slower.

"Whoa," says Bergamo.

We're surrounded by concrete as we drop amid a mechanical hum. Two sliding doors appear. They open the moment we come to a stop.

"Whoa," says Bergamo again, looking out at the room before us.

I'm thinking the same thing as we walk into the ultimate art collector's man cave. Echelon's basement could be described the same way, but this is different. The paintings hanging on the walls are recognizably by well-known artists—Banksy, Hockney, Warhol—all privately commissioned. For the very rich, art is an investment. For the superrich, it's simply about the pleasure of owning.

And no group seeks that pleasure more than Chinese billionaires. Shen is their go-between.

"Please," he says, pointing to two black leather sofas in the center of the room.

Bergamo and I sit. Shen walks over to a credenza and pours himself a finger of cognac. Not just any cognac—Louis XIII.

"Can I change my mind about that drink?" asks Bergamo, eyeing the bottle.

Shen doesn't respond. Maybe he didn't hear him or maybe he's choosing to pretend he didn't. Knowing Shen, I think it's the latter, but I don't let on. Bergamo looks at me, puzzled. I simply shrug.

Shen sits across from us, cradling the cognac in his palm. To Bergamo, he says, "This is the first time I've ever brought a stranger such as yourself down here." Every word is deliberate. He stares at Bergamo. "Do you know why?"

Bergamo's not sure if it's a rhetorical question. It isn't. Shen waits.

"It's because of Halston, I assume," says Bergamo.

"No." Shen raises the snifter to his lips, takes a sip. *"Xinrèn."*

Bergamo leans forward. "Excuse me?"

"That's the Chinese word for 'trust,'" says Shen. *"Xinrèn.* Because of the relationship you had with Halston's father and what transpired years ago, I'm choosing to show you first what I will now expect in return."

"Trust," says Bergamo.

Shen nods, takes another sip. "We have a buyer for the Picasso."

"Are we allowed to know who it is?" asks Bergamo.

"I'm afraid it doesn't work like that," says Shen.

What matters is that there's a buyer, not who it is. Bergamo nods. *"Xinrèn,"* he says. Trust.

Shen nods back. "The far more difficult task has been securing your request for—"

"Yes, such vases are very rare," says Bergamo. He's interrupted Shen. I reach over, place my hand on Bergamo's forearm. Now he gets it. "Oh. My apologies. I'm sorry."

Shen continues. "The difficulty is not securing the vases. The problem is who they're going to."

"You mean me," says Bergamo. "It's because of who I am."

"Not who you are but what you aren't."

"Chinese."

"It's not personal," says Shen. "Rest assured, your name has not once been mentioned."

"Still, what you're saying is that the idea of someone who isn't Chinese owning these vases from the Qing dynasty—it's, what, sacrilegious?"

"I would simply call it an issue of cultural differences."

"That's funny," says Bergamo, "because what I would call it is utter bullshit."

I'm about to unload on Bergamo, and Shen knows it. He calmly raises his palm, assuring me it's okay.

"I understand your frustration, Mr. Bergamo," says Shen, "which is why I have a proposal for you. Would you like to hear it?"

"That depends. Does it end with my getting the two vases?"

"Yes. But it will require one thing."

"What's that?"

Shen finishes the last of his cognac and smiles. *"Xinrèn,"* he says.

CHAPTER 52

BERGAMO FOLDS HIS arms tightly as we wait in the alley for his car to be brought around. He's looking straight ahead, trying his damnedest to ignore my stare. He can't do it.

"*What?*" he finally asks.

"I'm just making sure you understand," I say.

"Of course I understand. I told you I understood."

"No, you told Shen."

"That's right, and you heard me," he says.

"I need to hear it again," I tell him. "Shen brought you down into that basement of his to show you exactly what he meant. If you're to get those vases, they're for your eyes only. It can't ever get back to his people that someone other than their own now has them."

"It won't," says Bergamo.

His Porsche arrives; he tips the guy twenty bucks and proceeds to walk around to the front passenger seat.

"What are you doing?" I ask.

"What do you mean? You kicked my driver out of the car."

"That was just to get here."

"Good," he says. "Now get me back to him."

"Diva," I mumble under my breath.

"I heard that."

I settle in behind the wheel and pull out of the alley. We go a few blocks before we hit a red light. I look in the rearview mirror, then do a double take.

"What is it?" asks Bergamo.

"I'm not sure yet."

He starts to look, and I tell him to stop.

"You think we're being followed?" he asks.

"Like I said, I'm not sure yet."

"Well, let's get sure. Take the next right after the light."

"Not so fast," I say.

"What do you mean?"

"We need to know first."

He leans forward a bit, eyeing the side-view mirror. "Which car?"

"It's a van."

"The white one?"

"Yeah. When we came out of the alley, I saw it pull away from the curb after we passed it. It's been hanging back behind us ever since. Could just be a coincidence."

"Or it could be Nikolov...his thugs. Maybe he—"

"Knows what we did to him? If he did, we'd be dead already."

"Not if he wants the real Picasso."

"Decent point."

The light turns green and I continue straight up First Avenue, only a little slower.

"Still behind us?" asks Bergamo.

"Yeah. Still hanging back too. Keeping the same distance between us. Now we make those turns," I say. "Okay, you can look."

I hang a left at the next light. Bergamo stares over his shoulder. I can hear his breathing. He waits and watches, his eyes fixed out the back. "Shit."

We both see the white van make the turn. It's official. We're being followed.

CHAPTER 53

BERGAMO BEGINS TO panic. "What do we do?"

"We lose them. That's what we do," I say, speeding up. "We need to disappear."

"*Disappear?*" Bergamo hardly sounds convinced. "We should call the police," he counters. "Better yet, let's drive to a police station."

"Sure, and when we get there, we can tell them everything. Why you and I are together, where we came from tonight, and especially about the shipment from China we're expecting next week. That should go over real well."

"We don't have to tell them anything. Hell, we could simply be asking for directions."

"Then what?" I ask, checking the rearview mirror again. "Whoever's in that van can just park down the street and wait us out."

"Or maybe they don't," he says. "Maybe it scares them off."

"Fine. Hurry, then," I say. "Where's the nearest station?"

Bergamo takes out his cell, searches, his thumbs a blur as I dodge traffic. I've got one eye on the road, the other on the van's headlights. They look like two eyes staring at us in the night. I take a right on Third Avenue heading uptown, and the eyes turn with me.

"The Thirteenth Precinct," says Bergamo, scrolling. "That's the closest one. Straight up on East Twenty-First Street between Third and Second."

"Perfect," I say, darting around a cab. The driver honks in anger when I nearly cut him off, then flips me the bird.

We pass Sixth Street, then Seventh and Eighth, the lights cooperating—green, green, green. Up ahead at Ninth Street, the light turns yellow. I'm too far away to gun it. I jam on the brakes, screech to a stop.

"Where are they?" asks Bergamo.

"Far left lane, behind the bus," I say.

He looks again, craning his neck. "Fuck."

"What?" I ask, but I don't need to hear the answer. I can now see it. The van has veered out from behind the bus and is crossing lanes, heading straight for us.

"Go!" says Bergamo, his head still turned. His eyes are glued on the van. "Go now!"

"I can't!"

We're wedged between a Tesla and the cab I just passed. In front of the Tesla, people are in the crosswalk. There are cars driving by as well. Bergamo's head whips forward, taking it all in. We've got nowhere to go.

It's like a line of ducks. The Tesla, then us, then the cab. Behind the cab the van pulls to a stop. There are too many headlights in our eyes, so we can't even get a glimpse of who's behind the wheel.

"Oh no," says Bergamo.

"I see it." I see *them*. Two guys stepping out of the van. They're silhouettes but what they're doing is as clear as it gets. They're walking straight for us.

"*Go!*" yells Bergamo.

I still can't but that's not about to stop me. I hit the horn and shift the car into reverse to buy whatever space there is. It's a chain reaction. The cabbie honks back, thinking we're crazy, but by now I'm in drive again and I yank the wheel, edge out from behind the Tesla in front of us. *Move, Tesla!*

Or don't. I don't care. One way or another, we're getting around you. I hit the gas; Bergamo's Porsche lurches forward and squeezes out of the lane with no more than an inch to spare. People in the crosswalk are scattering, and the cars at the intersection screech to a halt to avoid smashing into us as we blow through the red light.

I'm gunning the engine, weaving through traffic. Bergamo's staring out the back.

"What are they doing?" I ask.

"They're getting back in the van."

The next light is green. "Now what?"

"They're not moving."

"Good."

"No, wait. Here they come."

We get green lights at Eleventh Street, then Twelfth, but the lights won't stay green forever. We can't make it to the precinct on Twenty-First without hitting another red, and there's too much traffic around us. I don't know for sure if I'll be able to run the light.

"What are you doing?" asks Bergamo.

"Plan B," I answer, taking a right onto Fourteenth Street.

You hear native New Yorkers boasting all the time that they know this town like the backs of their hands. Nonsense. They only think they do. Sure, they might be able to out-travel-guide me when it comes to restaurants and shopping, but, having grown up within a half an hour's drive of this city, I'll forever have them beat in one category.

Parking garages.

Before Bergamo can ask what plan B is, I'm turning into the twenty-four-hour garage on Fourteenth Street, the one my father used when we went to the Lilac Gallery so he could search for up-and-coming artists. I blow right by the attendant and loop down the familiar L-turn just far enough to ensure that no part of Bergamo's Porsche is visible from the street.

And—*poof!*—like magic, we've disappeared.

CHAPTER 54

BEFORE I EVEN walked through the front door of Echelon the next morning, word had spread. Like a virus.

No one actually says anything to me as I make my way through the cavernous lobby to the elevators. They don't have to. Their looks do all the talking, every stare saying the same thing: *How the hell did this girl get promoted to vice president?*

Except they already know. Smarmy Waxman made sure of it, strategically "leaking" his rationale to a few key Echelon executives, the ones who happen to have the biggest mouths. In chasing a thief through the streets, I almost literally ran my ass off for Echelon, and that's the kind of commitment and dedication that every CEO wants from his or her employees.

If they only knew the truth.

When I hit the up button on the elevator instead of the B for basement, I suddenly remember the internship fair that Columbia hosted just before the summer between my sophomore and junior years. All these HR people from leading companies descended on campus to pluck a few lucky undergrads for their prized programs, asking all the supposed curveball questions in their quick five-minute interviews that felt like one of those speed-dating events.

"So, Halston," said an interviewer from Condé Nast, double-checking my résumé to make sure she had my name right. "What would you say is your greatest weakness?"

"Why on earth would I ever reveal that to someone?" I answered. "I mean, did Superman go around tipping people off about kryptonite?"

News flash: I didn't get the internship.

"There she is, my new VP!" says Smarmy Waxman when he stops by my new office. "How are you settling in?"

If I'm going to be stuck at Echelon for a while, I might as well make the most of it, and that means getting the answer to a question that's been gnawing at me—and Skip—since the night of the auction. In fact, it's the first thing my brother mentioned when I told him about Waxman promoting me. The silver lining, he called it. A chance to solve the riddle. Who was the woman who was bidding against Bergamo?

There was something about her... something that doesn't sit quite right.

I tell Smarmy I'm settling in fine, and we make small talk. He even invites me to lunch later this week. I smile, nod, and say that's a great idea. I'm the new VP of BS.

Then, as he's about to leave, I hit him with the question. Almost as if it's an afterthought, I say, "Oh, I meant to ask you. Who was that woman bidding against Mr. Bergamo for the Picasso?"

If I'd blinked, I would've missed it. That's how fast it came and went, a very slight yet unmistakable flinch.

"Oh, her? She's a proxy for one of our clients," he says. He thinks for a moment, scratching his chin for added effect. "I can't remember the name."

"Of the client or the proxy?" I ask, even though I know exactly who he meant. He's stalling, trying to figure out a smooth way of not telling me the woman's name while not sounding suspicious.

"Huh? Oh, the proxy," he says. "Yeah, I've actually never met her. That's probably intentional. I do know that who she represents is incredibly private. He's the kind of member who doesn't want anyone knowing he's a member."

It certainly sounded smooth but it's too late. The flinch already gave him away. If I'm the VP of BS, he's the CEO.

Smarmy Waxman knows exactly who that proxy is.

Because that "member" she works for? It's him.

CHAPTER 55

"WHAT THE HELL are you doing here?"

"It's nice to see you too," I say, breezing past Bergamo and entering his corporate apartment in SoHo, which is conveniently—and secretly—located near his company's headquarters and flagship store on Spring Street. He claims only a half a dozen people know about the apartment. Make that seven now, including me. Lucky seven.

"You know what I mean," he says. "We agreed to lie low until next week, stay apart."

"And yet here I am, less than forty-eight hours later."

"Exactly. What's wrong? You said it was urgent."

Before closing the door, Bergamo peeks out into the hallway even though he shares the floor with only one other tenant.

"Don't worry, I wasn't followed," I tell him.

"So you say."

"So I know."

"How can you be sure?" he asks.

"Because I'm not the one they're following." I look around the apartment. Very swanky in all directions. "Do you have any water?"

"Wait. *What?*"

"Water," I say, pretending I didn't just drop a verbal grenade. "You know, to drink? Where's your kitchen?"

He's turning beet red, and I'm enjoying every moment of it. "What do you mean, you're not the one they're following?" he asks.

"I mean it's you. You're the one they're following."

"So you know who they are?"

"Nope."

"Then how do you know I'm the one they're following?"

"Because I've been following them," I say.

He laughs. He thinks I'm joking. I stare at him, straight-faced. "Hold on," he says. "You're actually serious?"

"Yes," I say. "Now, for real, can I get a water? Is the kitchen this way?"

I start walking down a hall off the foyer.

"Oh, for Christ's sake. It's the other way," he says.

I follow him into the kitchen, where I practically have to shield my eyes from the glare. The appliances, the counters, and the cabinets are all stainless steel. He grabs a bottle of Evian from the Sub-Zero, hastily hands it to me.

"Do you have anything else?" I ask. "Evian has a bit of an aftertaste."

He blinks. "Seriously?"

"Yeah. How about anything sparkling?"

Bergamo wants to scream, I can tell. He's keeping his cool only because he's desperate for me to keep talking. The Evian quickly gets switched for a bottle of San Pellegrino. "Okay," he says. "Now talk."

"There isn't much to tell beyond the headline. You're the target,"

I say, twisting off the cap of the Pellegrino. I take a sip. "It's funny. People who are following people never seem to look over their own shoulders."

"I've barely traveled anywhere in the past two days," he says.

"You traveled enough. Also, what's with the security team?" I ask.

"What about them?"

"They look like *GQ* models. Where'd you find them?"

"It was the best I could do at the last minute," he says. "They worked on Harry Styles's tour."

"Great. If you're attacked by a mob of teenage girls, you'll be safe."

"You think this is funny?"

"No, you're right," I say. "Sorry, I tend to crack jokes when I'm worried."

I take out my cell and show him a few pictures of the guys who are following him. They traded in the white van for a black Escalade.

"He sort of looks like that comedian," says Bergamo, pointing at one of them. "The one who had the TV show."

"Ray Romano," I say. "Yeah, I thought the same thing. Only this guy's been to the gym a little more."

"I'll ask it again," he says. "Do you think they're with Nikolov?"

"It's possible. But like I said, if Anton Nikolov truly suspected something, I think we'd know by now."

"You mean we'd be dead."

"Yeah. But maybe he's a little paranoid, so he's being overcareful, making sure of things," I say. "I know I'm paranoid, right?"

"And you were smart to be," he says.

"Good. I'm glad you think that." I wait a beat, taking another sip. "So you won't have a problem with what I'm about to suggest."

Bergamo already knows where I'm heading with this. It's as if he was just waiting for me to pivot.

"No chance," he says. "We're not calling this off. No way!"

"We don't have to call it off. We simply need to cool it for a bit."

"A distinction without a difference. Those vases—*my* vases—are on the water heading here as we speak. If we're not there to get them when they land, I'll never get them. Tell me I'm wrong."

I hesitate. My silence speaks volumes. I can see it on his face, the satisfaction of being right. "You're not wrong," I say.

"We need to alter the plan, not throw it out."

"In other words, we need to make sure you're not being followed when it matters most."

"Exactly," says Bergamo. "Any ideas?"

This is me pretending to think about it for a moment. When you hang around a guy like Bergamo long enough, you learn exactly what makes him tick. Greed. There was no way he was ever going to agree to *cool it for a bit*. The phrase isn't in his vocabulary.

"Well, there is one thing we could try," I say.

CHAPTER 56

A WEEK OF planning for a three-minute window.

That's how I explain it to Bergamo. I tell him I need to run the plan by Shen Wan first.

"Why?" asks Bergamo.

"Because it's Shen's window."

"What does that mean?"

"You'll see," I say. "Or maybe you won't. It will all depend on getting Shen's blessing."

I call Bergamo the following day. We got it, I tell him. Shen's on board.

A week of planning for a three-minute window.

One week later, at two thirty in the morning, I pick up Bergamo at a twenty-four-hour gas station a few blocks away from the Brooklyn Bridge entrance on Chambers Street. I'm driving a rental car with switched plates.

To make sure he wasn't followed, Bergamo took a taxi to a nearby

Greek diner, immediately exited through the kitchen, and got picked up by his driver, Nico, who then serpentined around the city for half an hour, running a couple of red lights along the way, before dropping him off at the gas station to meet me.

"Where is it?" Bergamo asks even before buckling his seat belt.

"Where else would it be? It's in the trunk," I say.

The idea of an original Picasso that just sold at auction for one hundred and forty-nine million dollars being stashed in the back of a dinged-up Toyota Camry from Avis clearly doesn't sit well with Bergamo. If his body language—mostly squirming—isn't enough of a giveaway, the tortured noise he lets out after we drive over a pothole leaves no doubt. He sounds like a wounded animal. This is killing him.

"We really couldn't take my car?" he asks.

"No. We really couldn't," I say. "The painting's fine, nice and snug in its case."

The drive out to the Brooklyn Shipyard takes about twenty minutes. We pass the main entrance with its brick gatehouse and go along the fenced-in container lot to another lot that is neither fenced in nor patrolled by any guards. It's basically a junkyard with a bunch of rusted-out forty-foot-high cube containers that made their last transatlantic voyage decades ago.

"This is perfect," says Bergamo, looking around as we pull in. "Creepy as shit, but perfect."

I cut the lights on the Camry and use the nearly full moon to slowly drive toward the water's edge. I stop next to a container flipped on its side and covered in graffiti, and when I shift into park, Bergamo reaches for the door handle.

"What are you doing?" I ask.

"I was getting out."

"What'd I tell you?"

"You didn't tell me anything."

"Exactly. So why would you think you should get out?" I hit the door locks, if only for effect. "Don't do anything unless I tell you to."

Bergamo nods, although he's clearly not happy about taking lip from me. Pissed is more like it. He mumbles something, nothing Hallmark would ever use in a card, but I'm not really listening to him. I'm not even looking at him. My eyes are trained about a hundred feet away on the water's edge.

A week of planning for a three-minute window.

Any minute now...

CHAPTER 57

BERGAMO CAN'T BEAR the silence. I can tell from his body language again—he can hardly sit still. "So what the hell are we doing?" he asks finally.

"We're waiting," I answer.

"For what?"

"The window."

This isn't Shen Wan's first rodeo at the Brooklyn Shipyard. Money and power can get you a lot of things, and in this case, it's three minutes of privacy. That's how long it takes for the surveillance cameras on the perimeter of the shipyard to reset after uploading the previous twenty-four hours of footage to the main server. It's a glitch in the matrix, something the outside security firm neglected to mention to shipyard management. But for the right price, one of the firm's technicians—supporting his family back in Gansu Province—was all too willing to share this intel with Shen Wan. Shen has utilized the loophole on a handful of occasions for his "special imports." The kind that don't show up on any manifest.

Like a couple of very rare artifacts from the Qing dynasty.

"Here he comes," I say.

Bergamo's looking for a car. "Where?" he asks.

I point out at the water. "There."

One if by land, two if by sea. The two vases. They were stashed on a dock in the shipyard upon their arrival from China yesterday and are being brought to us by boat within the three-minute window starting exactly at three in the morning, which is when the cameras aren't recording. I explain all this quickly to Bergamo.

"Well done," he says.

"It's not done yet." I pop the trunk. "Let's go."

Bergamo carries the case with the Picasso, hanging back a few steps behind me as we walk. "I'm going to need to see the vases first," he whispers.

"Second," I whisper back.

"Huh?"

"You're trading the painting for the vases. Not the other way around."

"Fair enough," he says. "First or second, as long as I see them."

"You will."

We get closer to the water, and the low hum of the motor on Shen Wan's Boston Whaler slices through the silence of the deserted lot. There's no dock, only a ladder. Shen cuts the engine and ties a rope around one of the rungs, and I drop to a knee and take the two steamer trunks that are housing the vases from him.

I set them down on the wood slats of a discarded pallet and glance at Bergamo. He looks like a kid on Christmas morning. Pure anticipation.

Shen climbs the ladder, greets me with a smile, and points at his

Rolex, keeping track of the three-minute window. "Seven seconds to spare," he says. "Lucky seven."

Shen and his boat are out of surveillance range when the cameras start rolling again at the shipyard, fresh off their reboot. We have all the time in the world now, if we want it.

We don't. No one says it; it's simply understood: *Let's be quick about this.* Bergamo lays the case on the pallet and opens it for Shen.

He looks at the painting, gives Bergamo a nod. "Beautiful," says Shen.

The word has barely left his mouth when the light hits his eyes. It's bright, blinding. I turn, trying to see where it's coming from, but the light is all I can see, a piercing white halo. No, make that two halos, side by side. They're like headlights except this isn't a car. It's two people. And, judging by their entrance, neither one is an angel.

"Beautiful indeed," says the first.

He dims his headlamp. He's still a silhouette but all any of us needs to see is the barrel of his gun as he steps forward.

We're being ambushed.

CHAPTER 58

THE SECOND ONE does the same thing as his partner, dimming his headlamp and stepping forward with his gun outstretched. He takes a few steps to his right to cut off any angles and ensure no one's making a run for it.

I don't even have to look at Bergamo to know that the thought of running isn't remotely close to entering his mind. He might be in shock. He might be scared for his life. But between the Picasso and the vases, there's more than two hundred million dollars' worth of art here, and there's no way in hell he's abandoning it. Not unless he absolutely has to. And not without at least trying to talk his way out of this.

"How much do you want?" Bergamo asks them.

The two smile behind their ski masks but only one answers. It's the one who spoke first, and it's clear he intends to have the last word.

"What do we want? Not much," he says. He points to the pallet. "Only what we can carry."

"You guys don't strike me as the art-collecting type," says Bergamo.

"We'll try not to be offended by that."

"What I mean," says Bergamo, "is that those things—the painting, what's in the trunks—they aren't easy to offload."

"Oh, crap. So you're saying we can't put them on eBay?"

Treating these guys like a couple of idiots isn't exactly the smartest strategy, and for the very first time since I've known Enzio Bergamo, he isn't sure what to say or do next.

Shen Wan calmly seizes on the silence. "I trust you know who you're stealing from," he says.

"I know who we're *not* stealing from. You're just the middleman. A very wealthy one, maybe, but still just the middleman."

"So you do know who I am," says Shen. "Which means you must also have some idea of who my partners are."

"Yes. They're even more wealthy than you, Mr. Shen. They'll be just fine."

Shen chuckles. "Is that what you really think? That what you're doing here will be only about money to them?"

The distance between Shen and their guns shortens. He's pissed both of them off. "Are you threatening us?"

"No," says Shen. "I'm trying to do you a favor."

"Is that so?"

"You don't have to do this. The two of you can turn around and go back to wherever it is you came from, no questions asked."

"That's your idea of a favor?"

"No," says Shen. "Letting you live is the favor."

"You have a strange idea of leverage, old man."

"It's not leverage," says Shen. "Do you really think this is the first time I've had a gun pointed at me?"

"Keep it up. Might just be your last."

I take a step forward, palms raised. "Let's all calm down a bit, shall we?"

"No one's talking to you, bitch. In fact, no more talking at all." He takes another step forward, point-blank range. "All of you, get down on your knees."

In the movies when people get told that, things don't usually end well.

"It's yours, all yours," says Bergamo, realizing the stakes have suddenly changed. "Just take them. Take everything. There's no need to—"

"Shut the fuck up." The first man cocks the gun's hammer. "I'm only going to say this one more time. *Down on your knees.*"

I look at Bergamo, pleading with my eyes: *Just do what he says.*

Shen drops to one knee, then two. I follow suit. Finally Bergamo does the same. We say nothing more as the second guy comes forward and closes the case holding the Picasso. He carries it to the edge of the water and comes back for the two vases in the trunks. After climbing down to Shen's boat, he speaks for the first time.

"Keys are on board," he says to the other man.

"In that case, we're good to go," says his partner. His arm is slowly bobbing through the air left to right, stopping and starting. He aims at each of us in turn, like eeny, meeny, miny, moe.

"You'll never get away with it," says Shen softly.

"I'm sorry. What was that?"

"Shen, please," I say. "Don't."

I know Shen hears me, but he's not listening. He clears his throat. "I said, you'll never get away with it."

The gun's no longer moving. The arm is straight, locked, aimed at Shen's chest.

"Maybe we will. Maybe we won't. But here's what I know for damn sure, old man. You won't be around to find out."

The echo of the shot drowns out my scream as Shen falls forward and hits the ground with a horrific thud.

"Jesus!" Bergamo cries.

"What was that? You've got something to say too?"

Bergamo stares at the barrel of the gun now pointed at him. His whole body is shaking. "No," he says. "Please. No."

"Yeah. I didn't think so." He nods at his partner, who's been watching from the top of the ladder. The boat's loaded up. Time to go. He walks past us, stepping over Shen's lifeless body, and stops next to the now-empty pallet. "I'm going to count to ten," he says. "If I can still see you, I'll shoot you."

CHAPTER 59

DO NOT WALK. *Run.*

Bergamo and I don't look back, not once. It's not a decision, it's instinct, a million years of Darwinism kicking in at once. Feet racing. Hearts racing faster.

"I can't breathe," says Bergamo as I start the engine, shift into drive, and speed away almost in one motion.

He's gasping from the sprint to my rented Camry but I know that's not what he means. He can't breathe because he's in shock.

I don't say anything. I focus on driving. Only when the shipyard disappears from my rearview mirror do my first words come. I'm talking to myself, thinking out loud. "They knew we'd be there, but how? We weren't followed. You and I didn't say anything over the phone. Hell, we never talked about any of this over the phone. All our texts were clean, spotless. No mention of the shipyard or Shen or anything. So how did they know? How? *How did they know?*"

"It was them. It had to be," says Bergamo. "The guys who were following me, right? The two guys in the white van?"

"I'm thinking the same thing."

"What about Shen, though?"

"What do you mean?" I ask.

"Whoever those two guys are, they knew beforehand how they were getting away. Shen's boat. Maybe it wasn't anything you and I did. Maybe they were also tracking Shen."

"You're right about the boat. They couldn't know about it from us."

I can feel Bergamo's anger building like a wave. It's overtaking his shock. "Why did he have to say anything? He should've just stayed quiet. What the hell was he thinking?"

"Stop it!" I yell at him. "Don't do that!"

"I know you were close to him, I get it. But he could've gotten us all killed."

I swerve off the road, jam the brakes. *"Shut up!"*

But he doesn't. He won't. "I don't really give a fuck about your feelings right now!" Bergamo yells back. "We need to focus. We need to figure out what we're going to do."

"There's only one thing we can do," I say. "We're going to the police."

I can hear the gears turning in his head. He's picturing how it would play out, start to finish. "No," he says. "We can't. We can't do that. We can't go to the police."

"Of course we can. We have to."

"Think about it."

"What's there to think about?"

"Everything."

"That night at Shen's casino, do you remember? When we were being followed afterward? That's all you wanted to do," I say. "Go to the police, go to the police."

"That was different and you know it."

"No. *This* is different. Shen was just killed right before our eyes."

"Yeah, I know. I was there, for Christ's sake," he says. "But what the hell are we going to tell them?"

"How about the truth?"

"Oh, really? Suddenly now that's what you want to do—tell them everything we've been up to, the whole plan?"

"It doesn't have to be everything."

He looks at me like I'm a dog chasing its tail. "I thought you were smart," he says. "Do you want to end up like your father? Because I sure don't."

"My father's in prison because he didn't tell the truth when he had the chance. *That's* why he's there, remember?"

"Yeah, all too well. But that was about money."

"And this isn't?" I ask.

"There's a dead body this time. Money's one thing, murder's another."

"What are you proposing?"

"We lie low," he says. "Just like we were doing."

"That's because we were being followed. Or, rather, you were," I say. "Everything's changed now."

"All the more reason to go about our lives as if nothing's happened. Because that's the least suspicious thing we can do."

"But all of our planning, the work we put in...I know you're covered on the Picasso with the insurance money, but—"

"After tonight, I don't give two shits about those two vases," he says. "And if we can get through this, consider your father's debt paid."

"I don't know, though. It might be a big risk to go to the police, but not going might be even bigger."

Bergamo stays silent. He knows I'm no longer talking to him. It's just me and my conscience. He also knows that he's already played his trump card: my father's debt to him. It's gone — *poof* — as long as I play this his way. That's twenty-five million dollars.

Enzio Bergamo has my number.

CHAPTER 60

THIS IS ME going about my life as if nothing happened.

I do everything as I normally would for the next couple of days. I even do the one thing I really don't want to do but can't avoid. I have lunch with Smarmy Waxman.

"May I start you off with something to drink?" asks our waiter at Le Chanteclair in Midtown, standing poised with pen and pad.

Smarmy lowers the wine list that he's buried his face in for the past few minutes and smiles at me. I'm getting creepy-uncle vibes. "You know, we have a very strict rule at Echelon about consuming alcohol during the workday." He leans forward and says, his voice dropping to a whisper, "But I won't tell the boss if you won't."

He thinks he's hilarious. It doesn't help that ever since he became CEO, every Echelon employee has been laughing at his dumb jokes in the name of career advancement. I'm already a VP at twenty-two but my dignity has no problem playing along.

"That's funny," I say, laughing.

Smarmy orders a bottle of Brunello, which I assume is ridiculously expensive given the way our waiter genuflects before bringing over a decanter.

"I'm glad we could do this, Halston," he says after we're alone again.

"Me too," I say, laughing for real on the inside. "Me too."

I don't expect him to get the joke. He's not supposed to. The guy is leveraging his power and position in the hope of getting into my pants. It's as if he were in a coma during the entire #MeToo movement.

Before I can even think of what to say next, we're interrupted. But not by our waiter. Not by any waiter. It's not even one person; it's two. They're dressed in ill-fitting, off-the-rack suits. One guy is standing slightly in front of the other, and he does all the talking. He makes no apology for interrupting.

"Are you Halston Graham?" he asks.

I look at him. I look at the two of them. They clearly don't work for the restaurant. In that case—"That depends," I say. "Who wants to know?"

I couldn't have teed him up better. This is the moment that all FBI agents must absolutely relish—getting to whip out the badge and hold it up like a gin card.

"I'm Agent Bryant," he says. He points to his partner. "And this is Agent Daniels."

"What's this about?" I ask.

"Yes," says Smarmy, echoing me. "What's this about?"

"Ms. Graham, we're hoping to get your cooperation with an ongoing Bureau investigation. We have some questions we'd like to ask you."

"Here? *Now?*"

"We went to your office and were told that you were here at lunch," he says. "As for the timing, yes, I'm afraid it's now. But it doesn't have to be here. In fact, we'd prefer that it not be."

"Where would it be?" I ask.

"At our field office downtown."

Smarmy goes from zero to irate in an instant. "You've got to be kidding me. You two march in here in the middle of our—"

"I'm sorry, who are you?" asks Agent Bryant.

"I'm Charles Waxman, CEO of the Echelon auction house and Ms. Graham's employer. And as far as I can tell, you're interrupting our lunch unnecessarily."

"I assure you, Mr. Waxman, we would never be standing here unnecessarily."

"Can you at least tell us what your investigation concerns?" I ask.

"As I said, I think it's best if we do this down at our office," says Agent Bryant.

Smarmy takes out his cell and holds it up like a grenade. "If you'd like to watch me call my lawyer, be my guest. But I can already tell you what he's going to say. If you don't inform Ms. Graham what this is about, she'll be finishing her lunch. Unless you're planning to arrest her, which I don't think you are."

"You're right," says Agent Bryant. "There'll be no handcuffs today, and hopefully not ever, for Ms. Graham. She's not the target of the investigation."

"Then who is?" asks Smarmy.

The two agents exchange glances as if giving each other the okay. "It's Enzio Bergamo," says Agent Bryant.

"Bergamo?"

"I take it you know him?"

"I do," says Smarmy. "What's he being investigated for?"

"I'm not at liberty to say, but you're welcome to ask him yourself if you'd like," says Agent Bryant. He pivots back to me. "In the meantime, it's important that we ask you some questions about him, Ms. Graham. Time is of the essence."

"Yeah, well, it can stay of the essence a little longer," says Smarmy, lifting his cell to his ear.

"What are you doing?" I ask.

"You can't talk to these clowns without a lawyer. I'm getting you one. Either mine or one from the firm."

"That won't be necessary," I say. "Please, you can put down the phone."

"You're entitled to have an attorney present," says Smarmy. He jabs his finger at Agent Bryant. "Go ahead, tell her, hotshot. She's allowed to have an attorney with her, right?"

Agent Bryant nods. "Damn skippy," he says. "You're welcome to have a lawyer with you, Ms. Graham. In fact, for your protection, I'd recommend it."

"I understand," I say. "But I don't need anyone's protection."

CHAPTER 61

I FOLLOW AGENTS Bryant and Daniels out of the restaurant. They don't say anything to me; I don't say anything to them.

Until we're outside.

"Seriously?" I turn to Agent Bryant. *"Damn skippy?"*

He laughs. "What? You don't like that expression?"

"Who says that? Like, on what planet does anyone say that?" I ask.

"Agent Bryant of the FBI's planet, apparently," he says.

"I rest my case. You don't exist."

"I did to your boss just now. He was thoroughly convinced."

"You're right, he was," I say. "Well done. What do you think, Agent Daniels?"

"Better than well done. We were awesome in there."

"Says the guy who didn't actually say anything," I point out.

"I've always been the strong, silent type. That's what people tell me."

"No, what people tell you is that you look like Ray Romano on steroids."

He shakes his head. "I still don't see the resemblance."

"You're in denial."

"I am not."

"You just denied being in denial," I say. We keep walking. "Where are you guys parked?"

They're just around the next corner, which means it's a good time to take one last look over my shoulder and make sure Smarmy didn't decide to follow us. I can picture him bolting out of the restaurant leveling fresh threats.

But the coast is clear. No Smarmy. There's still a half a bottle of Brunello at the table to be drunk. If he can't have me, he can at least have that.

Then he'll hopefully do the one thing I absolutely need him to do. It's what this whole charade today is about: getting him to call Bergamo and ask why the hell he's being investigated by the FBI and how on earth it involves me. Actually, forget the Brunello. Smarmy's probably making the call this very moment.

We turn the corner and I immediately see the limousine.

"Thanks, guys," I say. "My brother and I will be in touch."

They're not FBI agents. Their badges are as fake as their names. I stop at the limo and they keep right on walking. Their job is done.

I slide into the back seat. He's sitting across from me, drinking another cognac.

"You look pretty good for a dead guy," I say.

Shen Wan smiles, alive and well. "Are you ready to have some real fun now?" he asks.

CHAPTER 62

YOU JUST DON'T barge into the office of the US Attorney for the Eastern District of New York and demand to speak to the chief of the criminal division. You have to make an appointment.

And not just anyone can make an appointment. You have to be somebody, a big shot. I don't qualify but thankfully Shen Wan does.

There's a reason his casino has never been raided: Shen Wan is a one-man diplomatic back channel to the entire Chinese politburo. The US government looks to him from time to time to deliver sensitive messages. In return, it looks the other way on his various "business ventures."

"Shen, I was thinking," I say. "Maybe you want to pop in with me? You know, to make the introduction?"

"It will be fine," Shen assures me. "Just do your thing."

"You're right. I've got this." And yet I'm still not reaching for the door. I remain glued to the back seat of his limo.

Shen's chuckling a bit. "I think I've discovered young Halston's Achilles' heel," he says. "Contending with an older, accomplished woman who happens to be equally as smart as her. Men are much easier to manipulate, aren't they?"

"Not all men. Not even most men. Only the ones who let their libidos get in the way of logic."

"Are you sure that isn't most men?" He points to the door, smiling. "Now stop stalling and get out of the car. I don't want to miss my flight."

"It's your plane, Shen. I'm pretty sure your pilot will wait for you."

Shen's flying on his jet back to mainland China. He has business to attend to. There's also the fact that Bergamo thinks he's dead, and it's easier to lie low for a few weeks when you're sixty-eight hundred miles away.

"Good luck, Lucky Seven," he says.

It takes me about five minutes to get from the limo, up the steps, and through security to the US attorney's office in Brooklyn. From there it's another five minutes getting a visitor's pass and taking the elevator up to the third floor, where I check in with an assistant in the lobby. He instructs me to have a seat. Shen may have gotten me the meeting, but it's not as if Elise Joyce, chief of the criminal division, is the least bit happy about it. Lest there be any doubt of that, it's an hour before her assistant comes for me.

"You're still waiting to see Ms. Joyce, right?" the guy asks as if he's rubbing it in. "I can take you back to see her now."

Not all the way back, though.

Elise Joyce is standing in the middle of a long hallway next to an empty conference room. She's reading something in a file. Her assistant dumps me in front of her without so much as a word.

Joyce barely looks up from the file. "So you're my three o'clock favor, huh?"

"It's more like four o'clock now," I say.

That certainly gets her attention. I immediately regret being a smart-ass, but it's hard to suppress a reflex.

"That's funny," says Joyce, not laughing. At least she's looking at me now. "So why are you here?"

I glance around. We're the opposite of alone. There are at least a half a dozen staffers within earshot.

"Is there a place we can talk more privately?" I ask.

"Yes, there is."

I assume she's going to suggest her office or the conference room, the door to which is less than three feet away. She does neither. Elise Joyce simply stares at me, not saying another word.

"So, yes? There's a place?" I sound like a parrot, repeating myself. "There's somewhere we can talk more privately?"

"Yes, there's a place. No, we're not going there," she says. "Not until I know."

"Know what?"

"That you're not wasting my time."

Elise Joyce looks tall on television. She's even taller in person. Everything I've read about her is playing out in this very moment. She doesn't suffer fools easily, and is 100 percent the right man for her job—all the more so because she's a woman. An extremely attractive one, at that. No wonder she's dead set on becoming governor.

In three seconds, I know, this meeting will be over before it ever begins.

Unless I convince her otherwise.

CHAPTER 63

"ENZIO BERGAMO," I say.

"What about him?" asks Joyce.

"Do you know who he is?"

"I can't afford his clothes, but, yeah, of course I know who he is." She impatiently places a hand on her hip. "Once again, what about him?"

"He's using his company to launder money for the Lugieri crime family," I say.

Joyce narrows her eyes. She tilts her head, processing every word, but we both know what matters most in what I just told her is the name, and I don't mean Bergamo's.

"Lugieri, huh? Dominick Lugieri?"

I nod. "The one and only."

Bringing down the likes of Dominick Lugieri would be a major career coup for any criminal division chief at any US attorney's office. But for Elise Joyce, it's personal. *Very* personal. For years, she's had Lugieri in her crosshairs. Numerous prosecution attempts, no fewer than three trials. All to no avail.

"Follow me," she says, turning on her heel.

I fall in step behind her. "Okay."

We don't go into the conference room. We walk straight back to her office, where she closes the door and immediately points at the chair across from her desk. Looks like we're officially talking in private.

"How much?" she asks. "Bergamo and Lugieri. How much have they laundered?"

"Over two hundred million," I say.

She slides the keyboard on her desk to the side, lands her elbows on a scuffed-up leather blotter, and leans forward. Her eyes are trying to read my soul. "How do you know this?"

"That's not really relevant, is it?"

"It will be."

"But not yet," I say. "All you care about at this moment is whether I can prove it."

"So can you?"

"I wouldn't be here if I couldn't."

"But let me guess," she says. "You need my help."

"To get the evidence? No. Not really," I say. "Just set me up with a wire."

"You're that close to Bergamo?" she asks skeptically.

"I am."

"How is it that you're—" She stops, realizing that how and why I'm close to Bergamo isn't important. What matters is what I can get him to say on that wire. She changes her question. "How fast?"

"Shouldn't take more than a week," I say.

It's the right answer. Joyce leans back in her chair almost as if bracing herself for what comes next. She knows I'm not sitting in front of her purely out of a sense of civic duty.

"Okay. So what do you want?" she asks.

"You know what I want," I tell her.

"Yes, I do. But that's not something I can guarantee. I *can* promise you that—"

"Do you think I'm here to wrap pinkies with you, Ms. Joyce?" *Girl fight.*

"I know you think you have a little leverage right now, Halston, but you don't," she says. "Not one bit."

"I know what I have, and I know what I can deliver. And if you want it, you'll need to give me what I want and put it in writing."

"That's impossible. I can't do that."

"Of course you can," I say. "You're the boss."

"And you're in way over your head. I can force you to tell me everything you know. You understand that, right?"

"Yes, you can. But the one thing you can't do is force me to collect evidence for you by wearing that wire."

It's not a checkmate. It's more like a stalemate. I'm putting her in a tough spot. Like a used-car salesman, a US attorney doesn't do written guarantees. Not for what I'm asking.

But did I mention how *badly* Elise Joyce wants to bring down Dominick Lugieri?

She leans forward again, her elbows grinding into that desk blotter. "The evidence would need to be airtight."

"I understand," I say.

"The legal equivalent of a layup."

"Better yet, a slam dunk."

She cracks the slightest of smiles. It's not what I said, it's the confidence with which I said it.

My dad taught me that, told me time and time again: *Be confident or be nothing.*

"If you can deliver what I need, then you have my word…and I'll put it in writing," says Elise Joyce. "Your father will be a free man."

CHAPTER 64

"HI, DADDY."

"Hi, sweetheart."

"How do you feel?" I ask.

"Let's not talk about me today," says my father. His tired eyes stray for a moment to the one small glass-brick window in the visiting room. It lets sunlight in but you can't see out. "Tell me about your week. What have you been up to?"

"Not too much," I say.

"Whatever it is, it has to be more exciting than anything I'm doing."

"Well, there is something. I don't know how exciting it is, but I'm definitely a bit proud of myself. Remember how I mentioned that I wanted to read *Ulysses*?"

"Yes, it was one of your New Year's resolutions," he says.

"That's right. That and getting a cat."

"I'm guessing you still haven't gotten a cat."

"No, but I did finally read *Ulysses*."

"The whole thing?"

"Every word," I say. "You were absolutely right. That Joyce is one hell of a writer."

"So you liked it?"

"It's everything you told me it would be."

"Yes, Joyce can be quite the challenge. Good for you. Well done," he says. "So what's next on your reading list?"

"Next? *Ulysses* is over two hundred and fifty thousand words. Yes, I googled that, thank you very much. I need a break from reading. I'm going to binge-watch *The Wire*," I say. "Have you heard of that show?"

"Yes, absolutely."

"But I'm guessing you haven't seen it."

"Apparently the prison library doesn't have it," says my father. "Something about the way it portrays the police."

"Ha. As if anyone in here could have a lower opinion of law enforcement," I say.

"It's a good show, though, huh?"

"I'll tell you what—next week, I'll give you a full recap. How does that sound?"

My father looks at the small window again, at the light filtering through the glass brick. He smiles ever so slightly. "It sounds like a plan, sweetheart."

CHAPTER 65

THE STREAM OF calls from Bergamo begins that evening. They're not from his number and he doesn't leave a message, but I know it's him. He's using a burner phone. It's the right move but he's watched one too many spy movies. People are most vulnerable when they convince themselves they're being clever.

The calls continue into the next day. Instead of every few hours, he's ringing me every hour, like a bell tower. When I call in sick at Echelon, the messages from Smarmy start pouring in as well. First there's a voicemail, then a slew of texts. I can all but hear the conversation Smarmy had with Bergamo, pumping him for information under the guise of doing him a favor. *Just a heads-up, Enzio, that you're the target of a criminal investigation. Now tell me why.*

Smarmy probably thought he'd have the chance to ask me directly what those two feds at the restaurant wanted to know about Bergamo and to what extent the two of us were connected. For sure he didn't learn much from Bergamo. Enzio and his fresh new burner phone aren't about to share anything with Smarmy or anyone else.

I make both men wait. Men absolutely hate waiting.

For the second day I call in sick to Echelon. I don't respond to Smarmy's continued barrage of messages but the time comes for me to rendezvous with Bergamo. I text him. Burner or no burner, I have no intention of relaying anything over the phone. This makes Bergamo even more anxious to find out what's happening. He texts me back in all caps that he needs to see me **IMMEDIATELY.**

We take the same precautions, cloak-and-daggering around the city for a while on our own before Bergamo picks me up at noon along the east-west transverse through Central Park at Sixty-Fifth Street. He's in his company limousine with the same driver, Nico, behind the wheel. A stretch limo isn't exactly subtle but the tinted windows provide all the privacy we need.

"Hang here for a bit," he tells Nico and raises the partition. It's now just me, Bergamo, and an air of desperation.

"*What is it?* What do they have on us? For Christ's sake, what are they able to prove?" he asks like an impatient child, albeit one wearing a suit, shoes, and watch that easily total fifty grand.

"Relax," I tell him. "It was a ruse."

"What do you mean?"

"You're not the target of an FBI investigation. Smarmy is."

"Smarmy?"

I laugh. "Sorry. That's my nickname for him. It's Charles Waxman they're investigating."

Oh, the relief on Bergamo's face. But, still, he's confused. Of course he is. How could he not be? The FBI's targeting the head of Echelon and yet they're telling him they're going after someone else?

"Wait," says Bergamo. "At the restaurant, why did the agents—"

"Say it was you? Because they're trying to give Waxman a false sense of security while getting closer to him," I say.

"But why?"

"Do you remember that woman at the auction? The one who was trying to outbid you?"

"She almost did," he says.

"*Almost* is the operative word."

"What do you mean?"

"She was never going to win. She was a shill," I say. "She was planted."

"By Waxman?"

"That's right. Smarmy's been rigging the game, jacking up purchase prices to reap higher premiums. Apparently this wasn't the first time he's done it, or so the agents tell me."

"Why would the FBI involve you, though?" he asks.

"Because they learned I'm the new teacher's pet, which means I'm in a prime position to get the smoking-gun evidence they need. I'm literally a few doors down from Waxman's office now. I have access to files. Proximity."

"They were that sure you'd cooperate with them?"

"The short answer is no," I say.

"I mean, in a way, you'd be risking your career."

"Yeah, but I'm the girl who ran after the guy who stole your Picasso. That's their thinking. What wouldn't I risk in the name of doing the right thing?"

Bergamo leans back, taking it all in. "That son of a bitch Waxman," he says. "Rigging his auctions, huh?"

"Yep."

"How'd they even come to suspect him?"

"Turns out the woman Waxman hired to jack up the bidding is a high-priced escort who was just caught for tax evasion. To save herself, she sacrificed Waxman, sold him out."

"Talk about getting screwed," says Bergamo, laughing. "Jesus, I really thought this was all about—"

I cut him off, quickly raising an index finger to my lips: *Shh*. "I know. How could you not think it was about you? They literally used your name at the restaurant, told us you were the target," I say. "But that's only because they can connect me with you."

Bergamo stares at me. He's confused all over again. Why did I cut him off? Why didn't I want him to mention anything we've been up to?

This is why.

I tug down on my blouse, showing him. I'm wearing a wire.

CHAPTER 66

HE DOESN'T KNOW what to say or do. He's frozen. Speechless.

That same index finger covering my lips is now spinning in the air like one of those exercise wheels in a hamster cage. I'm telling Bergamo, imploring him, *Keep going! Don't stop! They're listening. We need to keep the conversation moving.*

"Anyway, so that's the story," I say. "Obviously, everything I just told you I shouldn't have, but I knew Waxman would be calling you after I got taken in for questioning and I didn't think it was fair that the FBI was using you to get to him."

Bergamo's still staring at me in shock, his brain trying to wrap itself around the fact that I'm wearing a wire. My finger's spinning even faster. *C'mon, c'mon, c'mon! This can't be a monologue, Enzio, you have to engage with me. This is a performance.*

He snaps out of it. "I...um...appreciate it," he says.

Acting-wise, it's not exactly Academy Award–caliber, but it's a start.

"Here's the thing, though," I say. "You've got to play it cool with Waxman. You can't let on that you know anything. If you do, the FBI will know it came from me."

"Sure. I understand."

"Do you, though?"

"Yes," he says. "I get it."

He thinks I'm doubting him, but I'm not; I'm stalling as I quickly type on my phone. "Okay, good. I believe you," I say, leaning over to show him my screen.

Ask if u can give me ride home

He nods, starting to get the hang of it. "So where can I drop you off, Halston? Do you want a ride back to your apartment?"

"Actually, I thought I'd visit the zoo since I'm up here. It's been years. I used to love going to see the sea lions as a kid."

Bergamo lowers the partition a few inches, clearing his throat. "Nico," he says. "Central Park Zoo."

The partition slides back up, and I talk a little more about the sea lions and how watching them remains one of my favorite memories. I'm going on and on. I'm killing time. Plus I'm preventing Bergamo from slipping up and saying something he shouldn't.

Within minutes we're pulling up to the zoo. I type quickly again on my phone, show him the screen. We say our goodbyes, and I watch from the curb as the limo drives off.

"How much is admission?" I ask the woman behind the glass at the zoo's ticket booth. The prices are posted two feet from my head but I have my reasons for playing dumb.

Soon, ticket in hand, I enter the zoo and head directly to the bathroom. From the bathroom I make a beeline for the exit and return to where Bergamo dropped me off. I'd told him to circle back in five minutes, and his limo is there waiting. I get back in and toss the wire with its transmitter into Bergamo's lap. The small strip of tape, fresh off my skin, is still attached to the microphone.

"What the hell is going on?" he asks. "What the hell are you doing?"

"Helping you," I answer. "Helping us."

"Why are you wearing a wire?"

"Because apparently you got greedy, which would have been fine if you hadn't also gotten sloppy."

"I have no idea what you're—"

"Don't even try that with me." I point at the transmitter in his lap. "Do you realize the risk I'm taking?"

He doesn't, not fully. Everything's happening so fast, he needs more time to think it through, but the headline should be a no-brainer: The FBI has it in for him. They know something. It's big.

"How much did they tell you?" he asks.

"Enough. They know you're laundering money for Dominick Lugieri. They just can't prove it beyond a reasonable doubt," I say. "And, by the way, are you insane? Getting mixed up with a guy like Lugieri?"

"You didn't seem to have a problem when it was Anton Nikolov. The Bulgarians, the Italians—what's the difference?"

"You were just as stupid to be in bed with Anton Nikolov. All I did was leverage it after the fact."

"You mean all *we* did." He catches himself. All this talk of connections. "Wait, hold on," he says. "How did the FBI even get to you?"

"How do you think? Through you. You were under surveillance and suddenly I showed up in the picture...literally. And not even those grainy black-and-white shots. Crystal-clear color. Video too. But they're so desperate to get their smoking gun on Lugieri that they're giving me a pass on whatever it is you and I are up to. As long as I cooperate."

"You actually trust them?"

"Of course not. But what choice do I have? What choice do *we* have?" I ask. "What matters now is making sure they keep trusting me."

"So what are you proposing?"

"For starters, how about a thank-you?"

Bergamo looks down at the transmitter again. I could have kept it on, trapped him, gotten him to incriminate himself. Instead, it's in his lap, no longer recording.

"Thank you," he says.

"As for what I'm proposing, it's simple. We need to give them Lugieri without giving you up."

"And how do we do that? More important, how do we do that without Lugieri finding out? Because if he does, I'm a dead man."

"Exactly," I say. "So whatever we do, it has to be good. Really good."

"You already have a plan?"

"No, not yet. But I will."

"When?" he asks.

"As soon as you tell me what exactly you do for him."

CHAPTER 67

MALCOLM HAD GAINED Dominick Lugieri's trust. He'd done it from the ground up, the only way it could be done, by being willing to hit harder and bleed more than anyone else in the ranks.

The best part was that Malcolm had made Lugieri look every bit the boss that he was and needed to be. After all, bringing in a non-Italian pretty boy wasn't exactly a natural fit for the family. Lugieri clearly knew what he was doing.

"Are you ready?" he asked Malcolm. He had summoned him back to his private dining room at Osteria Contorni, but this time Malcolm was invited to sit down with Lugieri and talk man to man. *Uomo a uomo.*

"Yeah, sure. I'm ready," said Malcolm. If you're the right guy for the job, you don't need to ask what the job is before agreeing to it.

Lugieri smiled, satisfied.

"I have this problem, right? It's one that usually only politicians have. Optics," said Lugieri. "As of late we've been using someone in the public eye to clean our money. The fact that he's a well-known person actually makes it easier. People like him travel a little more freely. Other people don't expect him to be associated with a man like me. But we've got a problem."

"Optics," said Malcolm.

"That's right. For every drop we make with him, every transfer, whoever it is we send from the crew stands out. You know what I mean? It doesn't matter how nice the suit — if you work for me, you look a certain way. But now you work for me."

"Who's the guy?" asked Malcolm.

"Enzio Bergamo, the fashion designer. You know who he is?"

"Yeah, of course."

"Your job is about protection. Protecting Bergamo and, more important, protecting us, the money. We started small with him, kind of like on a trial basis. Now we're stepping it up. At least, I want to. Tens of millions of dollars we're talking about. You're my armored truck, Malcolm. Thing is, you can't stand out like one, know what I'm saying? Not with the outlets that Bergamo uses to wash."

"Overseas, right?"

"Right. Paris, mainly. Not my backyard, for sure, and there are a shitload of motherfuckers to watch out for. Terrorists, drug cartels, and don't even get me started on the Ethiopians. So, like I said, are you ready?"

Malcolm watched as Lugieri waited for him to repeat his same confident answer: Yeah, sure, of course he was ready. But it wasn't coming.

"What is it?" asked Lugieri. "What's the concern?"

"Hopefully, there isn't one," said Malcolm. "But how well do you know Bergamo?"

"Well enough."

"So you trust him?"

"Situations like this, it's not really about trust."

"I guess what I'm asking is, how much do you really know about him?"

"How much do I need to know about him? He understands that if he screws me over, I kill him," said Lugieri. "Simple as that."

"But what if you never found out he was screwing you over? Or maybe when you do find out, it's too late."

"Too late for what?"

"In Afghanistan we never went through a door without knowing what was on the other side," said Malcolm. "Bots, drones, infrared, paid informants—we did whatever it took to find out. Because once you walk through the door, there's no turning back."

"What are you proposing?"

"Let me find out exactly what's behind the door with Bergamo. There's probably nothing to worry about. But just in case there is."

Lugieri mulled it over, running a finger up and down the side of his face. "He can't get wind that you're sniffing around him, though," he said.

"He won't."

"How can you be sure?"

"Did you?" asked Malcolm.

"Did I what?"

"Know that I was sniffing around you?"

"Oh, yeah?" Lugieri chuckled. "What'd you learn?"

Malcolm rattled off a nine-digit number.

"That's not my Social Security number," Lugieri said.

"No," said Malcolm. "It's Enzio Bergamo's."

Lugieri cocked his head as it dawned on him. "You already knew that Bergamo's been cleaning money for us? How'd you know that?"

"It's what I do."

"And I should do what I do. I should kill you for that."

"But you won't."

"You're right, I won't. That's the reason I brought you in, that type of mindset. So go ahead, do your checking on Bergamo. But make no goddamn mistake: From now on, what you know about me is only what I choose to tell you," said Lugieri. "Otherwise I'll kill you for sure."

CHAPTER 68

I SHOW UP unannounced at Bergamo's office above his flagship store in SoHo. He's pissed I didn't give him any heads-up and worries I might have been followed.

In another minute or so, these will be the least of his problems.

"Which do you want first, the good news or the bad?" I ask.

Before he answers, he stands up from behind his massive desk, comes around, and closes his door. As far as his two assistants out front are concerned, I'm here on behalf of Echelon.

"Start with the good news," he says, sitting back down. His desk chair, with its tufted leather and thick armrests, is like a throne. "Then maybe what follows won't seem so bad."

Fair enough. "The good news is that Elise Joyce got her search warrant."

Bergamo looks like a little boy whenever he frowns. "I was hoping for something better."

"Like what?" I ask.

"I don't know. I thought you told me that what I gave you would be enough for her to get the warrant."

"No, I *hoped* it would be enough, and not just for her but, more important, for the judge."

"Whatever," he says, rolling his eyes. "So when's it going to happen?"

"The raid? I'm not sure," I tell him. "They don't want Lugieri to be home at the time, that's all I know."

"That's easy. Just raid his house around dinner. The guy's out at that damn Italian restaurant almost every night," he says. "So what's the bad news?"

I glance around his office, hesitating. Near the windows are about a dozen full-body mannequins wearing Bergamo's latest dresses in preparation for his upcoming fall fashion show. The dresses are beautiful but the vibe is a bit unsettling; it's as if we have an audience.

"This morning while meeting with Elise Joyce, I overheard something I wasn't supposed to," I say. "One of the other attorneys in the room screwed up and let something slip. According to the FBI, someone in Lugieri's crew has been doing some digging on you."

"The FBI?"

"Their cyberterrorism unit or whatever they call it."

"I don't follow," he says.

"I don't blame you. It's crazy how they made the connection, but apparently whoever's doing the digging around your offshore accounts is using some pretty sophisticated software—as in military grade."

"And this guy, whoever he is, works for Lugieri?"

"Yeah."

Bergamo's shaking his head. "I still don't follow."

"Does Dominick Lugieri have any reason not to trust you?" I ask.

"He's a mob boss. He doesn't trust *anyone* outside his family."

"You know what I mean. You've given me account numbers and everything else Joyce could ask for to get her search warrant." I've been standing in front of his desk the whole time, and now I edge closer, my eyes boring into his. "She doesn't have to know, but I do. Are you skimming from Lugieri?"

"No," he says. "Of course not."

"Bullshit."

"Why are you bothering to ask if you're so sure?"

"Because I need to hear it from you," I say.

"What difference would it make? It doesn't affect you."

"No? What, you think the guy digging around in your finances wouldn't want to see who you're keeping company with these days, if there's anyone new?"

"You're giving yourself too much credit, Halston. You're just some kid working for an auction house. If anything Lugieri would think you're my..." He laughs. *"Goomah."*

"I'm glad you think this is funny."

"Relax. I told you, I've passed the audition. If there were any red flags, Lugieri would've found them. He didn't, which is why the next drop is what it is, a huge sum. He trusts me."

"I thought you said he doesn't trust anyone outside the family."

"Call it what you want," he says. "Lugieri's handing me eighty million dollars in cash to clean for him. What more do you need to know?"

Nothing more, Enzio. You've said enough for now.

CHAPTER 69

I WALK HALF a block south from Bergamo's offices, turn the corner, and stop at the back of the large delivery van parked at the curb, a repurposed UPS truck that's been painted white. I knock three times—twice fast, pause, then once. The doors split open immediately and I step inside, right back where I started. I'm a human boomerang.

"Did you get it?" I ask.

"Yeah," says Devin, the tech who wired me up. He's at the console wearing a backward Yankees cap, fidgeting with some knob. "We got it."

"The hell we did," says Elise Joyce.

"What's that supposed to mean?" I ask.

"You know exactly what it means. You could've gotten more from him. A lot more."

The fact that the chief of the criminal division of a US attorney's office is taking part in a field mission—that she's holed up in a surveillance van, no less—tells you all you need to know about how much Elise Joyce wants Dominick Lugieri's head on a platter. I can understand her impatience.

I just can't give in to it.

"More? *More?* You now have Bergamo on record saying he cleans money for Lugieri," I say. "He even said how much the next drop will be, eighty million."

"Yeah, but we don't know when and we don't know where," says Joyce.

"That's right, we don't. *Not yet.* That's what comes next."

"It could've come today."

"Bergamo's a lot of things, but he's not an idiot," I say. "All it takes is me asking one too many questions."

Devin, the tech, had outfitted me with a blazer that had a mic hidden in a button and the transmitter sewn into the lining. I take off the blazer and hand it to him while Joyce watches me with a suspicious eye. Already she's revved up her PR machine—a little tidbit of an online story here and a profile in the *Times* lined up there, an attempt to catch a massive media wave of attention that will propel her to the governor's mansion once she finally brings down Lugieri.

Female crime fighters make the best political candidates. Just ask any focus group. Elise Joyce sure has.

"If I didn't know better, Halston, I'd think you were stalling," she says.

"Thankfully, you do know better."

"I'm serious."

"So am I," I say. "Believe me, no one wants this to happen more than I do. You understand that, right?"

It's not my words that linger in the air, it's what I don't say. The subtext. The reason I came to Elise Joyce in the first place. This is a quid pro quo. I'm giving her what she wants in order to get what

I want. It's Dominick Lugieri's imprisonment in exchange for my father's release. The sooner the better.

But if Bergamo's no idiot, neither is Joyce. She's right, I am stalling. Just a little.

When you have only one shot at doing what should be impossible, the timing has to be perfect.

CHAPTER 70

JOYCE WANTS TO talk more, strategize, plan my next encounter with Bergamo. She has ideas, thoughts, everything short of a stack of color-coded index cards crammed with bullet points. Her entire focus is on recording as much dirt on Lugieri as possible.

But I tell her I have to go, that I need to be at work. It's the truth. What I don't tell her is why.

Smarmy's latest voicemail was waiting for me hours earlier when I woke up. You can ghost a guy like him for only so long. Eventually he figured out a way to get me in the office. Charles Waxman ain't the CEO of Echelon for nothing.

"I've been looking through your file," he announced after the beep. He spoke slowly, ominously, to ensure I paid attention to every word of his message. "Apparently our head of HR has been keeping a few secrets about you, Halston Graham. I mean Greer."

Really, Jacinda? In my file? You couldn't leave my past alone, or at least keep it inside your head? You had to put everything down in writing?

Apparently.

So off I go to meet Smarmy face to face. His office at noon, he told me. He ended his message with "Don't be late."

I'm not. I'm standing in his doorway at noon on the dot. He smiles broadly at the sight of me because that's what men like him do when they have the illusion of leverage.

"I want to apologize," I say after he motions me in. I close the door to his office even though he doesn't tell me to.

"Sorry for what, exactly?" he asks. "Not showing up to work? Not returning any of my calls? Or not being who you say you are?"

"I guess you can take your pick," I say.

"I intend to." He points for me to sit, not in the chair facing his desk but on his casting couch against the far wall. That figures.

I remain standing.

"If Jacinda wrote that in my file, she's wrong," I say. "I never lied about my name. I legally changed it to Graham."

"I know you did. But we'll get to that in a second. Now, please," he says, pointing again at his couch.

As soon as I sit, he walks over from his desk and sits in the armchair catty-corner to me, his bended knees only inches from mine. I can smell his mouthwash and cologne, a nauseating combo of mint and musk.

"I know you're curious about Bergamo," I say.

"*Curious?* No. Tonight when I go to dinner at Le Bernardin, I'll be curious about what the specials are. Bergamo is a member of Echelon who just made the single largest auction purchase in our history, and now he's being investigated by the FBI," he says, jaw tightening. I can see the tendons in his neck. "Believe me, I'm a little more than *curious*."

It's as if I've flipped a switch inside him. Or maybe this was his plan all along—simmering anger that builds into a rage.

"I understand," I say.

"Do you? Because it sure as hell doesn't seem that way. You have an obligation to Echelon. You have an obligation to me."

"I promised I wouldn't say anything."

"To whom did you promise that? The FBI?"

"What am I supposed to do? They said not to talk about the investigation with anyone."

"Of course they said that. But they didn't make you sign anything, did they? More important, they're not the ones who sign your paycheck," he says. "Or maybe you'd prefer to stop getting one."

"That's really not fair."

"Life isn't fair. But you already know that, Halston Greer. Why else would you try to hide from your past, from who you really are?"

If looks could kill, he'd be dead. "Leave my family out of this," I say. "And I told you, I didn't lie about my name."

"I wouldn't care if you did. What I care about is loyalty. That's what got you promoted," he says. "I'd hate to see it be the reason you get fired."

"Lucky for you, you don't have to," I tell him.

"What's that supposed to mean?"

CHAPTER 71

THE FEELING IS fleeting.

The joy of saying "I quit" to Smarmy disappears almost as fast as I storm out of his office.

It's strange. I needed a way to extract myself from Echelon after being promoted, and it all but fell into my lap. Problem solved. Smarmy going through my file was a gift. The moment he invoked my family and made it personal, my revised exit strategy was born. I should be happy.

Instead, I'm too busy being angry.

At Smarmy? Hell no. He's not worth it.

The elevator opens on the HR floor, and I make a beeline for Jacinda's office, blowing right by her assistant, Amanda, who doesn't even finish saying "You can't go in there" before I barge through Jacinda's door.

She's at her desk on the phone. "What the hell—"

"Hang up," I say.

"What?"

"Hang up!"

Jacinda freezes for a moment before whispering into her phone, "I'll have to call you back."

Amanda's in the doorway behind me, scared for her job. "I'm sorry, I tried to stop her," she says.

"It's okay," Jacinda tells her. "You can close the door."

"Are you sure?" asks Amanda.

"Yeah, she's sure," I say.

The door closes. I take a seat in front of Jacinda's desk. She eyes me as if I've just pulled the pin on a grenade.

"What are you doing?" she asks. "What is this?"

"It's my exit interview," I say. "Except I get to ask the first question: *Why?*"

"Why what?"

"Why did you put it all in my file?"

"I don't know what you're talking about," says Jacinda.

"Your boss does. Waxman knows all about my past, who my father is—you put it in my file, and he read it," I say.

"Are you serious?"

"Do I look like I'm not serious?"

"Let me rephrase that," she says. "Are you crazy? Why would I ever put that in writing?"

"You tell me."

"For one thing, I'd get fired." She blinks. "Wait, did he just fire you?"

"He was about to. I quit before he could."

Jacinda's waving her hands, confused. "Hold on, time-out. Waxman told you that he read your file and that I had notes in it about who your father is?"

"He was calling me Halston Greer," I say.

"That's impossible."

"So now I'm crazy *and* hearing things?"

Jacinda stands and walks to her file cabinet. She yanks it open, takes something out, and slams it shut even harder. Plop goes the file in my lap. The tab reads GRAHAM, HALSTON.

"Have at it," she says.

I don't bother opening the file. She's trying to prove there's nothing in there about my past other than my résumé.

"You knew we'd be having this conversation," I say.

"Sure, yeah, that's what happened. I took all the incriminating evidence out of the file ahead of time. I'm a genius."

"It wouldn't take a genius."

"Halston, think about it. If I put that stuff in your file without telling Waxman about it, I'm the one who gets fired," she says. "You know how he is, so protective of the Echelon image, demanding loyalty? He insists on knowing everything about everyone here, especially if it could affect things negatively."

"So you never mentioned anything to him? You never discussed it?"

"I told you it would stay between us. I gave you my word."

Short of hooking Jacinda up to a polygraph, I can't know for sure if she's telling the truth, but I believe her. "So if you didn't tell him and it wasn't in my file, how did he know?"

"I don't know, but no secret is safe around here with him," she says. She mumbles something else.

"What was that?" I ask.

"I said that no secret is—"

"No, after that. You said something under your breath."

"Just that it's uncanny."

"Oh my God."

"What?" she asks.

It's bizarre how the human brain works sometimes, how it can latch onto a part of a word and convert it into something else entirely in an instant.

The can.

"Do you remember where we were when we were first arguing about this? You came down to the valuations department and got me from Pierre's office," I say. "We were heading back to your office, right?"

"Yeah, but we never made it."

"Exactly. And where did we end up?"

It's dawning on Jacinda. The possibility. The very sick, creepy, and perverse possibility. "Wait, do you really think..." she asks.

"You said it yourself. *It's uncanny.*"

CHAPTER 72

I WALK AIMLESSLY around the Upper East Side for half an hour or maybe an hour; I have no idea. I'm pondering everything, and yet I'm unable to focus. All I know is that I couldn't get out of the Echelon building fast enough.

There's nothing from my office that I really need, and while I definitely want to say goodbye to a few people, that can wait. For now, my phone is on silent, Do Not Disturb, and I'm just walking and thinking.

Suddenly, I'm stopping.

My cell, which isn't supposed to ring, rings. That happens only if someone's desperately trying to get through to me, calling multiple times.

It's Miss D, the woman who runs Michelle's foster home. Something's wrong.

"Please tell me she's with you," says Miss D, panicked.

"With me? Why would Michelle be with me?" It's the middle of the week, not Saturday.

"She was in her bed last night but not this morning. We think she ran away. In fact, we're pretty sure of it."

Now we're both panicked. "How? Why?" I ask.

"There's this new girl here at the house who's caused some trouble," Miss D explains. "She apparently told Michelle that her mother would be away a lot longer than six months."

"Let me guess," I say. "Janet from Another Planet?"

"Ugh. Yeah, that's what they call her. Michelle told you about her, huh?"

"Janet said I was only spending time with Michelle because a judge made me."

"Some of these girls can be so cruel," says Miss D.

Almost as cruel as life has been to them.

"So, Michelle's just gone? She didn't tell anyone anything or leave a note behind?" I ask.

"Nothing. We didn't find anything but an empty bed. I was hoping, praying, that maybe she went to see you."

"Did you call the police yet?"

"That's my next call. I didn't want to get them involved until I knew for sure she was missing," she says.

"What about her mother?" I ask. "Michelle doesn't know which facility she's at, but that might not stop her from trying to figure it out and go there."

"The girl has no phone and little to no money on her."

"All she needs is the internet. That's as easy as finding an Apple store."

"If I know Michelle, the last thing she's doing right now is trying to find her mother. She's too mad at her. She thinks she's been lied to again. It's just one more betrayal stacked on all the others, and it's broken her," says Miss D. "Running away from the house is Michelle's way of running away from her mother.

She's confused, scared. Nothing in her world makes sense anymore."

Her last sentence echoes in my head. *That's it!* I think.

"Don't call the police," I say. "Not yet."

"Why not?"

"I think I know where she is."

CHAPTER 73

"FIFTH AVENUE AND Eighty-Second," I tell the cabdriver. "The Met."

The guy glances at me in his rearview mirror. It's subtle but unmistakable, the annoyance in his eyes: *Really, lady? It's only a dozen blocks. You can't walk it?*

No, buddy, I can't. Not right now. Because right now I need to get to that damn museum as fast as possible.

So many people believe in fate. I've never been one of them. Everything doesn't happen for a reason. It was nothing but a coincidence that I just happened to be wandering around the Upper East Side close to the Metropolitan Museum of Art at the exact moment that Miss D called me. Of all days and all times. Yeah, okay, on second thought...

I might believe in fate.

Twelve blocks later I hand the guy a twenty for a ten-dollar fare. I see a slight smile of forgiveness on his face before I jump out of his cab and sprint up the crowded steps of the Met.

One of the perks of working at the House of Echelon: free entry to all major museums in Manhattan.

I fumble for my employee ID and hold it up for the attendant, who scans the barcode on the back. Never mind that I quit my job a couple of hours ago.

I'm in and I'm walking. Then I'm running.

There are at least two places where you're not supposed to run: pools and museums. Let's just say lifeguards hated me when I was a kid.

I haven't reached the room yet, but I can picture Michelle as clearly as the painting: She's standing in front of Jackson Pollock's *Autumn Rhythm,* trying to block out the world around her and the anger that's grabbed her like a rip current. She's staring so intently...so desperately.

She's drowning.

I weave in and out of the throngs of people as they drift from one exhibit to the next. Finally I get to the room where the massive painting hangs. My eyes scan the crowd, and there she is.

Only she's not.

I look around again. I can see Michelle from head to toe, from her braids down to her pink Reeboks with the scuff marks. It's crystal clear in my mind. But nowhere else. She's not here.

I suddenly realize how crazy I am. *What were you thinking, Halston? Why would you think she'd be here, that this is where she'd run away to?*

And then I hear it.

"I knew you'd come," she says.

I spin around and see Michelle standing there, her eyes still red from crying. I hold her tight. If I hugged her any harder, she'd pass out.

"A lot of people are very worried about you," I say.

"I'm in trouble, aren't I?"

"No, everything's fine. As long as you're safe, that's all that matters."

"What about the museum people?" she asks.

"What do you mean?"

"I lied to get in here because I didn't have any money. I told the person taking tickets that I got separated from my cousins and I thought they'd gone outside."

It's not lost on me that she chose to say her cousins instead of her parents, but all I do is smile and hug her again. "That's more than okay, sweetheart. We'll just keep that between you and me," I say. I turn back to the Pollock painting, all those squiggly lines and drips of paint, the splatters and the splotches. "So did it help at all? Looking at it again?"

She bobs her head. "A little. I mean, it did make me stop crying."

"That's good."

"It's true, though, what Janet said, isn't it? About my mother being away a lot longer?"

We're surrounded by people, and all the benches in the room are taken. "Let's talk about that," I say. "I'll answer each and every one of your questions, and I promise to tell you the truth. But first it's me that gets to ask a question, okay?"

"Okay."

I whisper in her ear, "Hot dog or pretzel?"

She cracks a smile, and it's like the sun peeking through a cloud. "Hot dog," she says.

"Me too," I say. "I'm starving. There's a guy out front selling them. I saw his cart on the way in."

As we head out of the museum, I know I've got my work cut out for me. Words can fix only so much of a young girl's broken spirit. But right now, words are all I have.

"Hey, remember when I told you that you shouldn't call that Janet girl Janet from Another Planet?"

"Yeah, I remember," says Michelle.

"Well, from now on you can call her that anytime you want."

CHAPTER 74

MALCOLM HADN'T TIPPED his hand.

He didn't give Dominick Lugieri even a hint of a reason for wanting to meet with him. But the mere request said it all, and Lugieri knew it. The kid, Malcolm, wasn't showing up at Osteria Contorni again just to say he hadn't found anything on Bergamo. He most certainly had.

"Do you like clams Posillipo?" asked Lugieri, pouring himself a refill of Fontodi Chianti in his private dining room as Malcolm entered.

"Clams Posillipo? I've only had them once but they were pretty good," answered Malcolm, joining his boss at the table.

"Yeah, a lot of places do them pretty good. I like 'em here. You want some? I just ordered, I'll tell the kitchen to do another."

"No, thanks. I'm all set."

"My mother, God rest her soul, used to make clams Posillipo all the time. They were the best I ever had. Her sauce, I'm telling you—it was her sauce. You know what her secret was?" Lugieri leaned in and said, almost whispering, "A coffee filter."

"Like what you put in a coffee maker?" asked Malcolm. "That paper-cone thing?"

"Exactly. Most people, all the restaurants, they add a clam or fish stock from a can to the sauce. But not my mother. She took the water that she cooked the clams in, mixed it with a little white wine, and then carefully poured the leftover broth through not just a strainer but a strainer lined with a coffee filter. Did it take longer? Absolutely. But she didn't care. *She knew.* It's the little things in this damn life that matter. Attention to detail. That's what makes a sauce." Lugieri motioned to the manila envelope in Malcolm's hand. "So what little thing have you brought me today?"

Malcolm glanced at the other two men in the room standing by the wall. He knew them, knew their names. They'd been with him on the visit to those would-be weed kingpins from NYU, the Grass-Fed Pandas. From that day on, no one in Lugieri's crew had given Malcolm blowback on anything.

"Give us a minute, guys," said Lugieri.

Malcolm opened the envelope as the guys left the room. The first picture he put on the table was of Bergamo and a young woman talking at a party.

"Her name is Halston," said Malcolm, pointing directly at her head. "This was at Bergamo's beach house out in the Hamptons."

Lugieri leaned in for a closer look. "A pretty girl who isn't his wife," he said, knowing there was more to come. "Got it."

Malcolm placed the second photo on top of the first. "This is her walking into the building of Bergamo's apartment in SoHo near his headquarters." Out came the third photo. "And this is her getting into his limo another afternoon."

"So he's fucking her is what you're saying."

"Maybe. Maybe not," said Malcolm. "But I'm pretty sure she's fucking him."

"What do you mean? Who is she?"

"Halston Graham recently graduated from Columbia and now works for an art auction house on the Upper East Side."

The fourth photo was of her walking into the Echelon building.

"Bergamo's a member there," said Lugieri.

"That's right. I assume that's how the two of them met."

"So what does this have to do with me?"

"Up until this point, nothing," said Malcolm.

"But you said she's fucking him, right? Is she blackmailing him? Threatening to talk to his wife or something?"

"She's talking, all right." Malcolm removed the last two photos from the envelope, pushed the others aside, and placed them next to each other in front of Lugieri.

"Shit," said Lugieri, his eyes bouncing from one to the other.

"She was in the US attorney's office for over two hours," said Malcolm. "That's her entering, and that's her leaving."

"Who was she talking to?"

"I'm working on that, but it was someone in the criminal division."

"How do you know?"

Malcolm reached one last time into the manila envelope. He had no more pictures, but he brought out a visitor's pass with GRAHAM, HALSTON and CRIM. DIV. printed on it. Halston Graham was visiting the criminal division.

"She threw it in a garbage can outside the building," said Malcolm.

There was a knock on the door. One of Lugieri's guys popped his head in. "Your clams are here," he said.

"I've lost my appetite," said Lugieri.

His guy didn't know how to react.

"Just give us one more minute," said Malcolm.

His guy still didn't know how to react.

Lugieri nodded. "Yeah, another minute," he said. He took one more look at each picture on the table before leaning back in his chair.

"I figure, first things first, we find out who this girl was talking to," said Malcolm.

"Don't bother," said Lugieri. "It doesn't make a difference."

"Yeah, you're right," said Malcolm. "So what do you want to do?"

"What's her name again?"

"Halston. Halston Graham."

Lugieri nodded, folded his arms across his chest. "She's fucking with my sauce," he said. "I want her alive... and then I want her dead."

ACT IV

THIS WAY, THAT WAY, EVERY WAY

CHAPTER 75

I CALL BERGAMO and it goes to voicemail just as I walk into the Downhome Café a couple of blocks from my apartment.

The Downhome, cozy and quaint, is a neighborhood favorite, and there's usually a line out the door on the weekends, especially for breakfast, as the place is famous for their sausage pancakes. Yes, you read that right, and don't knock 'em until you try them. They mix diced homemade pork sausage into the batter, and each pancake is only a few inches wide. Piglets, they're called, and they come layered on your plate like a pyramid. Crazy-good, crazy-addictive.

"Good morning," says the hostess. I'm pretty sure she's a daughter of the owner. "Just yourself?"

"Just me," I say.

She'd never give a booth to only one person during the breakfast rush, but one of the benefits of being newly unemployed is that I'm here at eleven a.m. on a weekday, so there's no line and the place is only half full.

"Do you need a menu?" she asks.

"No, thanks."

The waiter comes over and I order the piglets and some coffee that I sip while answering a few texts and emails. My head's down the entire time. When I look up at the sound of footsteps, it's not the waiter with my pancakes.

"Mind if we join you?"

Before I can say a word, the two guys are sitting in my booth. "What the hell are you doing?" I ask.

"Now, that's funny. Because that's the exact same question we want to ask you, Halston."

The one doing the talking is all muscles and a crew cut, a US Army recruiting poster come to life. The one on my side of the booth, the guy who has me practically pinned against the wall, could've easily been the dude who killed Tony Soprano. I glance at his profile. His nose is crooked.

"What do you want?" I ask.

"We want to talk to you."

"So go ahead," I say. "Talk."

"Not here."

"Where, then?"

"You'll see."

"The hell I will," I say. "If you don't leave in the next five seconds I'm going to start screaming."

"No, you won't."

"Five... four... three..."

"So what is she, about eight or nine years old?"

"Excuse me?"

"That little girl from the foster home. What's her name — Michelle, right? What kind of a big sister would you be if something were to happen to her?"

I don't say a word. Timing is everything, and my food arrives. The waiter looks at the guys and has only one question. "You two need menus or are you ready to order?"

"Thanks, but we won't be staying."

But apparently they will be eating my pancakes. The silent one next to me, Signore Omertà, reaches for my fork, pours some syrup, and digs into my piglets.

Lo and behold, he speaks. "Shit, these are good," he says.

"What do you guys want?" I ask.

I watch as the military Ken doll across the table from me folds his arms and leans in. "I told you already," he says. "We want to talk to you."

"And the way you get me to talk to you is by threatening to hurt a little girl?"

"Would you say yes otherwise?" He takes out a wad of cash, pulls off two twenties, and places them under the saltshaker. "Shall we?"

One walks in front of me, the other behind, and we leave the diner. We don't go far. Just down the block is a Cadillac Escalade with tinted windows, the engine running. I get in the back seat, my escorts on either side of me. The driver, wearing aviator sunglasses, remains staring forward, motionless. The second he hears the doors close, he peels away from the curb.

The next second, my world goes black.

CHAPTER 76

IT'S DÉJÀ VU all over again.

The only difference this time is a higher thread count. The pillowcase pulled tight over my head doesn't feel like industrial-grade sandpaper against my face.

"Where are you taking me?"

Of course I ask that, and of course they don't answer. I can't see a thing. They tell me nothing. I'm just as I should be, completely in the dark.

We drive for about twenty minutes. Stoplights, turns, extended straightaways, but no bridges or highways. We're still in Manhattan. No one's talking; the radio's off. I can hear the sounds of the city— traffic, construction, the occasional voices cutting through the background hum of people walking about—but it's all just distant noise.

Then everything goes quiet as we take one last turn and slowly roll to a stop. There's silence, just the engine idling. I ask again where they're taking me, and again they don't tell me. Instead, I hear the clanking of chains and the flexing, metal-on-metal grind of hinges. It's a garage door being manually opened. We roll some more; the door closes behind us. *Poof!* I've disappeared.

The pillowcase gets yanked off my head, the doors of the Escalade open, and I get ushered into what could pass for an operating room, although I know we're not in a hospital.

No, this is where you get taken when going to the hospital isn't an option, and I don't mean because you don't have health insurance. If you listen closely, you can almost hear the echoes of lead clanking against stainless steel as, one after another, extracted bullets are dropped into a surgical bowl. When wiseguys get shot and still have a pulse, this is where they come. The mob doctor will see you now.

There's an operating table, an x-ray machine, and some monitors. I'm told to sit in a folding chair near the wall. My hands get zip-tied, wrist against wrist. The silent treatment continues; my two escorts don't say a word to me. They look to be waiting for something. Or someone.

I hear the footsteps before I see anything. Dress shoes against wooden stairs from above. The sound gets louder and louder until finally he appears, walking toward me and folding his arms tight against his barrel chest.

"You must be Halston," he says.

I don't answer. I look away from him.

He laughs, the laugh of someone who finds almost nothing funny. It's quick and to the point, a borderline grunt. "I'll take that as a yes." He leans forward. "Do you know who I am?"

I still don't answer.

He's done being amused. He grabs my face, his thick, bulky hand crushing my cheeks, and forces my head back toward him. "Look at me when I'm talking to you," he says through clenched teeth. "And answer me when I ask you a damn question. You got that?"

I nod. His vise-like grip eases, and he lets go of my face. I've never been punched, but my jaw now knows the feeling. "I know who you are," I say. "Everybody does."

"Because of what you see on TV and in the papers—is that what you mean?"

"Yes."

"That's the only way you know who I am, huh? From reading about me? Watching the news?"

"Yes."

"So how is it that I know about you, Halston?" he asks. "How the hell do I even know your name?"

"I don't know."

"Why do I not believe you?"

"I don't know that either," I say.

"You know what I think? I think you're lying to me."

"I'm not. I swear to God."

"You don't strike me as a very religious person."

"Okay, I swear on my life, then."

"Your life, huh? Now we're talking," he says.

Dominick Lugieri doesn't nod or motion with his hand. He simply stares at me, eyes burning into mine. I hear footsteps behind me but I don't turn. Only when I feel it do I say anything.

"Wait. Stop. What are you doing?"

There's a gun to my head.

"We're going to play a little game," says Lugieri. "Turns out, Malcolm here is like a human polygraph machine. Isn't that right, Malcolm?"

"Something like that," he says.

It's only three words but this Malcolm sounds different than he did when he was doing all the talking back at the Downhome diner. His voice is deeper, as if he's flipped a switch inside. Not on, but off. There's no emotion. He's soulless. Like a stone-cold killer.

"The rules are simple," says Lugieri. "Tell the truth and you might live. But lie to me one more time and you die."

CHAPTER 77

"ARE YOU READY to play?"

Lugieri takes a few steps back as he asks, because God forbid he gets any of my blood and brains splattered across his expensive suit.

"Please, no. *Please* don't do this," I beg.

He rolls his eyes. "Oh, for Christ's sake. Are you really going to start crying?"

I lift up my zip-tied hands to wipe the tears from my cheeks. "What do you expect?" I'm nearly shouting. "You've got a gun to my head!"

"No, Malcolm has a gun to your head. All I'm doing is asking the questions," he says. "For instance, what have you told the feds?"

"What do you mean?"

I feel the barrel of Malcolm's gun dig into my skull. He knows his boss well.

"That's a really bad start," says Lugieri. "One more time and it's game over, Halston. Now, who are you talking to at the US attorney's office?"

Deep breath. You've got this.

"Elise Joyce," I say softly.

Lugieri nods. He knew it. Of course he knew it. "The top bitch herself, huh? Man, that chick has such a hard-on for me. It's unbelievable."

"It has nothing to do with you."

He steps toward me again, his face turning beet red with rage. Screw his expensive suit, he's ready to pull the trigger himself. "*What the hell did I just tell you?* If you lie to me one more—"

"I'm not lying, I swear! It's Enzio Bergamo I'm giving them. Only him."

"Bullshit."

"Why would it be about you? That would be suicide." I tilt my head, reminding him there's a gun to it. "This is about my father... what Bergamo did to him."

Lugieri squints. "I'm listening," he says. For the first time, I feel as if I truly have his attention. *Now don't lose it, Halston. Hold on to it... for dear life.*

"My father's an art dealer. Or he was an art dealer. He's in jail right now because of Bergamo," I say. "Bergamo was a client and leveraged their relationship to get my father involved in a scheme that went south, to put it mildly."

"Wait," says Lugieri, palms raised. "Does Bergamo know that you know all this?"

"Of course not. If he did, I wouldn't have been able to get close to him."

"So you're setting him up?"

"Just like he did my father," I say.

"What was the scheme?"

"Bergamo has two passions when it comes to art: Qing dynasty vases and cubist paintings."

"Qing?"

"The period in China right after the Ming dynasty, mid-seventeenth century to the turn of the twentieth century."

"Forget I asked," he says.

"It doesn't matter. The scheme involved only paintings. Bergamo went to my father claiming to have a connection to a French attorney handling the estate of someone who had nearly a dozen never-before-seen Fernand Léger paintings in the attic of his home near Biot, in the south of France," I explain. "This was a huge coup for my father."

"And he took Bergamo at his word? He trusted him that much?"

"My father didn't trust anyone. But Bergamo put his money where his mouth was, buying one of the Léger paintings for himself, using my father as the broker for a private sale. When the French attorney saw he could offload these paintings discreetly through my father, they were in business. My father began brokering private sales for his other clients. There was just one problem."

"The paintings were fake," says Lugieri.

"Exactly."

"But didn't your father have them checked out?"

"Authenticating is a little tricky when the paintings don't officially exist. There aren't many secrets in the art world. Word would've gotten out if he'd hired someone. So my father did the best he could on his own to verify them," I say. "But he'd be the first to admit that he desperately wanted those paintings to be real, and that probably affected his judgment. He never intended to rip anyone off. It was an honest mistake. Or at least it should've been."

"What's that supposed to mean?"

"After selling about six paintings and banking huge commissions, my father suddenly heard the voice of his own father in his head saying something he used to say a lot when my dad was a kid: *An easy buck is the devil's paycheck.* My father just had this gut feeling that something wasn't right, so he anonymously arranged to have one of the paintings examined by a black-market authenticator. And that's when he found out he'd been selling fakes."

"You said he was in jail. So what happened?" asks Lugieri. "He turned himself in or something?"

"I wish," I say. "*He* wishes. No, he made a really bad decision. Coming clean would have ruined my father's reputation, ended his career. He would've been okay with that if it weren't for the most important thing in his life: his family. All he could think about was how they would suffer, not just financially but in every way. They'd forever be the wife and kids of that art-scam guy. So my father convinced himself that he had good reasons to not reveal the truth."

"Are you sure it wasn't just greed?"

"Greed would be if he kept selling the paintings. He didn't. In fact, he went to Bergamo and explained they'd been cheated. Bergamo wanted to get his money back from the French attorney but the lawyer refused, citing buyer beware—*caveat emptor*—along with the complexities of a US citizen filing a lawsuit against a French citizen living in France. It wasn't impossible to do. It was just impossible to do without it becoming an international news story. To prevent that from happening, my father promised to make Bergamo whole on the transaction. He would basically give him all of his commissions to cover the twenty-five million that Bergamo had paid for one of the paintings."

"Let me guess," says Lugieri. "He never got the chance."

"My father assumed that one of his other clients discovered the painting he'd bought was a fake and turned him in. The FBI never revealed their source. It was only after the trial, after my father was already serving his sentence, that we learned that Bergamo had been behind the whole thing. It was his scam. There was never a French attorney. Bergamo commissioned the fake Légers and conspired to defraud my father's clients for over two hundred million dollars," I say. "And the worst part? Bergamo was the FBI's source. Only they didn't know it. After my father learned that the paintings were fake and went to Bergamo—his supposed friend—Bergamo made the anonymous tip to the FBI."

"To cover his ass."

"In every way possible. He knew my father would protect him. Sure enough, my father never mentioned Bergamo to the FBI. He knew the damage it would do to Bergamo's brand just to have his name connected with the investigation."

I watch as Lugieri folds his arms, nodding along with my last words.

"Wow," he says. "That is one fucked-up, crazy story. And the craziest part? I actually believe every word of it."

"I told you," I say.

"Yes, you did. Thanks for telling me the truth, Halston." He mulls things over for a moment and then shrugs. "Unfortunately, we still need to kill you."

CHAPTER 78

I'M IN A place where no one can hear me scream but I scream anyway. It's pointless. I'm not changing anyone's mind.

Then it's as if Lugieri's guy, Malcolm, can read mine. His free hand, sans gun to my head, comes slamming down on my shoulder the split second I try desperately to get up from the chair and run. Where I'd be going, I don't know. Neither does Lugieri. He looks at me.

"Why?" I ask. *"Why?"*

"Because I do business with the idiot, that's why. You're a loose end, and loose ends are bad for business," says Lugieri. "That's me telling you the truth."

He nods at Malcolm. That's all it takes. My death sentence isn't even a word. It isn't even a countdown. The only thing I have time to do is close my eyes.

Click.

More like a half a click, really. I open my eyes. I'm still alive.

The gun's no longer pressed against my head. I turn to look behind me.

"Shit," mumbles Malcolm. He's trying to adjust the hammer.

"What the hell?" asks Lugieri.

"It's jammed," says Malcolm.

That gets a chuckle out of the other guy from the diner, whatever his name is, in the corner.

"Shut the fuck up," Lugieri tells him.

"Sammy, give me your gun," says Malcolm.

He has a name. Sammy. How much of a brain he has remains unclear. "What?" he asks.

"I said, let me have your piece," says Malcolm.

"Oh," says Sammy. "Yeah, sure thing."

He pulls out the gun tucked at his waist, walks over to Malcolm, and nearly drops it while handing it over.

"For Christ's sake," says Lugieri, rolling his eyes. He turns to head back up the stairs. He's had enough of his Keystone Cops. Apparently he doesn't need to watch me being murdered.

"You pussy!" I scream. "You can't even stick around for it, huh?"

He spins. "What the hell did you just say?"

"You heard me."

"You're right, I did," he says. He points at Malcolm, who now has Sammy's gun pressed against my head. "Fuckin' blow her brains out."

"One last thing," I say. "There's one question you didn't ask me: How did we know?"

"Know what?"

"You didn't ask how we knew Bergamo was the anonymous source for the FBI, that he was the one who set my father up."

"Why would I give a shit?"

"You told me yourself that you do business with Bergamo," I say. "He launders your money for you."

"How do you know that?" asks Lugieri.

"My brother told me," I say. "He knows a lot of things about you, all the bad stuff. In fact, do you know what my brother would do if he were here right now?"

"I do," says Malcolm. "It might look something like this."

CHAPTER 79

I FEEL THE barrel of Sammy's gun leave the back of my head and the breeze of Malcolm's arms whipping out wide, a gun in each hand.

Oh, the look on Sammy's face. He's staring at his own Glock aimed square at his chest. *That's right, Sammy boy, you gave us your own gun. You just up and handed it over.*

But Lugieri's look takes the cake. His initial shock gives way to the kind of anger that comes only when you realize you've been taken down by a long con. Suddenly, he gets that his trusted Malcolm is a mole. He's been played from the very second they met, the allegiance as fake as the jammed hammer on Malcolm's gun.

"You're a dead man," says Lugieri. "You know that, don't you?"

"It's funny," says Malcolm, "the only guys who say that are the ones on the wrong end of the gun." He pauses, smiles. "You know that, don't you?"

I'd love to sit around and enjoy the moment, soak it all in, but there's still work to do. I spring up from the chair and do one of the few things I can do with my hands zip-tied: I press the button on the wall. The garage door opens like a curtain to reveal the supporting cast who've been outside all along, listening and waiting for their cue.

Three of the four cops have their guns drawn. The fourth has a pair of small cable cutters to get me out of the zip ties. When my arms are free, I hand over the wire and transmitter from underneath my sweatshirt. I'm pretty good now at removing them. Practice makes perfect.

"You get it?" I ask. But I'm not talking to the cop.

"Every word," says Elise Joyce, who's standing behind him. She wouldn't have missed this moment for the world. "Nicely done. You and your brother."

I started calling my older brother "Skip" when I was in kindergarten and Malcolm told me that he was skipping the fifth grade, going straight from fourth to sixth. The smarty-pants. He was already doing advanced algebra and could write computer code. He also could bench-press me ten times with one hand, which was why no one ever called him a nerd—not to his face, at least, because they knew they'd get their own faces rearranged.

Only when both Sammy and Lugieri have been cuffed and read their rights does Skip lower his weapons. He's still watching them both, though. Still gripping both guns.

Elise Joyce walks over to Lugieri, the happiest ten feet of her life.

"How you doing, Dominick?" she asks. "Nice to see you again."

Lugieri can't even look at her. "Enjoy this while you can," he says.

"Oh, I plan to."

"Once again, you'll never get a conviction."

"Something tells me this time will be a little different," says Joyce. "You know what that something is? You, Dominick. Because this time you've done all the heavy lifting for me."

"We'll see about that." But the words don't pack a punch, and he knows it. He's going over all the things that Malcolm knows about him, including what he witnessed with his own eyes. For instance, when Lugieri killed a member of his crew right in front of him at Osteria Contorni.

"You know what the most amusing part is, Dominick?" Joyce motions at the cops. "We didn't need to bring more. Do you know what I mean by that?"

Lugieri looks at her for the first time. "Fuck you," he says.

"Careful there, Dom. You've already been read your rights. But we both know what I'm talking about. We didn't need an army because you left yours behind—you didn't want any of them to know that your decision to do business with a sloppy, loose-lipped, and debt-ridden character like Enzio Bergamo had put your entire operation and every man working for it in jeopardy. That's right, you left them all behind...in every sense of the word."

Elise Joyce is smiling a little too widely. So are a couple of the cops. Even before I look over at my brother, I know what he's doing: rolling his eyes. There's only one reason he's sheep-dipping from army intelligence and it's not to stand around and listen to grandstanding like this.

sheep-dipping
verb
Taking a temporary leave from the military to pull a covert job as a civilian.

I clear my throat, and the sudden sound of it serves its purpose. Joyce turns to me and sees my look, the message in my stare.

We've still got places to go, people to see.

CHAPTER 80

SKIP AND I head for the back seat of an official vehicle of the US attorney's office. You'd think the car would be something plain-Jane like a Ford or Honda. Think again. Elise Joyce and her top staffers get to roll through the Eastern District of New York in Tesla Model 3s when they're on official business. Drivers included.

The more I rub the back of my head, the more Skip ignores me.

"Okay," he says finally. "You can stop now. I get it. Very funny."

"You didn't need to press that hard," I say.

"Actually, I did."

"Well, then, you didn't need to enjoy it so much."

"Who said I enjoyed it? I never said that."

"Putting a gun to your little sister's head? It goes without saying."

Skip and I both catch the eyes of the driver looking at us in the rearview mirror. *What'd she just say? A gun to her head?* He quickly looks back at the road.

"She's kidding. It wasn't a real gun," Skip assures him.

"Yes, it was," I say.

"I mean, it wasn't loaded."

"Yes, it was."

The driver's not sure what the hell to think. He looks at us again with a nervous smile. "I've also got a little sister," he says.

Skip laughs. "Is she also annoying?"

"Don't answer that," I tell the driver.

We hit a red light. Skip pulls his sleeve back to look at the Casio G-Shock he's been wearing since West Point. "Do these events usually start on time?" he asks.

"Almost never," I say.

"And you know that because you've been to, like, what? Zero fashion events?"

"First of all, they're called fashion *shows,* not events. Second, unless you live in a cave, everyone knows that. Oh, wait, that's right. You've actually lived in a cave."

My brother just loves it when I reference his time in the hills of Afghanistan, especially in public. He glances at our driver again before giving me his patented put-a-sock-in-it sidelong glare, as if the man might be a Russian intelligence agent.

"You're a riot," says Skip. "Real funny, metalhead."

That earns him an elbow to the ribs, which triggers his trying to flick my earlobe. We're officially two kids in the back seat who need to be separated.

Are we there yet?

Ten blocks later we pull up in front of Spring Studios on Varick Street in Tribeca. The paparazzi and Kardashian fan clubs have dispersed, and the fashion beat reporters have made their way inside, but the red carpet remains. We step out and I call the senior of the two cops who arrived ahead of us to make sure they're in place.

"Here," I say, handing Skip his lanyard.

He gives it a look and chuckles before hanging it around his neck. "VIPs, huh?"

"I know. Gotta love the irony."

Bergamo has not only invited us to his own demise; he's given us backstage passes.

CHAPTER 81

"HEY, IS THAT Anna Wintour?" someone says.

I don't have time to look as an usher hurries us along the side wall of the jam-packed studio, the long runway for the models parting the crowd down the middle like a neon-white glow stick. There's a buzz to the room, an energetic hum. But it's nothing compared to backstage.

This is chaos. Everyone's moving all at once. This way, that way. Every model, every dress each one is wearing—all of them are getting the last-minute finishing touches by a hive of workers wielding bobby pins, hair dryers, mascara wands, and lipstick.

"What?" demands a woman with a headset, stopping the usher as soon as we get three steps past the black velvet curtain. There's no *Hello,* no *How can I help you?* Nothing but one word and a nasty look of complete annoyance. She repeats herself, hand on hip. *"What?"*

"Hi," I say, stepping in front of the usher. Skip does the same. "We're here to see Enzio."

"So is everyone else," says the woman, seamlessly transitioning from resting-bitch face to active-bitch face. She gives me a quick head-to-toe and delivers an even quicker sniff-like sound as if to suggest she wouldn't be caught dead wearing what I'm wearing, especially at an Enzio Bergamo fashion show.

I realize I'm going to enjoy this even more than I thought.

"Yes, I saw the crowd out front. He's the man of the hour, all right. Who wouldn't want to be at a Bergamo fashion *event,*" I say, putting a hand on Skip's shoulder. "Now, can you please tell Enzio that Halston is here and urgently needs to speak with him? I promise you that he'll want to see me."

There's that sniff-like sound again but it's followed by the desired result. The woman pivots on her heel and goes off in search of Enzio.

"I think she likes you," says Skip.

I turn to thank the usher for his time but he's already disappeared. Can't blame him in the least, although he'll regret not sticking around.

Quickly, the woman returns with Bergamo. He dismisses her with a wave of his hand. It's incredibly rude, but I can't lie, it's also incredibly fun to watch.

"What the hell are you doing here right now?" asks Bergamo.

"What do you mean? You invited me," I say.

"The show's literally starting in two minutes," he says. "That's what I mean."

"Maybe we just wanted to wish you good luck."

Bergamo looks over and up at Skip. There's a hint of recognition. Or maybe it's just the first twinge of unease.

"Oh, that's right," I say. "You've never met my brother. When you first started doing business with our father, Skip was already off at Valley Forge. Military prep school — go figure."

"Two minutes!" a stagehand yells. "Two minutes to show!"

Bergamo anxiously looks over his shoulder. Models and makeup artists are gathering, waiting for his final approval. "I'm needed, but thanks for wishing me luck on the show," he says.

"The show? No, that's not what we're wishing you luck on," I say. "We're referring to the trial."

"Excuse me?"

"You know, the trial," says Skip.

"What trial?" asks Bergamo.

"Yours, of course," I say.

"What are you talking about?"

"You were willing to sacrifice our father for money, so we suggested a trade of our own with the US attorney's office."

"Call it a prisoner swap," says Skip. "You for our father."

"There was just one problem, though," I say. "Although we knew that you set up our father, we didn't actually have the proof."

"You're damn right. Because it never happened," says Bergamo.

"But it did, Enzio. You know what also happened? Your laundering money for Dominick Lugieri. Now, there's something that can be proven," I say.

Bergamo steps toward me, enraged, the tendons in his neck bulging above his collar. He wants to strangle me, kill me, but he can't even reach me, as Skip steps in the way. Big brothers are the best. In Skip's case, really big. He towers over Bergamo, who immediately backs off.

Still, I can see the wheels in Bergamo's mind turning as he races to figure out the argument, the angle, the right-back-atcha moment.

As quick as a smirk, he thinks he's got us.

CHAPTER 82

"YOU'RE NOT THAT stupid," he says. "Or are you? All the work to set me up, pretending we were partners, making me think you were repaying your father's debt—and where did it get you?"

"You tell me," I say.

Bergamo shrugs with the subtlety of a B movie actor. "It's nothing more than a case of 'he said, she said.'"

"You mean my word against yours?"

"No, I mean your word against his," he says. "I'm talking about *him*."

"Who? Lugieri?" I ask.

"That's right. Which means you don't have an endgame, Halston. At least, not one that doesn't end with your funeral," he says. He jabs a finger at Skip. "Same for you, big brother."

Bergamo's so pleased with himself for delivering his gotcha line, the threat that Skip and I will end up being fitted for cement shoes. He's grinning so widely, I can see all the way to his molars. But there's something about the way I smile back at him that makes his begin to wither.

"Yeah, I get it. Lugieri's a dangerous guy," I say. "It sort of makes me wonder why you were doing business with him in the first place. Seriously, Enzio, what were you thinking? Laundering money for the mob?"

"You don't know what you're talking about."

"Yeah, that's pretty much what Lugieri was saying—right before he was arrested this morning."

"Bullshit," says Bergamo. "There's no way."

"Are you sure about that?"

"I would've heard."

"You just did," I say, holding up my phone. The picture's a little blurry but it's definitely Lugieri. It's also definitely him in handcuffs.

"One minute! One minute to show!" yells the stage manager.

The throng of people behind Bergamo grows. Everyone needs him for something. He doesn't even have to look over his shoulder; he can feel the pressure building, spiraling. His grin is long gone. His teeth are clenched, his jaw tightening like a drum.

"Can we talk about this after the show?" he asks, his voice barely cutting through the chatter around him.

"No," I say. "We actually can't."

"Why not?"

"Because you won't be here after the show."

Bergamo fakes a laugh, desperately clinging to the idea that he still has some leverage. "Oh, so now you're a cop too? What, you're here to arrest me?"

"No," I say, pointing, "but I think those guys are."

Now he looks. Now he sees them. Two of New York's Finest take their cue, slice through the crowd, and head right toward him.

There's no more facade or false bravado, just sheer, unmitigated panic.

And panic can make a person do crazy things.

CHAPTER 83

"PLAY IT AGAIN," I tell Skip in a conference room at the First Precinct downtown in Tribeca. There're just the two of us on one side of the table, sitting and waiting.

Within minutes of Bergamo's arrest, the videos started popping up on TikTok, Instagram, YouTube, you name it. The much anticipated debut of Enzio Bergamo's fall fashion line kicked off with none other than the designer himself frantically sprinting from backstage and onto the runway with two cops—wearing classic dark navy with clean lines—in hot pursuit.

Skip taps his phone again and we watch the best angle yet. The other clips were from the side, peekaboo angles from the back. This one, somehow, was filmed from straight on, almost directly at the end of the runway. "The Fall of Bergamo," reads the title.

Neither svelte nor in shape, Enzio was no match for the two cops. But just as he was about to be tackled mid-runway, he tripped over his own feet, fell flat on his face, and let out the kind of high-pitched yelp destined to be a meme unto itself.

As if his day could get any worse.

Skip checks the time on his Casio G-Shock. We've had our fill of Bergamo blowing up the internet. My brother's bored. We both are. The Greer kids aren't good with inertia, though we know that the longer this afternoon drags on, the more likely it is that things will unfold as we expect.

"At least the sodas are cheap," says Skip, taking a last sip of his Diet Coke from the First Precinct's subsidized vending machine. A dollar a can, what a bargain.

"Do you want another?" I ask.

The door opens before he can answer, and Elise Joyce walks in like she owns the place. Depending on who you talk to, she sort of does.

"You lied to me, Halston Greer," she announces, taking a seat across from us at the table.

That's Skip's cue to remain silent. He leans back, folding his arms. I'm leaning in. "Lied to you? About what?" I ask.

"Bergamo and his fifteen-hundred-dollar-an-hour attorney just shared a lot of interesting information about how you set him up," says Joyce.

"So what you really mean is that I lied to Bergamo."

"No, you lied to me too."

"Name one thing I told you that wasn't true," I say.

"Call it a sin of omission, then."

"Is that a crime?"

"No, but fraud is," she says.

"You're the expert, but for there to be a crime, I think there needs to be a victim. I don't see one."

"I'm sure Anton Nikolov and his beautiful fake Picasso would beg to differ. Do you want to tell him it's a fake or shall I? On second thought, it shouldn't be you, given that nasty Bulgarian temper of his. I guess I'll do it. He'll thank me in the end."

"Great. I can picture the billboards now: 'Elise Joyce, friend of organized crime,'" I say, adding air quotes for good measure.

"That's funny," she says.

"It's also no way to get to the governor's mansion, now, is it?"

Joyce smiles like a heavyweight champ after taking a good punch — stung but far from beaten. I'll give the woman this: She has no fear... or shame.

"Oh, I'll be in that mansion one day. You can count on it," she says. "In fact, thanks to you two, I'll be there even sooner than anyone thinks."

"Great, congratulations. Now, if you could just release our father, we'll be on our way and you can get busy campaigning," I say. "Glad we could help you out."

"But that's just it," she says. "You're not done helping."

I rest my forearms on the table. "You'd better not be saying what I think you're saying."

Joyce edges forward, matching me forearm for forearm. "Or else what?"

That's all it takes to get Skip involved. "Wait a minute," he says. "You can't do this."

But she can, and we all know it.

"We delivered Lugieri as promised. Now you hold up your end of the bargain," I say. "You release our father."

"For the record, my end of the bargain assumed you weren't engaged in breaking the law. I should've known, though. Art fraud? It runs in the family, apparently."

I'm about to lunge across the table when I feel Skip's hand holding me back.

"Easy, Halston. Let's not do anything that might keep you here for the night," says Joyce.

"What do you want from us?" asks Skip.

"Like I said, thanks to you two, I now have the opportunity to bring down Dominick Lugieri *and* Anton Nikolov. It's a field day on the mob. In fact, I can picture the actual billboards," she says, breaking into a smile. " 'Elise Joyce. No one's tougher on crime.' "

"You still haven't answered my question," says Skip. "What do you want?"

"Just a little more cooperation to seal the deal on Nikolov, that's all. Once you do that, your father's a free man."

"That wasn't the deal," I say.

"It is now," she says. "Take it or leave it."

"We'll leave it."

Skip turns to me. "Halston—"

"No, screw it," I say. "Screw her."

"I think you're overlooking something," says Joyce. "There's something else you'd be getting besides your father."

"What's that?" asks Skip.

"Immunity," she says.

"The minute I strapped on that wire for you, we already had it," I say.

Joyce gives me a pitying sigh. "You're an Ivy League grad, Halston. But you're definitely no lawyer."

"I don't need to be. In fact, I don't need to be here listening to this bullshit." I stand.

"That's fine," says Joyce. "Trust me, the immunity offer is in spite of you, not because of you. It's only on the table because of your brother and his military service."

"Great. Maybe you can put him in one of your campaign ads." I turn to Skip. "Are you coming or what?"

Skip isn't moving. He's just staring at me, his eyes narrowed in indecision. "Halston—"

I cut him off. "Seriously? You're going to sit here and put up with this crap?" It looks like he is, and that leaves me with only one move. "Screw you both!" I say and bolt out of the room.

CHAPTER 84

I'M PISSED. FUMING. Livid. Cursing out loud.

I keep it up along the hall, down the stairs, and straight through the lobby of the First Precinct—anyone and everyone I pass bears witness to my fury, and they're all thinking the same thing: *Wow, that girl is absolutely, positively ticked off about something.*

It's enough to make me smile the second I hit the street.

An hour later, when I'm sitting in my Jeep exactly where I need to be, my phone rings. "Hi, I'm looking for Meryl Streep," says Skip.

I can't help but laugh. "Very funny."

"And very believable, sis. Well done."

I'm *sis* when my brother's genuinely impressed. I'm *metalhead* the other 99 percent of the time.

"So she bought it?" I ask.

"Right now Elise Joyce is thinking you're in dire need of therapy."

"She should talk."

"She joked afterward about your needing an anger-management

class," says Skip. "Apparently you also made quite the impression on a few cops while leaving the building."

"Go big or go home, right? So she bought my routine. What about yours?" I ask. "Any chance she saw through it?"

"No chance," he assures me. "The leading cause of blindness will forever be the pursuit of power."

"Who said that? Mark Twain?"

"No, a bartender in Kabul."

There's something beautifully ironic about pulling off a good-cop, bad-cop routine in a police precinct. The moment I stormed out of that conference room was the moment Elise Joyce realized that she desperately needed Skip's cooperation. So he played right into it. He pitched the plan that could deliver Anton Nikolov in addition to Lugieri, giving her a double hit on organized crime. A mob massacre, the press would call it, the kind of coup that could propel a budding politician into the highest realms of power.

All that was needed was the help of a man so hell-bent on avoiding jail that he'd do almost anything.

"How long did Bergamo mull it over?" I ask.

"Two seconds. Three, tops," says Skip.

"And that fifteen-hundred-dollar-an-hour attorney of his?"

"I think the guy used the phrase *suicide mission* but Bergamo didn't care. So now we're waiting for the paperwork, just like you thought. The attorney insisted."

"I told you," I say. "No one does a deal with Elise Joyce on a handshake. Always get it in writing. Although a lot of good that did us, right?"

"Again, just like you thought, sis."

"Wow, that's the second *sis* in two minutes, brother."

"Don't get cocky, metalhead."

"It was so predictable, though, right? I knew Joyce would use Dad as a hostage if we gave her the chance."

"And now she thinks she owns me," he says. "So, are you ready?"

"As I'll ever be."

"I don't like that you're doing this part alone."

"It's the only way, and you know it."

"Yeah, but I still don't like it."

"I'll be fine," I say.

"Where's he now?"

"Hold on, let me check." I swipe over to the tracking software. Courtesy of Nikolov's own cell phone, we've known where he is every minute from the first time I met him. The GPS is accurate to a hundred feet. "He's either in Macy's, Starbucks, or a Sunglass Hut."

"Are you serious? He's in a mall?"

"Yep. The Mall at Short Hills in Millburn."

"That's actually good. It's near his home," says Skip. "Now you just have to get him back there."

"That's the plan," I say.

But it's the way I say it, with the kind of tone that only my brother can pick up on.

"I know what you're thinking," he says.

"No, you don't," I say. "You definitely don't."

"You want to see the expression on his face."

Damn. "Okay, maybe you do."

"Don't do it," says Skip. "Do you hear me? Stay in the car."

"You're starting to break up on me," I say, making some static noises.

"I'm serious."

"And I'm touched. But don't worry about my end, just take care of yours, okay? How much more time do you need?"

"An hour and a half," he says. "Ninety minutes."

"That's too long."

"You haven't even made the call yet."

"Yeah, but the second I do, the clock starts ticking and there's no turning back. He's either with us or he's not," I say.

"You mean he's either with us or he kills you."

"Tomayto, tomahto."

"For real," he says. "Be careful, Halston."

My brother doesn't often call me by my actual name, though I have vivid memories of two times he did. One was the day our mother killed herself. The other was the day our father was sentenced to prison.

"I'll be careful," I say. "I promise."

Skip laughs all too knowingly. "Now uncross your fingers and tell me that again."

CHAPTER 85

NIKOLOV LETS MY first call go to voicemail. Of course he does. He doesn't recognize the number.

"It's Halston," I say after the beep. It's all that's needed.

He's not in Macy's and he's not buying a new pair of Ray-Bans at the Sunglass Hut. Ever the man of the people, even in a cashmere sweater, Anton Nikolov is sipping a coffee at a table in Starbucks. Sitting with him, of course, is his ever-present shadow, Blaggy.

Does Blaggy ever get a day off? What's the schedule for a lead henchman of a Bulgarian mob boss?

I watch as Nikolov listens to my message; he turns to Blaggy the second he hears my voice.

I immediately call again. Nikolov answers before the second ring. He sounds a lot more Bulgarian when he's angry.

"How the hell did you get this number?" he asks.

"No *Hello*? No *How are you*?"

"Fuck your hello, and I don't care how you are. How do you think I am?"

Say what you will about Anton Nikolov, but he doesn't waste time with polite chitchat.

"So you've heard the news about Bergamo?" I ask.

"More like seen it," he says. "Along with everyone damn else in the world."

"A literal fall from grace, huh?"

"You think this is funny? 'Cause I don't."

"I get it," I say.

"I don't think you do."

"Why do you think I'm calling? We need to talk."

"So talk," he says.

"In person."

"Are you sure you want to do that?"

"What's that supposed to mean?" I ask.

"It means you just became a liability," he says. "Bergamo will do or say anything to avoid going to jail. You realize that, right?"

"So?"

"So who's to say you won't do the same?"

"That's why I wanted to talk to you," I say.

"And that's why I'd sooner just kill you and be done with it."

"You have to find me before you can kill me."

"Oh, I can find you, all right," he says.

"Oh yeah?"

"Anytime, anywhere. So fast, it will make your head spin, Halston."

"Right back atcha, Anton," I say. "By the way, I hear the pumpkin-spice latte is really good. Is that what you're having?"

And there it is. The head-on-a-swivel, eyes-darting, oh-shit moment that I've come to witness in person. And the best part is he can't see me. Though it's not for lack of trying. Nikolov immediately springs up from his chair and runs out the door of Starbucks, leaving his shadow behind. Blaggy races to catch up with him, asks what the hell is happening.

Now that I have your attention, Anton.

"Where are you?" asks Nikolov, frantically looking left and right. But the Short Hills mall is packed as usual, people crossing in front of him, his view obstructed no matter which way he turns. He'd have better luck finding Waldo.

"I didn't figure you for a mall kind of guy," I say.

"Clever. Very clever. A busy public place to ensure your safety. So what do you want?"

"I told you—we need to talk."

"So stop with the games," he says. "Come out from wherever you are and we'll talk."

"Not here."

"Where, then?"

"Your house," I say.

He laughs. "Maybe you're not as clever as I thought. My house?"

"Head there now, and I'll do the same."

"What's the catch?" he asks.

"No catch. Just a conversation," I say. "And if you don't like what I tell you, you can kill me as many times as you want."

CHAPTER 86

I'VE MADE HIM an offer he can't refuse.

I'm so convinced, I don't wait for him to agree or say another word. *Click*. I'm gone.

So is Nikolov. Twenty minutes later, he and Blaggy are arriving at his house in Millburn, New Jersey, rolling up in a black Cadillac Escalade with tinted windows. I know this because I'm there in my Jeep, waiting at the gate.

I follow them up the long driveway lined with tall trees and park in front of Nikolov's gaudy brick mansion. The two humongous bear topiaries are still flanking the front door, as are a couple of guys with AR-15s.

Before Blaggy even begins walking toward me, I step out, cell phone in hand, and spread my arms. He's patting me more for a wire than a weapon. Blaggy turns to his boss with a nod, signaling I'm clean.

"So what do you have to tell me that's so important?" asks Nikolov.

"In your driveway? Nothing," I say. "Let's go inside."

"We're fine right here," he says.

No, we're not. "Is the painting inside?"

He doesn't have to ask which one. "Why?"

"It's not a trick question," I say. "It's a beautiful painting, a Picasso in his prime, and I miss looking at it. That's why. I was an art history major, after all. So is it inside?"

"Of course it is," he says. "You can't freeport a painting that everyone thinks was destroyed. We all know it doesn't exist, right?"

That's right, Anton. That's why I knew it would be here.

"I'm thinking you keep it in one of two places," I say. "It's in your office or in some mystery safe room like you see in the movies."

Nikolov nods at his guys with AR-15s. "My whole house is a safe room."

With that, he puffs his chest out, turns, and walks inside. Blaggy points a thick finger at Nikolov, and I fall in line.

I can tell Blaggy's even more pissed at me than his boss is because this is now twice I'm walking into this house on my own terms. The first time I'd orchestrated my own kidnapping and tricked Blaggy into introducing me to Nikolov. This time I managed to tail Nikolov without Blaggy knowing. This guy's got one job: to watch his boss's back, guard his six. And he still didn't see me coming. He knows it.

I follow Nikolov through his foyer. The shine on the white marble floor is near blinding. "I never thought I'd be back here," I say.

"That makes two of us," says Nikolov.

"If I'm not mistaken, the last time we were together with Bergamo, it was in your apartment in the city and you had a gun to my head."

"Yeah, right after you kicked Bergamo in the balls."

"He deserved it," I say.

"And you deserved the gun to your head."

"We'll agree to disagree on that, but we both don't like the guy. Am I wrong?"

Nikolov stops in his tracks halfway through his living room and angrily turns to me. "For your sake, there better be more to this conversation than you and I just thinking the guy's a prick," he says.

"There is."

"So let's have it."

"I want to see the painting first."

"Damn, you're annoying." He starts walking again, muttering over his shoulder, "If you weren't a girl..."

It's not in his office or in a safe. The Picasso hangs over a fireplace in a mahogany-paneled room complete with a bar, a poker table, and an entire wall of game-hunting receipts, among them the heads of the African big five: a lion, a leopard, a buffalo, an elephant, and a rhinoceros.

But I barely look at them. I only have eyes for Pablo.

"There you go," says Nikolov. "Have a good, long look. Soak it in, there, art history major."

Which is exactly what I do. "It's quite something." I fall into a deep silence as I stare at his beloved Picasso, knowing I'm driving him nuts.

Finally he can't help himself. "Oh, for fuck's sake," he says. "Are you ready to talk now or what?"

"Almost. Just a little bit longer." I'm humming a tune to myself. Something light, upbeat. It's killing him. I can feel his glare on my back and Blaggy's glare as well. Blaggy, standing in the doorway, is surely thinking of all the fun and creative ways he could torture me.

Eventually I turn around and stare at Nikolov with just a hint of a smile. "You know, if I weren't a girl, I wouldn't be wearing heels," I say.

"What's that supposed to mean?" he asks.

It means this.

Faster than a gunslinger, I reach down for one of my new Jimmy Choos I bought with my winnings from courtsiding his gambling site. The shoe's off my foot and in my hand in the blink of an eye, and before Nikolov can finish screaming "Nooooo!" I lodge the stiletto heel right smack in the middle of the painting, leaving a gaping hole in the canvas.

"Now let's talk," I say.

CHAPTER 87

THEY'RE BOTH COMING at me at once.

Nikolov has his arms out, ready to strangle me, but it's only Blaggy I have to worry about. He's an actual gunslinger, and in his outstretched hands is his Glock, quicker than quick.

There are only two words that can keep me alive right now, and they're not *Don't shoot*.

"It's fake!" I yell.

Nikolov freezes. Blaggy does too. For a moment, my one chance to explain, they remain as still as statues. In Blaggy's case, he's a statue of a guy with his Glock aimed at my chest.

"Talk," says Nikolov.

Adrenaline speeds up everything in the body but I've got to fight it. Fast talkers are bullshit artists, and I'm not getting a second chance to explain why there was never a real Picasso.

Deep breath. In...out...go!

"I needed you to bring down Bergamo," I begin, then explain what Bergamo did to my father.

Nikolov squints, taking it all in. "So he screwed over your dad," he says, "and your genius idea is to screw over me?"

"But that's the thing," I say. "You're not getting screwed over. What you're about to get is a gift."

"A gift, huh?" Nikolov folds his arms. "I can hardly wait."

"I don't blame you for not believing me," I say. "You have no reason to trust me anymore."

"I never trusted you. You had something I wanted." Nikolov motions to the wall. "The first thing I did when I brought that painting home was shine one of those black lights over the entire thing, the same light your buddy Werewolf used at the museum."

"Wolfgang."

"Whatever his name is," he says. "The point being—"

"You wanted to know for sure. Yeah, I figured you might do that so I got Wolfgang to swallow his pride when he was making your copy. What you have is an unsigned duplicate of an original Wolfgang forgery." I point at the gaping hole in the canvas. "And it's worth just as much now as it was when I walked into this room."

I watch as Nikolov nods, smiling. He thinks he's got me pegged. "You're telling me all this because you know Bergamo's willing to do anything to avoid jail. He'll cut a deal, spill his guts. So this is your Hail Mary. Because you knew that once I found out you and Bergamo set me up, you'd be as good as dead. Which is why you're here desperately trying to cut your own deal—so I don't kill you. But you've got nothing I want in return, Halston. Absolutely nothing."

"That's where you're wrong," I say. "In fact, you've got it all wrong."

CHAPTER 88

QUICK, WHAT'S THE best way to fool someone?

Make him think he's fooling someone else.

This is what I tell Nikolov, giving him a glimpse of my playbook. Not so I can brag, not like some brash twenty-two-year-old poised to take a victory lap, but simply to explain: This is how I tricked the guy who burned my father into trusting me.

"Bergamo thought I was repaying my father's debt to him," I say, "and he was so focused on getting you to hang a fake Picasso on your wall—on making a fool of you—that he didn't see what was really happening."

"And what was really happening?" asks Nikolov.

"You've seen the videos. The whole world has now. Bergamo's fashion empire, built entirely on his name, is about to crumble," I say. "Worse, he's about to be locked up for a long time and forced to wear nothing but blue denim on a daily basis. Unless, of course..."

"Unless he cuts a deal, like I said."

"But not just any deal. He's got to give the US attorney something special. I'm just a kid; I'm not a trophy," I say, nodding at the stuffed heads on his hunting wall. "But do you know who is? You."

"Bergamo might be desperate, but he's not that dumb," says Nikolov.

"Exactly. He knows he can't rat on you. Besides, if anything, you come off as the victim in this whole scheme," I say. "But what if instead of ratting you out, Bergamo was setting you up?"

"What do you mean?"

"Look at your phone."

"Why?" he asks.

"Because you're going to see a text from Bergamo asking you to call him immediately."

"How come a text? Why wouldn't he just call me?"

"Are you going to keep asking me questions or are you going to look at your phone?"

Nikolov takes out his cell. He sees the text, shakes his head, and says, almost as if he's trying to reassure himself, "No. No way. He's still not that dumb."

"That's why Bergamo's convinced he'll get away with it, because he knows that's exactly what you'll think—that he wouldn't do it because he doesn't have a death wish. That's his leverage, his ace in the hole. That and the fact that it's actually a really good plan."

"How do you know?"

"Because it's my plan," I say.

"Hold on. *Bergamo knows you're here?*"

"No. He has no clue. Just like he has no clue that he's doing exactly what we need him to."

"Which is what?" asks Nikolov.

"Call him and find out."

"How do I know you're not still working with him?"

"Because he's in jail right now," I say.

"So?"

"So when you call him, he's going to tell you the big secret, that your Picasso is a fake. He doesn't know you already know that. Meanwhile, he's known all along but he won't confess that. He'll claim that I set both of you up, and he'll try to make you so angry, so full of rage, that you'll decide that the sole mission in your life is to end mine. Because that's when you'll give the US attorney the smoking gun: attempted murder."

"That's your plan? You want me to kill you?"

"No. Elise Joyce wants you to kill me. Or try. That way, she can stop you just before you do."

"She'd love that, wouldn't she? Taking me down?"

"You don't know the half of it." I wait for his look. "Oh, you haven't heard?" I turn to Blaggy. He's already frisked me but I still point at my pocket, letting him know that I'm only reaching for my phone. The picture is cued up, ready to show: Dominick Lugieri in handcuffs. I walk it over to Nikolov.

"Holy shit," he says. "When?"

"This morning."

"How?"

Nikolov hates Lugieri. Or, rather, he hates the stranglehold Lugieri has over some New York unions.

"How is a story for another time," I say. "But it's like I told you — you're not getting screwed, you're getting a gift. Two gifts, actually. This is the first: Lugieri out of your way."

"How do you propose to pull off the second?" he asks.

"It starts with you calling Bergamo," I say. "You give him an Oscar-worthy performance. You're shocked—*shocked!*—to learn the Picasso is a fake, and you vow to kill me."

"Then what?"

"You kill me."

"You mean so Elise Joyce can swoop in and save the day?"

"Exactly."

"But you're telling me this all in advance," he says. "So are you working with her or against her?"

"What do you think?"

CHAPTER 89

"HI, DAD."

"I'm so glad you're here."

"Me too."

"I've been worried about you."

"And I've been worried about you. How do you feel?"

"I'm fine. All good."

"You just looked away when you said that."

"So?"

"So that's the biggest tell in poker. Every time you do that, you're trying to bluff me."

"Nonsense. And that's enough talk about me. Your turn. What's new with you? How goes it in the outside world?"

"Honestly? Sometimes I think you might actually be safer in here than out there. It's a complicated world."

"I try not to look at the news much in here. The cinder block is depressing enough."

"What about movies? Are you still watching a lot of those?"

"There'll never be a better way to pass the time. Any new recommendations?"

"Well, I finally got around to watching that *Yellowstone* series. Better late than never, I figured. It got me thinking about some of Kevin Costner's other stuff, movies he did when he was younger. I came across one I somehow missed. It's called *Revenge*. Ever see it?"

"No, I don't think so. I must have missed it too. Who else is in it?"

"Anthony Quinn. You remember him, right?"

"Of course. *Zorba the Greek*."

"Yeah, although it's interesting. In this *Revenge* movie he plays a wealthy Mexican businessman, but he reminds me more of a mob boss."

"Why's that?"

"He commands a lot of loyalty from his men."

"Meaning there's little they wouldn't do for him."

"Exactly."

"Remember *The Untouchables*? That's probably my favorite Kevin Costner movie."

"Probably mine as well."

"The best part is when he recruits his team to bring down Al Capone, the people he knows for sure he can trust. He has to go outside the department, think outside the box."

"Exactly."

"Yeah, that was a great movie, all right, although it probably appeals more to men. I mean, it's safe to say a certain someone in our family hasn't seen it."

"Very safe."

"Come to think of it, she's never been a big fan of men-saving-the-day stories, has she?"

"No, not at all. I wouldn't even recommend *The Bodyguard* to her."

"That's your sister, all right. But she's the only one you've got, son."

"Trust me, Dad, I know."

CHAPTER 90

SKIP RARELY PLAYS the combat card or any card related to his role with Special Forces. So if he's telling you a story about a certain mission he was part of, rest assured there's an ulterior motive lurking.

"I'm only here because my brother told me you wanted to apologize," I say, sitting across from Elise Joyce in her Brooklyn office. Her window overlooks the Korean War Veterans Plaza where Fulton and Tillary Streets meet.

Joyce, sitting behind her desk, laughs loudly, mocking me. "And you believed him?"

I look over at Skip and his lying eyes and then spring up from my chair to do exactly what I did the last time the three of us were together—storm out.

Only this time I don't even make it to the door. I barely make it out of my seat. As soon as I stand up, Skip puts his big-brother hand on my shoulder and pushes me back down.

"There was this one time in Fallujah," he says, his hand still on my shoulder, "our Persian interpreter, who spoke both Dari and Pashto, came down with the chicken pox, of all things. There was no other interpreter embedded with us in our unit, but it's not like we could just call a time-out in the war. We had a sweep planned—when we literally go door to door in the neighborhood searching for weapons—and while a few of us knew a couple of words and phrases, no one was even close to fluent in either dialect. So we had to scramble, and what we did was find a Sunni carpenter who spoke Pashto but wasn't a Taliban sympathizer, and we paired him with a Hazara farmer who was fluent in Hazaragi, which is very close to Dari. Now, normally these two guys would hate each other's guts, but as it turns out, their fathers had fought together against the Soviets. In other words, having a common enemy had allowed their fathers to put aside their differences, and these men did the same—at least long enough for us to complete our sweep without anyone getting their freakin' head blown off. Do you two understand what I'm getting at?"

"That depends," I say. "Am I supposed to be the Sunni carpenter or the Hazara farmer?"

Skip's answer is a quick, hard pinch of my clavicle, which is what he used to do to me when I was a kid and he wanted me to shut up. The death grip, I called it. It still works.

"Can we talk about the common enemy now?" asks Joyce. "And this plan of yours?"

"You mean *ours*," says Skip. "It's our plan now."

"That depends," says Joyce.

"On what?" he asks.

"Whether or not it works," she says. "Because it's my ass on the line if it doesn't."

It's my turn to laugh in her face. "Your ass? *Your* ass? If this plan doesn't work, I'm as good as dead," I say. "Literally."

"So let's make sure that doesn't happen," says Skip.

Joyce picks up the printout sitting on her desk and holds it like it's a live grenade. "I've changed my mind. I need to know how you're able to intercept Nikolov's calls," she says.

"No, your first instinct was right," says Skip. "The less you know—"

"Yeah, I get it. Plausible deniability." She stares at the transcript. "But still."

"I showed you how we could track Nikolov's movements by his phone," says Skip. "Let's just say, once that trapdoor is open, the possibilities are near endless."

"In other words," says Joyce, "it's military software and you're not about to give me details."

Skip grins. "Something like that."

"Speaking of military," she says.

"There'll be a team of two staked out at the warehouse in Jersey," says Skip. "They're both former SEALs, private contractors now."

"Will they be enough?" asks Joyce. "Only two?"

"You're footing the bill, you tell me," he says.

"You won't know what you're walking into. What if Nikolov has a dozen of his guys in that warehouse?"

Skip points at me. "To kill one skinny little girl?"

"That's real funny," I say.

"Seriously, though," says Joyce. "You could easily be outnumbered."

"Outnumbered, maybe, but not outmanned," says Skip. "My guys and I will be just fine."

"It's not you she's worried about," I say. "In fact, you never worry about anyone other than yourself, do you?"

"You'll have to forgive my sister—"

"No, she's right," says Joyce without even a hint of shame. "This is just a transaction. A deal. You're getting me what I want, and in return you get what you want. Your father."

"No, that was our last deal," I say. "What you're doing now is extortion."

"Call it whatever you want," she says. "Ask me if I give a shit."

I'm shooting daggers. "You're a piece of work, you know that?"

"And you're just pissed off because you're not the smartest chick in the room," says Joyce.

I've got a thousand comebacks but I leave them all unsaid. After all, I know what she knows—or at least what she thinks. Releasing my father from prison is entirely her call.

So I sit there and take it.

Of course I do.

CHAPTER 91

I THINK I read this in a Malcolm Gladwell book. No, wait. On second thought, it might have been a fortune cookie.

Routine can be the secret of life... or the kiss of death.

I leave my apartment at twenty minutes before ten for my regular Sunday-morning barre class at Radiant1 Fitness, after which I'll stop at Juice It Up for my usual mango, banana, and pineapple smoothie. I barely make it down the block before the two guys approach me.

"Don't run," says the first.

"Don't scream," says the second.

To make sure I do neither, they both flash their gun-tucked-into-the-belt ensembles before pointing at the black Escalade idling at the curb.

Still, it's not as if I'd let myself get abducted off the streets of Manhattan without asking a few questions.

"What the hell's going on?" I say. Yeah, that seems pretty spot-on.

Of course I don't get a straight answer. "Somebody wants to talk to you," says the first guy.

"Who?" I ask.

"Just get in the damn car," says the second guy. "Or we can help you get in, if you'd like."

And that's that. The story of how I'm going for a ride.

Just like Anton Nikolov told me it would happen. His guys, his plan.

I don't say much in the car. Neither does anyone else. The driver has two earrings in each ear and knuckle tattoos that spell out *hell* on the left hand and *fury* on the right. I'm not sure which one delivers the harder punch, hell or fury, but considering the driver's hulking frame and how the top of his head is scraping the roof of the Escalade, it's a safe bet that those who have tried to find out over the years immediately regretted it.

He misses the turnoff for the Manhattan Bridge.

I clear my throat. No one notices. I clear my throat again, louder. They all notice but no one says anything. We're heading farther south, toward the financial district instead of over to New Jersey. Shit. Never have I been so upset about not going to Newark.

I need to say something, except I can't.

But I have to.

Which leaves me no choice. Everyone in the car is supposed to know I'm wearing a wire. What the hell.

I start yelling, "What are you doing? Stop! Get your hands off me!"

No one has their hands on me. No one's doing a thing beyond staring at the crazy girl in the middle seat reaching up under her own sweatshirt. I rip the tape from my skin, detaching the wire. Here goes nothing.

"What the hell, guys? What are we doing?"

The driver tightens his grip on the wheel, flexing his *hell* and *fury*, before saying in a Bulgarian accent, "Change of plans."

CHAPTER 92

"GO FASTER, YOU'RE losing them!" barked Elise Joyce from the back seat.

She was not supposed to be riding with him in the first place, so the last thing she was going to do was sit in the front seat and risk being seen.

"I'm not losing them," said Skip calmly. "And this is the right distance."

"Yeah, until we lose them," said Joyce.

Skip gave her a glare in the rearview mirror. "For the record, I've done this before."

"And I haven't. That's the whole point. We can't screw this up."

"Which is exactly what happens if we get too close," he said.

That shut Joyce up for a few blocks. With her baseball cap pulled down so low on her head, all Skip could really see was her disapproving clenched jaw.

A few blocks later she was back at it. "Why is it so damn quiet?" she asked. "Is the volume up? Did you mess with the dial?"

Skip pointed at the dash. The radio of his sister's Jeep Cherokee was broadcasting her wire transmitter via the link to his phone. "The volume's fine."

"Why isn't anyone talking, then?" she asked. "They talked on the street when they took her, so why not now?"

"They have her. What more is there to talk about?"

"They're mob guys, they're always going on about something."

"Maybe if they were alone," he said.

"What do they care what Halston hears? They think they're about to kill her."

Skip wanted to remind Elise Joyce that this wasn't *The Sopranos* and that not all mob guys engaged in witty banter while on a job. Of course, the irony was that Nikolov's men, in the same kind of Cadillac Escalade that Tony Soprano drove, were about to cross the Manhattan Bridge over to New Jersey.

Until.

Joyce shot forward from the back seat and yelled practically in Skip's ear, "*What happened?* They didn't turn."

"No, they didn't."

"That was the turn for the bridge—they should've turned," she said.

"You're right."

"Why didn't they—"

"Sit back," Skip told her.

It was the way he said it—the tone, the edge. He was no longer talking to the chief of the criminal division at the US attorney's office. From that moment on, from the very second the mission went off script, Elise Joyce was a civilian. And as she sat back without saying a word, Joyce knew it.

Skip sped up. To hell with keeping a proper distance.

"*What are you doing? Stop! Get your hands off me!*" his sister was suddenly yelling, her voice blaring through the Jeep's speakers. The volume was definitely up and working.

Then came the sounds. Rustling, static, a struggle...ending with an abrupt silence.

"Shit. They found the wire," said Joyce.

Skip shot her a look over his shoulder: *You think?*

CHAPTER 93

I'M TRAPPED IN a car with a bunch of human brick walls.

Everything I say bounces off them. They don't take the bait, not once. I try over and over to get one of these goons to tell me where we're heading, and each time I'm met with silence. Nothing works. Logic, sympathy, deadpan humor—I exhaust all angles.

Well, almost all.

The angle I avoid, the arrow that stays in my quiver, is the outright reminder. Four words: *We're not alone, guys.*

I don't use it because they already know my brother's in the trail car, and for some damn reason they don't seem to give a crap. If I had to guess, I'd say these guys are just putting too much faith in their elementary math skills. There're three of them and only one Skip. Three is greater than one. Easy-peasy, right?

I hate to break it to them, but they're on the wrong side of that equation.

Or so I keep telling myself.

The Escalade speeds up, merges onto the West Side Highway, and zigzags through traffic, and that voice in my head sounds a little less confident. These brick walls know something that I don't, and that's the very definition of *leverage*.

I turn to look out the back, checking to see where Skip is in my Jeep, and they don't try to stop me. I'm free to gaze all I want. The less they care, the more worried I get.

My instincts kick in. *Test the boundaries, push the envelope, find the ceiling.* I reach for my phone. Not quickly, just casually.

Ceiling found. No sooner does my phone appear from my pocket than it gets ripped out of my hand. I expect it to be tossed out the window, since that's what would happen in the movies, but life rarely imitates art. Goon number 1 simply holds on to my phone, but he utters something for the first time in the car. It's not a word; it's a sound. A satisfied grunt.

No matter. As long as the phone stays in the car, Skip can track us. But as I look at the dash and see our speed topping eighty, the question becomes whether he can keep up with us.

Hell and Fury behind the wheel is fearless — or maybe just flat-out crazy. With every lane change, every swerve, he's mere inches from clipping the bumper of another car. I'm holding on to the seat so hard, my fingernails are about to tear into the leather. Forget about where they're taking me; I just hope we get there in one piece.

Be careful what you wish for.

We take the next exit off the highway. We're no longer going eighty but my mind's still racing. After a few turns, I know our destination even though we're not there yet — it's the last of the undeveloped land in downtown Manhattan, a block-long stretch of vacant lots and abandoned warehouses just above the financial district.

I turn to look again over my shoulder, desperate to find Skip. I can't see him. Or — wait, maybe that's him. I don't know, I can't tell. Way, way back... that looks like my Jeep. Sort of.

The Escalade swerves again, then turns, and I whip my head back around to see what's happening. We're pulling in between two warehouses on a potholed stretch of pavement only about twenty feet wide. I immediately get a bad feeling. We're hidden, out of sight. The feeling only gets worse when I spot the Lincoln Town Car parked up ahead, its engine running.

The Escalade slows to a stop alongside the Town Car. I look over, but the windows are tinted; I can't see inside.

At first, no one does anything. It's as if they're waiting on something.

Then all at once, doors begin to open and I'm getting dragged out. It's so fast, there's no time to scream.

Still, nothing's happening with the Town Car next to us. The doors are closed, windows up, engine idling. Then I see it. The trunk pops; the lid rises. It's like a giant shark opening its jaws, ready to swallow me whole.

Now I'm screaming, but not for long. This has all been planned out. Duct tape gets slapped over my mouth, silencing me. All I can do now is kick and squirm, but I'm no match for Nikolov's goons. They hoist me up and into the trunk like I'm a feather. My arms are yanked behind my back and I'm hit with more duct tape — wrists, then ankles. So much for pulling the emergency latch.

Slam! The trunk goes black. Whatever's about to happen next, I'm not meant to see it.

But apparently someone else is.

CHAPTER 94

ELISE JOYCE WAS at it yet again in the back seat, her voice piercing Skip's ears as he weaved through traffic. She was worried, pissed off, anxious.

She was also no idiot. Joyce was looking ahead. Not just at the Escalade widening the gap between them but at the whole situation, which was now threatening to implode as fast as Nikolov's guys were turning the West Side Highway into their own autobahn.

She was gaming the outcomes in her head, recalculating the risk, and the more she did, the less she was liking the results. Only minutes ago, everything was progressing as planned. Now everything was going to hell in a handbasket. Including, possibly, her entire career. Which was why Elise Joyce was done taking a back seat to the soldier behind the wheel. She was a US attorney, for Christ's sake, chief of the entire criminal division. She gave the orders, not the other way around.

"I'm using your phone!" she barked as she grabbed it from the cup holder next to him.

Skip was in the middle of a triple lane change at eighty miles an hour, so there was no taking a hand off the wheel to stop her. "What are you doing?" he asked.

"Calling Nikolov, finding out what the hell's going on," she said. It was a call that she could make on Skip's phone but not hers. Her phone records were a matter of public record.

"Yeah, you do that," said Skip, heavy on the sarcasm. "I'm sure Nikolov will answer right away and explain everything to your satisfaction."

"Hey, maybe he doesn't even know," said Joyce. "Have you thought of that?"

"You mean, like, his guys have suddenly just gone rogue, hatched their own plan?" Skip didn't bother rolling his eyes. "Uh-huh, that's probably exactly what's happening right now. Hurry and give their boss the heads-up."

"You got any better ideas?" she asked.

"We're doing it."

"Not very well. Can't this piece of shit go any faster?"

Technically, yes. Realistically, no. The Jeep's engine—no, the entire Jeep was screaming its age, every rusted bolt and lug nut rattling in unison.

Skip didn't answer Joyce's question. He didn't have to. "Look, they're getting off the highway," he said, pointing.

So were a lot of other cars, but at least Skip could make up some lost ground. Instead of a distant dot, the Escalade was close enough that there was no losing it through the crosstown traffic.

"Where the hell are they taking her?" asked Joyce.

"I've got a pretty good idea," said Skip. "And if I'm right, this has Nikolov's fingerprints all over it."

"What do you mean?"

"It's his own little depreciation write-off. Only not so little. He owns a couple of abandoned warehouses a few blocks from here."

"How do you know that?"

"I do my homework."

Skip watched Joyce in the rearview mirror as she processed everything. She made a weird face when she was deep in thought, as if she'd just eaten something from the fridge that might or might not have been past its expiration date.

"Forget calling Nikolov," she said, putting his phone back and reaching for her own. "What we need is backup."

"It's too late for that."

"Why?"

"Because whatever this is, it's about to go down."

"Yeah, but—"

"No buts. This is what I need you to do," said Skip. Up ahead, the Escalade made another turn. The warehouses were in sight, only a block away. "The second I get out of the car, you start recording on your phone. Do you understand? Whatever happens, keep recording."

"What are you going to do?" she asked.

"You'll see. Just *keep* recording."

"Then what?"

"Then we all live happily ever after."

"You better be right."

"I will be," he said. "But in case I'm not, what will you be doing?"

She didn't answer. He glanced at her over his shoulder, and his eyes made clear that this wasn't a rhetorical question.

"Okay, I got it. I'll be recording," she said.

"And then what?"

"What do you mean?"

"I mean if things go sideways," he said, "if that happens, make sure you record it and then get the hell out of here."

Joyce was processing again, and this time, judging from the look on her face, the milk in the fridge had definitely gone bad. The idea of things going sideways was sending her into a panicked tailspin.

"Shit," she said. "Shit, shit, shit."

"Yeah, no shit," he said.

CHAPTER 95

SKIP PUMPED THE brakes about fifty yards behind the Escalade as it pulled up in the alley alongside a Lincoln Town Car, the engine idling. Even from that distance, Skip could see the trail of smoke from the exhaust.

Out came his Glock 19. He immediately checked the magazine, a ritual of his, popping the release and jamming the extended floor plate against his palm all in one motion, then turned around to Joyce. Her face was flushed red. Her panic had morphed into anger.

"This is all your fault," she said. "All your goddamn fault."

"That's a funny way of wishing me luck," he said. "Now, listen. When I get out, you get out."

"Why?" asked Joyce.

"So you can get behind the wheel."

"Yeah, whatever."

He ignored her petulant teenage attitude; her nod was all that mattered. Skip nodded back. "Good talk, Rusty," he said, opening the door.

He didn't look back but he knew she was doing exactly what she'd been told to do. He heard her door open and then, seconds later, the driver's door closing. She was behind the wheel, engine running. He'd left the key fob in the cup holder where he'd had his phone. His phone he'd taken with him.

Skip walked slowly down the alley, his Glock tucked at the small of his back. Jeans and a belt were still the best holster out of uniform.

Everyone in that Escalade knew he'd been following them; he wasn't sneaking up on anyone. Still, his right hand—his shooting hand—barely swung with each stride. It stayed tight to his hip, ready to reach behind him in a heartbeat.

He watched it all unfold before his eyes.

The doors of the Escalade opened, as did the trunk of the Town Car. Halston was moved like a piece of luggage. It was quick, organized, and choreographed. She didn't have time to struggle, and she couldn't even yell, thanks to the duct tape.

Skip didn't yell either. Yelling altered your sight line on the battlefield and shifted your focus. He kept walking, only now the hand by his hip held a loaded weapon. Soon, he wouldn't care if these guys saw him or his gun.

But not yet.

He took cover behind a dumpster and waited a few seconds for them to look his way. But they didn't.

Time to announce his arrival.

"Hey!" he called out.

They all turned. They all saw his Glock drawn. And they all didn't move a muscle.

Skip pierced the silence, yelling, "Open the trunk. Now!"

They still didn't move. They were statues, staring back at him. Except for one; his eyes, for a split second, shifted across the alley. Not in front of Skip... behind him.

Skip turned but it was too late. The guy had gotten the jump on him, springing out of a side door of the warehouse exactly as one does in an ambush. It happened so fast.

The last thing Skip heard before falling to the ground was his own gun firing. That's because the second-to-last thing he heard was the sound of the other guy's gun. Timing is everything, whether you're courtsiding or trading bullets.

Down the alley, behind the wheel of the Jeep, Elise Joyce gasped and fumbled the phone in her hands. She'd zoomed in as she recorded and got everything—Skip and the vehicles and the men moving Halston—right up until the sound of the shots and Skip going down.

Instinctively, she ducked for cover in her seat. She wasn't sure exactly what had happened, but she stole a quick peek over the dash and saw that Skip was still on the ground by the dumpster. He wasn't moving.

Well, she sure as hell was.

She threw the Jeep into reverse, slammed her foot on the gas, and peeled out, tires screeching, her heart racing, her head swiveling. Frantically, she kept looking from the front to the back, trying to navigate the narrow alley while checking to see if they were coming after her.

Everything was a blur, and yet amid all the adrenaline and fearing for her life, the Jeep barreling backward with the engine redlining, Elise Joyce still managed one gleeful thought as she glanced at her phone, knowing the evidence it contained.

I'm gonna be the next damn governor of New York.

CHAPTER 96

THE TRUNK IS pitch-black; there's no light for my eyes to adjust to. The seals are seamless, no illumination getting in from anywhere. I'm blind.

But I'm not deaf. One of the guys says something nearby, but I can't make it out. His voice is muffled. Another guy responds—same deal. They're talking, but I can't understand the words. Where are they taking me?

Nowhere in a hurry. As fast as they moved me into the trunk, there's now nothing happening. The car's still just idling. Even the talking has stopped.

Then I hear exactly what I've been waiting for—Skip to the rescue. There's nothing muffled about his voice. I can tell he's calling out from a distance but every word is booming, crystal clear.

"Hey! Open the trunk. Now!" he demands.

That's my brother, quick and to the point. I can picture him taking cover somewhere in the alley, his Glock drawn. *Okay, guys. Do what he says. Open the trunk.*

I'm lying here waiting, in the dark in every sense of the word. I don't hear anything. Nothing's happening.

Then everything happens.

All at once I hear two shots. And all I can tell is that they're from two different guns.

My mouth is taped but still I try to scream. *Skip! Skip!* I'm pounding on the lid of the trunk. No one's saying anything, no one's moving.

Wait.

I stop pounding when I hear the sound of tires peeling out, the sickly roar of the engine...I know those sounds well. It's my Jeep. It's leaving, fast, and I'm back to hearing nothing. What the hell's happening?

My lungs are burning, the duct tape sending all my screams back down my throat. *Skip! Skip!*

The trunk suddenly opens, the light and everything else hitting me all at once.

"Hey, metalhead."

I'm looking up at my brother. He's smiling. I'm speechless. Even after he pulls off the duct tape, I'm still at a loss. I manage three words. "What the hell?"

"You okay?" he asks.

"Am I okay? *Am I okay?* You scared me to death."

"Yeah, sorry about that." He helps me out of the trunk. "Had to be done, though."

Skip cuts my hands free of the tape and I immediately punch him in the shoulder as hard as I can, which is never hard enough with him.

"I'll tell you what has to be done," I say. "I'm going to kill you, that's what has to be done."

"You can't," he says. "I'm already dead. We both are."

CHAPTER 97

SKIP CALLED AN audible. The simple question is why?

Of course, I have my own unique way of asking it. "Are you fucking crazy? Why the hell did you need me in an alley locked in a trunk with my mouth taped?"

"I got a tip from our friends," Skip answers.

"First of all, don't call them that," I say. "They're not our friends."

"What would you prefer I call them?"

"Feds, agents, G-men—anything but our friends."

"They're doing right by us, making good on a mistake. They've also been watching your six. My six as well. Which is how I got the tip and why you ended up in that trunk today," he says, pointing over my shoulder.

The Lincoln Town Car, engine still idling, is the only vehicle remaining in the alley. No sooner did Skip help me out of the trunk than Nikolov's guys disappeared in the Escalade. More on that in a minute.

"Oh, great," I say. "You've officially drunk their Kool-Aid. Those so-called friends of ours are just protecting their investment—that's it, nothing more. All we are to them is a means to an end. If it weren't for what they're getting out of this whole thing, the FBI wouldn't give a shit about your six or mine."

"I think I liked it better when your mouth was taped," says Skip.

"And I think you still haven't told me anything."

"Maybe if you'd let me?"

"I'm listening," I say.

He points again over my shoulder. "I'll explain on the way there."

"Where?"

"You'll see," he says. "We can't hang around here any longer."

That much he doesn't have to explain. In a few minutes Elise Joyce will be back with an entire SWAT team and detectives.

Skip gets behind the wheel of the Town Car, and I grab shotgun. He peels out and I turn to him, all ears.

"I was able to identify every key guy in Lugieri's crew," he begins.

What makes someone a key guy? The answer's very straightforward for my brother. If you're someone, anyone, who might want revenge on Lugieri, congratulations, you're officially a key guy.

But with every foolproof plan to bring down a mob boss, there's still the possibility of a fool you didn't count on. When Skip walked into Osteria Contorni to meet Dominick Lugieri for the first time, he had no idea that Lugieri would be killing one of his crew in cold blood. Mind you, the victim was hardly innocent. The only thing uglier than the guy himself was his rap sheet, says Skip. Meth dealing, aggravated assault, endangering a minor...the world hardly weeps for him.

Save for one person.

Lugieri's private dining room at Osteria Contorni is supposed to be like Vegas: What happens in there, stays in there. And it would've too. No one would've known about the murder had Lugieri not foolishly gotten in bed with Bergamo to launder oodles of money. But once he did, all bets were off. The room was no longer Vegas. The truth escaped.

And landed squarely on Antonio Franchero.

"Who's that?" I ask.

"The brother of the guy Lugieri killed," says Skip. "And for the record, he's just as ugly. And he blames me for his brother's death."

"But Lugieri pulled the trigger. Why's the brother blaming you?"

"He's blaming everybody. But he can't get to Lugieri, especially with him in custody. You and me, on the other hand, he can get to."

I know Skip's not worried about himself. "You mean he can get to me," I say.

"Whatever. The brother wants us both dead, and according to our *friends,* the chatter they've picked up on, he's willing to die trying."

"So you figured—"

"He can't kill us if we've already been killed," he says. "And all we needed was a reliable witness."

"The next governor from the great state of New York, huh?"

Skip nods. "She recorded the whole thing."

Our original plan was good old-fashioned entrapment. Elise Joyce was supposed to waltz into that warehouse in New Jersey thinking she was taking down Anton Nikolov for the planned murder of one Halston Graham, aka Halston Greer, aka me.

Surprise. The only one who'd be getting arrested was her. The two men backing up Skip in the warehouse were FBI, and the mistake they were correcting on behalf of the Bureau was allowing—or, more accurately, being oblivious to—the lead prosecutor in our father's case to suppress evidence that would've supported the defense. Of course, that prosecutor was Elise Joyce, and the evidence was a series of email exchanges between our father and Enzio Bergamo that suggested Dad wasn't initially aware he was participating in a major art scam.

But instead of being taken to a warehouse, I was taken to an alley, stashed in a trunk with my mouth taped, and made to think that my brother had either abandoned me or, worse, been shot and killed. So it pains me to admit this:

As audibles go, this one was genius.

Skip looks over at me when he's done explaining. "I can tell," he says. "You're seeing the endgame, right? The way this plays out?"

"It'll be like a zombie movie," I say.

"Exactly."

"But in the meantime, we're dead. So now what?"

He's timed it perfectly, turning into a parking garage on Eldridge Street on the Lower East Side. The attendant takes one look at the car and nods.

"We're here," says Skip.

CHAPTER 98

WE DRIVE PAST the attendant, around a tight corner, and into a metal-cage car elevator that takes us up two levels; there, we park in a spot reserved for CIOCIOLA & CO. Right next to the spot is a locked door with rusted hinges, a sign that warns about high voltage, and a keypad. Skip puts in a code, and we enter a narrow hallway, at the end of which is another door and a keypad that requires a different code, or so Skip tells me.

Finally we're inside.

"What is this place?" I ask.

"It's a safe house. Well, more like a safe apartment," says Skip.

The furnishings are sparse, just the essentials. There's somewhere to sit, somewhere to eat, somewhere to sleep. A bathroom with a shower. Besides a lone flat-screen TV, the walls are bare, not a personal touch to be found anywhere, although nothing looks temporary either, the way it might if the place had been set up only for this assignment... or whatever the FBI is calling it these days. Originally, this was Operation Austin, named not for the city in Texas but rather for the golfer

Mike Austin, who holds the world record for the longest drive off a tee in a professional tournament. In other words, what we've been doing, Operation Austin, has been all about the long game.

Maybe they're still calling it that, I don't know. Once the game started, any contact with the FBI stopped. Not that there was too much before. There's a fine line between trust and distrust, and I've been straddling it with the Bureau from day one. In all fairness, though, and as Skip keeps reminding me, we approached them, not the other way around.

Now we're waiting on them, stashed in a safe house. Scratch that, a safe apartment. "I'm hungry," I announce.

"There's some food in the fridge," says Skip. "A couple of sandwiches."

"For real?"

"It's not like we can order Uber Eats."

"Good point."

I'm halfway through a turkey and cheddar on wheat when Skip's phone pings. He looks. It's one of the agents texting. "They're on their way," says Skip.

Agents Sigma and Tau walk through the door about twenty minutes later, both looking exactly as they did the first and only time I met them a few months ago. There really isn't one word that captures the feeling they give you. In fact, I don't think any words apply. It's more like an emotion. When you look at them, you immediately feel the weight of everything they've encountered in all their years as field agents. They wear it on their faces, their bodies. They still joke and banter, but it's done with an air of detachment. Even when they're right in front of you, they still seem far away.

"Tomorrow," says Tau, grabbing a bottled water from the fridge and joining us at a table near the kitchen. "She would've done it today, but it's Sunday. Less press coverage. Bad TV."

She, of course, is Elise Joyce. And the *it* is her arresting Nikolov.

As soon as Joyce returned to the scene of the crime, as it were, and saw no evidence of anything she witnessed in that alley, the decision was made. This is what Tau and Sigma tell us, courtesy of their guy at the organized crime task force. Joyce is obliged to notify the OCTF in a situation like this.

"She has an unmarked staked out near the end of Nikolov's driveway in case he tries to go anywhere before dawn," says Tau.

"Is that when she wants to bring him in?" asks Skip. "Bright and early?"

"There's something about arresting a mob boss in his pajamas," says Sigma.

"She's planning for six a.m.," says Tau, "so we want to be in place at Nikolov's home around five, which means we'll be picking you up here at four."

"There goes my beauty sleep," says Sigma with the awareness of a guy who knows he'll never be mistaken for a male model. He points at Skip and then me. "Although I am looking forward to seeing Joyce's face when she walks in and sees the two of you back from the dead."

"Who's wearing the bodycam?" asks Skip.

"There'll be two arresting officers in addition to us," says Tau. "Both will have cameras."

I can't help thinking of how satisfying it will be when the footage goes viral. Sure, for total clicks, it will never top Bergamo's face-plant on the runway of his own fashion show, but the effect will be the same, and that's all that matters. Elise Joyce, who broke the law to put my father in jail, is finally going down.

I'm so wrapped up in picturing it in my head that I barely hear Sigma's phone ring. He steps away from the table to answer it. I'm not paying attention. No one is.

"Fuck!" yells Sigma.

Now we're all paying attention.

CHAPTER 99

WHATEVER IT IS, it's not good.

Sigma confirms as much when he returns to the table. "Joyce isn't making the trip to Nikolov's house," he says. "She's not coming for the arrest."

"That's impossible," I say.

"Apparently, it isn't," says Sigma.

"How?" I ask. "*Why?* Why isn't she going?"

"We don't know, but word got back to the task force."

"It might be a safety thing," says Skip. "She saw me get shot and killed this morning and is convinced Halston met the same fate. In her mind it's not as if Nikolov will be rolling out the red carpet for her."

It's hard to push back on that, especially having seen all of Nikolov's security. Joyce has no idea that his guys and their loaded AR-15s will be standing down. And, yeah, after what she "witnessed" in the alley, maybe she's a little gun-shy.

But still.

"She's wanted to be in on everything. *Everything*," I say. "Every setup, every wire worn. And I don't mean just in the loop. She wanted to be right there where it was happening, on the scene, on the front lines. She didn't have to ride with Skip this morning when he followed me, but she insisted. That's her thing, what she thinks will get her to the governor's mansion: 'Vote for Elise Joyce, the fearless female.'"

"What can I tell you? She's taking a pass," says Sigma. "She's not going to Nikolov's house."

"She's not passing on all the glory, that's for sure," says Tau. "The way she was beaming from that podium last week announcing Lugieri's arrest along with Bergamo's? She knows good TV from bad, that's for sure."

"Okay, so plan B," says Skip. "We need to figure out a way that Joyce changes her mind and joins the raid on Nikolov's house."

I hear every word Skip says but it's only two words that echo in my head: *Good TV*.

"No," I blurt out. And now I've got three guys staring at me. *No? What do you mean, no?* They're waiting on me to explain. Here goes. "I mean, there's another way to go about this. But I would need to visit Nikolov beforehand."

"First of all, he's under surveillance," says Skip. "Second, you're dead, remember? You can't be seeing or talking to anyone."

"But what if I weren't?" I ask.

Skip squints. "Weren't what?"

"Dead," I say. "What if I escaped from that trunk before Nikolov's guys killed me?"

Skip has seen this look in my eyes many times since we were kids, the spark of an idea taking hold.

"Where are you going with this?" he asks.

"Not *where* but *who*. Who would most want to hear the story I'd have to tell, the sister grieving the cold-blooded murder of her brother, hell-bent on revenge and bringing all the receipts? You know what that would be, don't you?"

"Yeah," says Skip with the same look in his eyes. "Good TV."

CHAPTER 100

WE'VE GOT TWELVE hours, tops. But all that matters is the next sixty minutes.

"You want me to do *what*?" asks Nikolov.

We're using Agent Sigma's 128-bit encrypted satellite phone. No one can listen in, there's no tapping the line, but if anyone could, they would hear me telling Nikolov to give himself up.

"You have your attorney reach out to Joyce's office and say he's caught wind of your impending arrest. But you're so confident of your innocence that you're willing to come in voluntarily for questioning. As much as Joyce would prefer the headline that she raided your house at the crack of dawn, she knows she can't turn down this offer because it's admissible in court. So she agrees to it."

"Then what?" asks Nikolov. "So I go in... and then what happens?"

"You go in, answer all her questions, and make it abundantly clear that you had nothing to do with whatever she thinks you did."

"Yeah, okay. *And then what?*"

"Then she arrests you," I say.

He laughs. "You're fucking crazy. Why would I ever do that?"

"I'll tell you why," I say.

Thirty minutes later, the real crazy begins.

"You want me to do *what*?" asks Skip.

"I want you to punch me in the face," I say.

He has no intention of hitting me, even though he knows why I'm asking. "No chance, sis," he says.

"C'mon, I'm not talking full strength, just something that will bruise up quickly. You told me Amir punched you before you first met Lugieri. It's my turn to take one for the team."

"Nice speech. Still not going to happen," says Skip.

I turn to Agents Sigma and Tau. "Don't look at us," they say in unison.

"Fine. I'll do it myself."

But there's no way I'm about to pull an Edward Norton from *Fight Club* and start beating myself up. It's one thing to take a punch; it's an entirely different thing to be the one also delivering it.

"What, you don't think Joyce will believe you unless you're banged up?" asks Tau.

"Yeah," says Sigma. "Of course she'll believe you. She saw you get put into that trunk and now suddenly you're alive—what's not to believe?"

I mull it over for a moment. "I guess you're right," I say.

If time heals all wounds, how long do you have to wait to make new ones? I figure ten minutes.

We move on, discussing how I'll contact Joyce and from where. Presumably, Nikolov's guys took my cell phone. Also, how did I escape? Do I have further evidence proving Nikolov was the one who ordered the hit on Skip? The both of us? I need to have all the details locked down.

"I'll be right back," I say, heading off to the bathroom.

I partially close the door and stand behind it about six inches away. The laws of physics are very clear on what will happen next.

I shut my eyes, lean in forehead first, and brace myself for when they come running. On your mark, get set...

"Help!" I scream.

CHAPTER 101

I MEET ELISE Joyce in the back of a bodega a few blocks from her office. I'm battered, bruised, and hysterical. Unexpectedly, she hugs me.

Not because she's so relieved I'm alive or because she thinks I'm in desperate need of emotional support after losing my brother. No, her embrace—and her fake tears and bullshit words of sympathy—comes from sheer joy. She's like a rich kid waking up on Christmas morning: There's no doubt in her mind that she's about to get everything she wants.

The governor's mansion, wrapped in a bow.

I tell her everything that happened with my equally fake tears. How I was able to use the sharp edge of the interior catch on the Town Car trunk's lock to cut through the tape around my wrists. They started driving, and when they were at a stoplight, I popped the emergency latch and made a break for it. I ran and ultimately lost them in a crowded subway station.

"As soon as I saw a train coming, I jumped the turnstile and caught the train just as the doors closed. I switched trains twice and then took the L train out here to Brooklyn. That's when I borrowed someone's phone and called you."

"I thought for sure you were dead," she says.

"What about my brother?" I ask. "You told me on the phone that they killed him. Those were the gunshots I heard while in the trunk?"

"Yes."

"So you saw it happen?"

Joyce nods, hesitates. "I more than just saw it. Before he got out of your Jeep, he insisted that I record everything. I didn't want to tell you but—"

"It's evidence. I understand, I get it," I say. "And I'm glad you got it. It's important." Deep breath. "Where is he now? At the morgue?"

Again, she hesitates. "I obviously got the hell out of that alley as fast as possible. I called it in to the First Precinct and when we came back, there was nothing to see. They'd taken your brother."

I turn and fix my gaze on a nearby refrigerated display case stocked with every conceivable energy drink. There are four shelves of Red Bulls alone.

I can feel Joyce staring at me, thinking of what to say next. More to the point, she's trying to figure out how to get what she needs from me.

"That's some shiner, by the way," she says.

I turn back to her. "I wish I could say you should see the other guys."

"Don't worry, I'll be seeing them, all right. But I'm going to need your help."

And there it is. The ask.

"Whatever it takes," I say.

"Nikolov has already lawyered up."

"What do you mean?"

"Word somehow leaked that he was about to be arrested, or maybe he just assumed as much once you escaped," she says. "Either way, his attorney reached out about an hour ago and offered up Nikolov for questioning."

"When?"

"Tomorrow."

"What's the angle?" I ask.

"I don't care. It doesn't matter," she says. "They don't know I have the recording. We'll listen to everything Nikolov says, and when he's done, he'll be arrested. And you can start getting some justice."

You can say that again.

CHAPTER 102

THE PRESS ROOM is packed, standing room only. Even out in the hall I can hear the buzz. They're all talking about the same thing, the rumor. Another high-profile arrest?

Wow, that Elise Joyce is having the best week of her professional career. First it was Dominick Lugieri and Enzio Bergamo. Now she's bringing down none other than Anton Nikolov? She's no longer a rising star. She's a supernova.

And she's taking the stage in thirty seconds.

According to Joyce, I don't have a speaking role. Not that she actually says that. She just tells me everything she's going to do and asks that I stand behind her at the podium, well within the frame of all the news cameras so everyone can see me looking forlorn and heartbroken. I'm a prop. Exhibit A.

Exhibit B is the large photo of Skip in uniform projected on a screen with MALCOLM GREER, US ARMY SPECIAL FORCES in boldface type at the bottom.

Exhibit C, *c* as in the *coup de grâce*, is her cell phone video of Skip's murder in the alley. Joyce absolutely, positively can't wait to show it.

She's so excited that she rushes through her opening statement, confirming the rumor that, yes, Anton Nikolov has been arrested for Malcolm Greer's murder. Nikolov might not have pulled the trigger, she declares, but he for sure pulled all the strings. And she can prove it.

"But that's for the courtroom," she says. "I'm not blind to the court of public opinion, however, which is why it's so important to show you the following video, no matter how graphic and disturbing it might be."

She looks over at one of her aides, and the woman immediately hits a button on a remote. The video plays. Even in a roomful of jaded reporters who have seen it all in their careers, there are still a few audible gasps when Skip gets shot.

Hands rocket up once the video ends but Joyce has one more thing to say before taking questions.

"I just want everyone to know that I had every intention of editing this video, blacking out Captain Greer's image, but his sister," she says, pointing at me, "insisted that it be shown as is. She's more committed to the whole truth and nothing but than I am."

You have no idea, Counselor.

Joyce takes questions, answering each one directly or deftly pivoting as she sees fit. She has a set narrative that this was all part of a sting operation, which gives her the cover to say that certain facts and details can't be revealed at this time. Q and As with the US attorney are always a cat-and-mouse game, and the press are used to it. Reporters rarely ask pointed follow-ups for fear they'll get shut out in the future. Those who have the podium have the leverage.

"Yes, you in the back," says Joyce, pointing.

The young man in his mid-twenties stands, clears his throat. "If you're not willing to reveal how the video was obtained or who shot it, why should we assume it's real?"

Joyce blinks. *"Real?"*

"Yes," he says. "What guarantee do we have that it's legitimate?"

"What more of a guarantee would you like? I don't know if you've heard but I am a US attorney and chief of the criminal division."

That elicits a few smirking chuckles from the room. Joyce calls for the next question.

The reporter remains standing. "I'm sorry, that wasn't an answer," he says loudly. "That was just your résumé."

"Excuse me?" asks Joyce.

The entire press corps turns to look at the reporter. So do all the cameras, swiveling on their stands.

The balls on this young guy, everyone's thinking. *Who the hell is he? What paper or network is he from? And what's up with those muttonchops?*

I suppress a smile, thinking of Wolfgang's response when I called him. *Halston, if I can fake a one-hundred-forty-nine-million-dollar Picasso, I'm pretty sure I can swing a media badge.*

I was pretty sure as well.

"You've arrested Anton Nikolov for ordering a hit on Malcolm Greer," Wolfgang continues. "The video purports to show him being shot—"

"Purports?" Joyce's face flashes red.

"I'm just saying that murder cases usually require a dead body for evidence, and you don't have that."

"No, what I have—what you all have—is my word that we possess all the evidence we need to convict Mr. Nikolov."

"But if you're wrong, you've destroyed a man's reputation."

"Which is why I'm willing to stake mine that I'm not wrong," says Joyce.

"Are you sure about that?" asks Wolfgang.

The word *yes* is only one syllable but Joyce can barely get it out of her mouth before every jaw in the room drops. She turns around from the podium to see what everyone's staring at. It's her entire career going down in flames.

"What the hell?"

"You mind if my sister and I say a few words?" asks Malcolm.

CHAPTER 103

THOSE WHO HAVE the podium have the power.

For the first time in a long while, Elise Joyce has no clue what to do next. She stammers, she nearly trips over her own feet, and ultimately she storms out of the press conference without completing another sentence, which is fitting because waiting for her backstage are Agents Sigma and Tau, who will promptly inform her of her right to remain silent.

"While we have you all here," begins Skip as I join him at the podium.

Every face looking back at us has the same expression: Shock. Disbelief. The immediate desire to figure out what the hell is happening. How is Malcolm Greer back from the grave? Of course the answer is plain to see. He was never dead.

Skip and I take turns laying out the case against Joyce, quickly highlighting the past few weeks before getting to the smoking gun—the evidence she suppressed during our father's trial. And just to make sure every reporter digests every last detail, Skip gives the address of a website he created just for the occasion. He didn't get overly snarky with the name; it's very straightforward: joycebrokethelaw.com.

No one waits for us to open the floor for questions. The room erupts before Skip can finish saying *dot-com,* everyone yelling over one another. We answer what we want to and deflect what we don't. Ultimately, it's an FBI sting operation, we explain, and they'll be announcing their own press conference later today. No one needs to know—not now and hopefully not ever—that Skip and I are the ones who first approached the Bureau. Of course, that won't stop a few reporters with pit-bull blood from chasing down their suspicions, and they can have at it.

The one thing they'll never know is how we hacked into Elise Joyce's private email server that she used to skirt her transparency requirements at the US attorney's office. How did we even know she had one?

Years back, when the FBI raided our home, they took my father's laptop, which contained screenshots of text exchanges with Bergamo, demonstrating my father wasn't originally involved in the forgery scam. He wasn't comfortable having the texts just sitting on his phone so he made the pdf copies and erased the entire thread. During discovery, my father's attorney requested these copies but was told by Joyce they weren't on the hard drive. A digital forensics expert even backed up her claim.

So, once again, how did we know Joyce was using a private email server for official business?

For a long time we didn't, but it always bugged me that those screenshots went "missing." Joyce had to be behind it; the question was how. Then, during my senior year at Columbia, I met Vikram. He was a computer science major. He also had the second-highest GPA in our graduating class. Second behind me—until I messed up on my art history final.

I asked Vikram how someone in Joyce's position, knowing that my father's hard drive would be examined by a digital forensics expert, could delete files from the drive without leaving a footprint.

"The short answer is that she almost certainly couldn't," said Vikram.

"What's the long answer?" I asked. "The one that explains why you said *almost*."

Vikram explained the concept of mirroring, an AI program that could mimic the activity on a server in real time. "Or with half a millisecond of lag time, if you want to be precise about it," he said.

Mirroring basically allowed someone to create two realities, one public and the other private, and then alter a digital footprint in a way that 99 percent of forensics experts wouldn't be able to detect.

"Vikram, please tell me you're in the one percent," I said.

He was.

And so was whomever Joyce had used to install the mirroring program on the criminal division's server at the US attorney's office. Or at least, that's what Vikram believed—right after he was able to trace a backdoor portal to a private email account registered to a fictitious name but having the same IP address as...wait for it...the modem in Elise Joyce's Upper East Side apartment.

"Thanks, but no, thanks," said Vikram after I offered to pay him for his help. No matter how much I insisted, he refused to accept any money from me. Ironically, that was the thrust of his valedictorian speech at graduation:

Doing right in this world should be reward enough.

CHAPTER 104

"HI, DADDY."

I can't remember the last time I said those words without being surrounded by cinder block. That's how long it's been. But today there're no walls around us and nothing but blue sky above. My father's a free man.

He hugs me. He hugs my brother. "Hi, Dad," says Skip.

My father hugs Amir, who insisted on driving us immediately after the press conference. Normally I'd feel a little self-conscious about showing up at a state penitentiary in a white Rolls-Royce Phantom. I even said as much to Amir, which was when he reminded me of his early days in Pakistan after escaping Iran in 1979.

"My wife and I slept in an old sewage drainpipe for a month before upgrading to the concrete floor of a storage room," he said. "I wasn't ashamed of what I didn't have then, and I'm not ashamed of what I do have now."

What Amir has now, after coming to America and initially finding work as an assistant mechanic, is over two dozen luxury-car dealerships in the tristate area. One of my father's first clients, he was also a victim of the scam. Right before sentencing, though, my father transferred every penny of every remaining asset he had to Amir in an effort to make good on his debt. It was my father's way of saying *I'm sorry*.

And this was Amir's way of saying *Apology accepted*. He and his wife took me in after my mother's suicide, and once he learned the truth behind the scam, he was all in on engineering my father's release. "I want to be there for your dad," Amir told me from the start. It was only fitting that on this particular day, he would literally show up for him.

So off we went in his Rolls. For the record, it rides like silk.

"Do you mind if Fred here takes it for a quick spin?" my father asks.

"Of course not," says Amir, tossing Fred the keys.

It's no surprise that Fred, the only security guard who truly looked out for me—and my father—over the years, is the one who escorted him out of the prison. Early on, Fred whispered to me, "The walls have ears," right before I was about to head into the visitation room. It's the best tip-off I ever got.

Fred laughs in his deep baritone voice. "I really can't," he says, about to hand back the keys.

"Of course you can," says Amir.

"Yeah. C'mon, Fred," says my father. "Trust me, you only live once."

That seals the deal. Fred witnessed the heart attack that almost claimed my father. It resonated even more with him because Fred's own father had died from one.

"Okay, maybe just a quick spin," says Fred. We're outside the walls of the prison; he's got no one to guard. He climbs behind the wheel and pulls away, flashing the world's biggest smile.

Make that the second-biggest smile.

My dad's got him beat. "Today's a good day," he says, hugging Skip and me again. "A very good day indeed."

Unlike Elise Joyce, the FBI agents were true to their word. If Skip and I did as we promised, they said, our father would be released. Of course we knew Joyce would renege, which was why it was part of our plan.

There'll be no declaration of a mistrial. No need for a new one either. Officially, it's "time served" for Mr. Conrad Greer, inmate number 47296. That's what the paperwork says. What it doesn't say is that the FBI, when duly motivated, has extraordinary pull with the penal system.

My father turns around to take one last look at the prison that's now behind him in every sense. He'll never get those years back, none of us will, and all that time he spent inside will stay with him for the rest of his life. But at least starting today, he gets to decide where that will be, the place he'll call home, and I guarantee you there won't be a cinder block in sight.

"Who's hungry?" my father asks. "Fred tells me there's a good diner a few miles south of here. Big menu, they make everything."

"What are you in the mood for?" I ask.

My father looks at me. We both know he's scheduled to have a stent inserted in his right coronary artery in two days, and we both know I'm not about to give him a hard time about fat and cholesterol, given the moment. He smiles again. "Did I ever tell you what my favorite Jimmy Buffett song is?"

"We don't have to speak in code anymore, Dad," says Skip.

"Maybe not, but I'm going to order the same," I say.

"Me too," says Amir. "And I don't even know what it is yet."

Fred returns in the Rolls, thanks Amir, and turns to my father. Guards aren't supposed to hug prisoners upon their release but Fred doesn't seem to care too much about protocol today. "Screw it," he says, wrapping his big arms around my father. "Take care of yourself, okay?"

"You too."

And off we go, taking Fred's suggestion and going to the diner down the road. It's only a few miles away, but to my father it feels like another planet. We grab a booth in the back and start chipping away on all the things we have to catch up on—what's happened and what lies ahead. I've still got another thing on my plate but that's for another day.

"What'll you have?" asks the waitress.

"A cheeseburger in paradise," says my father.

Make that four.

EPILOGUE

AUTUMN RHYTHM

CHAPTER 105

I LOVE FALL in New York City.

For all the same reasons you hear about. I don't care if they're clichés. The leaves turning in Central Park. The crisp, cool nights. The drumbeat of the sidewalks with everyone rushing—quick, quick, quick—to all the places they need to be. There's definitely a rhythm to it. Chaos in control.

And all of New York City seems to love the fall of Elise Joyce.

It's not as if she were a household name. At least, not before. What resonated with people, beyond the facts of what she'd done, was the perception that she had no remorse. Consumed by ambition, she'd managed to rationalize the very behavior she was tasked with rooting out as a US attorney. Worse, she wasn't one among many, a foot soldier who got out of line—she was the one in charge. In the days that followed, some of those pit-bull reporters managed to uncover a few more instances in which she bent the law so far, she might have broken it. Time will tell. Or, more accurately, a jury will.

Yeah, if I had a nickel for every time I either heard or read someone quote the British historian Lord Acton on the heels of the press conference. But that's the thing about clichés, and why I don't mind them. They're invoked so often because they're always true.

Power tends to corrupt; absolute power corrupts absolutely.

If I had to bet, Enzio Bergamo, currently out on bail and wearing the world's least fashionable ankle bracelet, will ultimately accept some type of plea bargain in exchange for pleading guilty.

As for Dominick Lugieri, there'll be no bargains on the table. He'll remain in custody, awaiting trial, along with eleven guys in his crew against whom the state was able to bring charges. That alone was enough to warrant my being placed in the Witness Protection Program, but apparently we've also got to contend with the brother of the guy Lugieri killed at Osteria Contorni—although before he left the country, my brother no longer seemed too concerned about him, and it wasn't simply because Skip would be flying in a C-27J Spartan to rejoin his unit embedded somewhere in the Middle East. He knew something about the brother that I didn't, and I was fairly certain it was the kind of something that I—and every other civilian on the planet—would never know.

Never you mind, metalhead, I knew he'd say if I ventured to ask. I didn't.

After my father's successful stent procedure and after our family spent a few additional days reconnecting at an "undisclosed location," Skip was off. I followed the next day, but not before my father and I had one more conversation.

"I'm proud of you," he said. "Even though you didn't listen to me."

"I always listen to you. But it's like you used to say to us: Be confident or be nothing. So maybe I'm just a little stubborn with my ideas."

My father hadn't wanted Skip and me to do what we did. He thought it was too risky, too ambitious. "I don't mind a game of solitaire," he'd told me one Sunday afternoon in the prisoners' visiting room, "but I'm not a big fan of dominoes."

Meaning: Did we really have to take down everyone who'd screwed him over all at once?

In my mind, it was the only way.

"Speaking of stubborn," he said, "that's what I wanted to talk to you about."

I knew what was coming. "It's about Mom, isn't it?"

"It's more about you, sweetheart. Because there's nothing your mother can do anymore to change. She'll always be exactly as you remember her."

"I know."

"You never talk about her. You never even mention her name."

"I know that too," I said. "It's hard."

"Of course it is. And Lord knows you excel at holding a grudge—as Bergamo, Lugieri, and Joyce know," he said. "But this particular grudge you need to let go. And if you can't do it for yourself, can you do it for me?"

"I'm not sure I even know how."

"It doesn't have to be all at once. But maybe with each passing day you can try to be a little less mad at her, not blame her as much for giving up on herself... for giving up on us."

I took my father's hand, squeezed it tight. "I promise you I'll try," I said.

"Good. Now go do what you told me about," he whispered. "Make me even prouder."

CHAPTER 106

AGENTS SIGMA AND Tau are assigned to drive me to the airport. I don't mention the unscheduled stop I want to make until I click my seat belt inside their Chevy Suburban. They, of course, immediately say no, not a chance. Then I tell them why, and they have a change of heart.

Sigma turns to me from the front passenger seat. "Why didn't you say so?"

"I just did, you knuckleheads."

He chuckles. They both do. "Yeah, we're really going to miss you, Halston," says Tau.

Sarcasm truly is a lost art. These two are a couple of Picassos.

Deena Maxwell—Miss D—greets me in the foyer of the Sisterhood Foster Home. She knew I was coming, so she made sure Michelle would be there. It is a Friday, not our usual day. Of course, after going viral at Elise Joyce's press conference, I am anything but usual.

I'm sure Miss D has a lot of questions after watching me at the podium with my brother, but she doesn't ask a single one. This visit isn't about her or the two of us, and someone with the compassion and fortitude to oversee an entire foster home understands that.

"Hey, Michelle!" she calls upstairs. "Halston's here!"

I hear the footsteps before I see her scuffed-up pink Reeboks turning the corner around the banister on the second floor. Michelle had been told I was coming, but that's all.

"Hi, Halston!" She practically leaps into my arms. "What's happening? Are we going somewhere today instead of tomorrow? Huh? Are we?"

"Halston just wanted to stop by for a quick visit," says Miss D. "Why don't you show her what you were working on in the art room? I'm sure she'll want to see it."

Michelle's eyes light up at the idea. She spins around and motions for me to follow. I mouth *Thank you* to Miss D, and she shoots me back a wink. I had asked her if there was somewhere in the house where I could talk to Michelle alone, and she knew just the place.

"Wow, this is cool," I say, walking behind Michelle into a den that has been converted into an arts and crafts free-for-all. Every inch of wall space, every tabletop, everywhere you look, there is some sort of creation. Paintings, collages, sculptures, hanging mobiles—and yet I am still able to spot it immediately, pinned to a large corkboard.

"Can you guess which one's mine?" asks Michelle.

"I don't have to guess," I say, pointing. "Did you really paint that?"

Of course she did. The squiggly lines and drips of paint, the splatters and the splotches. I am looking at a nine-year-old's homage to Jackson Pollock, made with all the colors of the rainbow instead of just black and white and brown. I wouldn't want it any other way.

"Do you like it?" she asks.

"I love it!"

"Do you see what I did with all the lines, the way they go zig-zag-zig?"

"I think that's my favorite part," I say.

"Mine too." She folds her arms, smiling. "Miss D called it a masterpiece!"

"I agree."

"Oh, and guess who didn't like it?"

"Janet from Another Planet."

"She was just jealous, right?"

"Totally."

"I can't wait to show it to my mother," she says. "And I can't wait for you to meet her!"

It is an easy segue. Unfortunately, it isn't an easy conversation. "I wanted to talk to you about that," I say.

Michelle can hear something in my voice. "Is something wrong?" she asks.

"I can't wait to meet your mother too. I just won't be able to when she comes and visits."

"Why not?"

"I have to go away for a little while," I say. "It's, like, a business trip."

"For how long?"

"I'm not sure exactly, but at least a few months."

"You mean I won't get to see you every Saturday?"

I watch as her eyes well up with tears. I know exactly what she is thinking: *Why does everyone leave me?*

"I promise you I'll be back," I say. "And I'll make you another promise. When I do come back, you're going to have a lot to tell me about. A lot of really good things."

"How do you know?" she asks.

It would be so simple to be the hero. I could tell her about the job waiting for her mother when she gets out of rehab, as a receptionist at one of Amir's dealerships in Midtown Manhattan. Or about the rent-free apartment in one of the many buildings that Shen Wan owns in and around Chinatown and the Lower East Side. Michelle will have her own bedroom, where she can hang as many paintings as she wants.

The biggest gateway drug in the world is poverty, Miss D had said. I'll be damned if I'm going to let that gate open again.

"How do I know about all these good things? I just know," I say to Michelle, wiping a tear from her cheek. "But it's a promise. You trust me, don't you?"

She nods. "Yes."

I know she does, which is another reason I can't be the hero. It has to be her mother. She is the one who needs to earn back Michelle's trust. She has to stay clean and stay focused on being there for her daughter. Always and forever.

"I'll miss you, sweetheart, but I'm going to write you letters, and you'll write back, and it will be just like we're hanging out together," I say. "And soon we will be again, okay?"

Michelle wipes away her remaining tears. She unpins her painting from the corkboard. "Here," she says, handing it to me. "I want you to take this with you."

"But don't you want to show it to your mother?"

"I'm going to make another. It will be a special one just for her."

"I think that's a great idea," I say.

We hug so tightly, I don't want to let go. But I know I have to, and it isn't just because there is a plane to catch.

I get back in the Suburban, and for the entire ride to the airport, I stare at Michelle's masterpiece. Her own *Autumn Rhythm*. My finger traces all the lines going zig-zag-zig.

Life rarely comes at you straight, and the shortcuts are few and far between. Sometimes, to get where you want to go, you need to take the long way. It's the unexpected path, or at least the path that no one else expects.

If you're looking for me, I'll be off the grid for a while longer. But eventually I'll be back around. This isn't bye forever.

It's just bye for now.

ABOUT THE AUTHORS

JAMES PATTERSON is the most popular storyteller of our time. He is the creator of unforgettable characters and series, including Alex Cross, the Women's Murder Club, Jane Smith, and Maximum Ride, and of breathtaking true stories about the Kennedys, John Lennon, and Tiger Woods, as well as our military heroes, police officers, and ER nurses. Patterson has coauthored #1 bestselling novels with Bill Clinton, Dolly Parton, and Michael Crichton. He has told the story of his own life in *James Patterson by James Patterson* and received an Edgar Award, ten Emmy Awards, the Literarian Award from the National Book Foundation, and the National Humanities Medal.

HOWARD ROUGHAN has cowritten several books with James Patterson and is the author of *The Promise of a Lie* and *The Up and Comer*. He lives in Florida with his wife and son.

Elinor Gilbert is

THE INVISIBLE WOMAN

—but *not* the kind who can walk through walls. As she joins a special FBI surveillance detail, she discovers why a person living in the shadows might want to *reappear*.

Read on for a sneak peek.

MY NAME IS Elinor Gilbert. And I am the Invisible Woman.

No, not the kind that can make a deck of cards look like it's shuffling itself.

The other kind.

Five years at the same dry cleaner, and he still asks my name when I drop something off.

Eleven years at the same drugstore, and I doubt the pharmacist could pick me out of a lineup.

My kind of invisible isn't fantasy or science fiction. It's real. It happens slowly, over time. And you won't even know it's happening.

Then one day you're in line at Whole Foods, feeling good about yourself and your healthy life choices—a cart full of plant-based ground meat, oat milk, fat-free yogurt, and organic broccoli (and deftly hidden under all that, a chocolate fudge cake that serves four)—when some guy scoots in front of you. So you say, very nicely, "Excuse me. I think I was next."

And the jerk says, "Oh, sorry, lady. I didn't even *see* you."

Say *what*?

That's when you start to notice how things have changed.

Those annoying wolf whistles from construction workers that you found so demeaning at the time? Gone.

Those makeup ladies in Bloomingdale's who tried to spritz you with the latest Eau de Something New and Fabulous? History.

Sure, those nice-looking guys on the bus are still there. And they still try to catch your eye. But now, it's to offer you their seat.

Somehow, when I wasn't looking, I seem to have passed my sell-by date. And there's nothing I can do about it.

Well, except for that chocolate fudge cake.

THE GRIDDLER IS technically a coffee shop. But the staff lets you sit for hours, even if you're not working on a screenplay.

Another plus: They make a great Cobb salad. Huge homemade croutons, chunks of free-range roast chicken, and a giant crispy X of bacon across the top.

My waiter today, Desmond, takes my order as if he's doing me a favor. My guess is he's an actor wannabe, hoping to be noticed by all the screenwriter wannabes nearby. He's sized me up and decided I can do nothing to further his career.

But a simple snub won't spoil this glorious Sunday in late September.

As I nurse my last glass of summer rosé, something Eleanor Roosevelt once said pops into my head: *No one can make you feel inferior without your consent.* That Eleanor. What a trouper. She had a mother-in-law who hated her and a skirt-chasing husband who humiliated her with a gaggle of willing women and one in particular:

Missy LeHand. His tall, beautiful, very *public* private secretary who, according to rumor, made FDR's Warm Springs summer cottage quite a bit warmer.

But Eleanor was not one for pity parties. I raise my glass and silently toast her and her dignity as Desmond shows up with my salad and a bowl of blue cheese dressing on the side.

I look around. Except for the usual handful of scruffy writers typing away on laptops, I have the place pretty much to myself. So it surprises me to see an older man swivel from the cash register, bypass all the empty tables, and head in my direction with a cup of coffee. I don't have my distance glasses on, but he seems to be smiling. At me? The Invisible Woman? Maybe he didn't get the memo.

But as he gets closer, I see it's not a smile at all. It's a smirk.

I'd know that smirk anywhere.

It's Alan Metcalf. Somebody I used to work with. Somebody from my days at the FBI. Somebody who—

Well, rather than use some really ugly expletives here, I'll just say this: He's the guy who threw me under the bus.

"Elinor dear," he says, drawing it out in that slow Southern drawl he affects to sound sexy. (Now it's my turn to smirk. I know he grew up in New Jersey.) I'm delighted to see that the years have not been kind to him. What he's lost in hair, he's more than made up for in belly fat. But Metcalf is still pretty much as I remember him: a small man who has convinced himself that arrogance makes him look taller.

"It's been a while," he says.

Not long enough, I think. He eyes the empty seat at my table, hoping I'll ask him to join me. I don't.

"May I?" he finally says. Before I can reply, he pulls the chair out to sit and spills coffee on his sleeve. I try not to laugh.

"You're looking well," he says. He doesn't mean it. He'd say the same thing to a leper. "This is quite the coincidence," he adds. Lie number two.

"No, Metcalf," I say. "Thomas Jefferson and John Adams dying within hours of each other on the Fourth of July? *That's* a coincidence. You being here is not."

"You know me too well," he says. Wrong. I know the *FBI* too well. I know that when they want something, nothing will stand in their way.

"So—to what do I owe this honor?" I ask.

He looks around cautiously to make sure none of the scruffy writers are eavesdropping on what an even scruffier middle-management government guy in a cheap suit has to say.

"We need you," he says. "We have a surveillance assignment. And you're the perfect person to help us out."

Is he kidding?

"Love to help you out," I say. "But I gotta go home and shampoo a rug."

"Now, listen—"

"No. *You* listen," I say. "I'm sure several of the ten thousand FBI agents out there would jump at the chance to work for someone with your level of integrity."

Metcalf's so vain, he probably considers that a compliment.

I return to my salad and spear a particularly crisp piece of bacon, hoping he'll leave me alone. Or die. Whichever comes sooner.

"At least hear me out," he says. "This is something you'd be great at."

Am I curious? Of course. But I'll be damned if I'll let him see that.

"Whatever it is, Metcalf, I'm all wrong for it now. Fact is, I've got a new career I love."

He laughs. "I'd hardly call what you have now a *career*," he says. "You've been teaching music to a bunch of overprivileged private school kids you can't stand. The only thing you love about it is getting summers off."

"Look, I'm really not—"

"Which means you can get a job at a music camp every July, then pop over to Europe every August. You've got a friend from college living in Paris and an ex-beau in Rome."

"Very good," I say. "Now, for your ten-point-bonus question: What was my mother's maiden name?"

I can't believe this guy. Does he really expect me to jump all over him with gratitude?

As Metcalf shakes his head, pondering his next move, his jowls sway like drapes. "Okay. You win," he says at last. "Go back to your lunch. But let me just say: If you can see your way clear to letting bygones be bygones, this assignment is very important to us. Do this, and we'll make it worth your while. And as far as your *reputation* goes..."

I put my fork down with a clunk. There they are. The magic words. *My reputation.*

"Okay. Tell me about it."

"Not here," he says. "This job is way too under the radar, and there's a lot of backstory. Come by my office tomorrow, and I'll tell you everything. Around ten?"

"And what if I say no?"

"You won't," he says. He crushes his cardboard coffee cup and leaves it on my table. One final smirk, and he's gone.

And once again, just like the old days, I'm the one who has to clean up his garbage.

CLEANING UP ALAN Metcalf's garbage. That's what ruined my life.

I entered the New York City job market with a BA in medieval literature and a minor in music theory. Absolutely nothing of any use to any human resources director anywhere. I might as well have majored in Ping-Pong.

So when I saw an opening for a management assistant at the local FBI office, I jumped at the chance. True, *management assistant* was just FBI-speak for *secretary*. But still. I'd seen all the movies. I was sure it was going to be exciting, being assigned to a real live FBI special agent GS-5 who worked in domestic terrorism.

Even back then, Alan Metcalf was gruff and aggressive, overly ambitious, and out for blood. But so were the Knights of the Round Table. I felt right at home.

Eventually, I applied to be an agent myself. It took a few years and several months at Quantico. But then I was promoted, assigned to white-collar crime. Metcalf always bragged that he was the one who first saw my potential. In truth, he was annoyed about losing me as his assistant. He was pissed the day I told him my promotion had come through.

Many years later, Metcalf came to me for a favor. A big one. He wanted me to share the name of a certain confidential informant I had worked with.

Both of us knew he shouldn't be asking for this. You don't just swap out informants like playing cards. There's a whole legal protocol involved. Still, when I said no, he was furious.

Through court records, Metcalf found the guy's name and accidentally disclosed it to the wrong people. A massive security breach. The poor informant had to be whisked away to witness protection. The FBI lost a cherished source. And to save his own ass, Metcalf accused me of outing the guy.

Oh, well. Ancient history.

Today, I've got an important decision to make. What do I wear to an interview for a job I don't think I want?

In the back of my closet is an old Halloween costume from my salad days, a sexy nun outfit with a convertible butt-flap. That could be fun if I were absolutely *sure* I didn't want the job.

Am I?

I settle on jeans, a well-worn sweatshirt, and simple gold hoop earrings I know will be way too small to set off the FBI metal detector. It's the perfect outfit for an undercover surveillance assignment if I want the job.

Do I?

I keep coming back to one simple question: Do I want to go back to work for a man who refers to the most harrowing event in my life as a *bygone*?

Before I can begin to wrestle with that Talmudic question, my phone rings. I assume it's Metcalf's current assistant calling to confirm my appointment with her boss. I can picture her now—a young woman (it's always a woman) Metcalf hired using the same criteria as he did with all the others before and after me: a solid liberal arts background, a tendency toward hero worship, and a minimum bra size of 34C.

But it's not Metcalf's assistant du jour calling. It's my friend Vicky. We met when we were kids. Of all my friends, Vicky's the one I've known and loved the longest.

"Still on for dinner Wednesday?" she asks.

"Wouldn't miss it."

"Great. What do you feel like having?"

It always amuses me when people ask this. How do I know what I'm going to be in the mood for on Wednesday? I'm still wrestling with what to defrost tonight.

"Anything. Your call."

"Maybe that Italian place again?" she suggests. She means Luciano's, an elegant little spot in the West Village with lobster ravioli to die for.

"Perfect," I say. And everything would have been perfect if I hadn't added, "Hey, you'll never guess who I saw yesterday when I was—"

I stop midsentence.

"Who?" Vicky asks.

What was I thinking?

Vicky was privy to the whole Metcalf saga twenty years ago. She hates him almost as much as I do. This is not the time to open that can of worms. Thinking fast, I pull a name out of our collective past. "Uh, Liza Zurndorfer."

"Liza?"

"Remember her, from elementary school? We used to call her ZZ? She looked great."

"Really? I heard she died."

"Oh." *Busted!* "Well, I guess it wasn't her, then."

"Gotta run. Editorial meeting in five. Six thirty Wednesday okay?" she says. Vicky, a high-powered editorial director in a small publishing house, is constantly running to or from a meeting. Our conversations are always short. This time I'm grateful.

She hangs up before I can say something else stupid.

AS I EXIT the subway at the City Hall station, I'm still conflicted. The FBI's New York field office is at 26 Federal Plaza, two blocks away. I start walking, and my phone beeps. It's a text from Metcalf. Could I meet him at a coffee shop on the corner of Warren Street and Broadway, a couple of blocks in the other direction?

Really?

It's unusual to meet off campus, but I don't question it. Maybe this gig is more undercover than I realized. I head north, wending my way past hundreds of men and women in charcoal suits—lawyers, judges, and government workers, all rushing off to jobs that must seem important. Just as mine once did.

I spot Metcalf at a booth way in the back. He's frowning at a corn muffin. Who could be annoyed at a corn muffin? It doesn't take much to set this guy off. Years ago, when I worked for him, someone taped a hand-lettered sign to his door: EASILY IRRITATED. We all thought the guy who did it would be fired. He wasn't. Turned out, Metcalf enjoyed being known as a dick.

I slide in opposite him.

"What do you know about the art world?" he asks.

"And good morning to you too," I say. The art world? I've got a couple of *Happy Birthday, Miss Gilbert* finger paintings from my music students taped to my refrigerator. That's about it.

"We got an anonymous tip," he says. "Some guy who runs an art gallery in Mamaroneck may be laundering money for a Mexican cartel. Las Serpientes," he says. "You look surprised," he adds.

I am. "A small art gallery? In a small Westchester County suburb? Hardly sounds like it would be worth a cartel's time."

Metcalf sneers just a bit.

Uh-oh. My first demerit. I backpedal. "What I mean is, if it was one of those established New York galleries—"

"Then it wouldn't be under the radar, would it?" he says. He breaks off a piece of corn muffin and butters it. "C'mon, Elinor. You should know how these things work. You've been to the rodeo before."

Now I'm the one who's EASILY IRRITATED. True, I worked in fraud for a while, but never in money laundering. Still, I know how huge a problem it is. At one point, the Medellín Cartel had so much cash, they spent two thousand a month just on rubber bands.

"The guy is an art dealer named Ben Harrison," Metcalf says. "We think the cartel is buying art from Harrison, then holding it in storage."

"In Westchester?"

"Westchester, Geneva, could be anywhere. When they're ready, they sell it for wildly inflated prices. Harrison gets a cut on both ends, dirty money gets clean, and some rich sucker somewhere owns a piece of art he thinks is valuable because he trusted a sketchy dealer. So everybody's happy. Well, except the US government."

"And my job would be..."

"Find proof. We want to know everything about Ben Harrison. Who he meets. Who he talks to. Neighbors he's suing. Hookers he's screwing. Habits, hobbies, fetishes. Anything we can use to flip him.

Hell," he says, taking his final bite of the corn muffin and brushing crumbs off his green-and-yellow polyester tie, "if he has an unusual bowel movement, we want to know about it."

"You're a classy guy, Metcalf, you know that?" Most people would be insulted by this. But Metcalf is not most people. He smiles.

Surveillance gigs usually mean sitting in a car outside a suspect's home or digging through phone records and checking credit histories. But there's only so much you can glean from that.

"And, uh, exactly how close do you want me to get to this guy?" I ask.

"You'll be living with him."

"*What?*"

"Don't flatter yourself," he says. "He's married. Second marriage. Trophy wife. New baby."

"So I'll be — what? His social secretary?"

"No."

I hope he doesn't ask me to be the guy's personal chef. I use my oven to store sweaters.

"Actually, we'd be putting you in there as a baby nanny."

I start to laugh. "You gotta be kidding. I don't know anything about babies."

"You'll learn," he says.

He takes a book out of his briefcase and slides it over to me: *What to Expect the First Year*. *This* is my official FBI briefing? I mean, I know the government has a thirty-four-trillion-dollar budget deficit. But still.

"People have been taking care of babies since the cavemen," he says.

"Cave*women*," I say. I slide the book back to him.

"Men, women, what's the difference? Everybody likes babies. You do too, don't you?"

"Sure I do. Love 'em. In other people's arms or homes or uteruses. Just not mine."

"Elinor, you're being unreasonable."

"Metcalf, this is nuts. There's gotta be someone else more suited for this. Some bright-eyed young summer intern who wants to jump-start her career."

"True," he says. And is it my imagination, or is he starting to smile? "But at your age, you'll be able to dig around without being noticed."

Of course. I'm the Invisible Woman. For a moment I almost forgot.

He pulls a thick envelope from his briefcase. "Here," he says, handing it to me. "A license plate for your car..."

"I don't have a car."

"...plus two new credit cards and the burner phone you'll use from now on. It has end-to-end encryption."

"Meaning?"

"Only you and me can read our texts. Hide your old cell someplace. In a shoe, under your vibrator, I don't care where. Just get rid of it."

"Listen, Metcalf—"

"You graduated from Penn State in 1992."

"No, I—"

"It's already part of your Instagram account."

"I don't have an Instagram account."

"You do now," he says. "An account on Facebook too. Your new name is Caroline Babulewicz. Feel free to google it."

"That's a terrible name. I don't even know how to spell it."

"Check your new driver's license. That's in here too. Oh, and I already notified the school where you work that you've had a family emergency and won't be coming back for a while. Tomorrow, we'll fit you for your new uniform. You'll go for an interview the next day and start the day after that," he says.

"I'm out of here," I say.

I start to stand but Metcalf grabs my wrist. He holds it tight. Too tight.

The coffee shop is filling up now. A lot more people. Lots more noise. He leans in a little closer so that when he speaks, I'll hear every word.

"It's an FBI-DOJ-approved Group Two undercover operation," he says. "Do this for us, and we'll rehire you and pay you what you would have been making now had you stayed at the FBI all these years, including benefits."

"Metcalf, let go of my wrist—"

"Plus we'll reinstate your pension and backdate it. It'll be like you never left."

"I said let go. You're hurting me."

"The previous twenty years? Let's just call that an extended sabbatical. That's all anyone has to know. Oh, and we'll throw in a GOV starting right now. What do you think?"

I hate what I'm thinking.

Cash. My pension back. Health insurance. Long-term disability. A chance to reclaim my reputation. And a government-owned vehicle.

Even with all that, I want to say no. But I can't. And I'm embarrassed to say what finally tips the scales in his favor.

I'm a New Yorker. He agreed to throw in free garage parking.

For a complete list of books by
JAMES PATTERSON

VISIT
JamesPatterson.com

Follow James Patterson on Facebook
JamesPatterson

Follow James Patterson on X
@JP_Books

Follow James Patterson on Instagram
@jamespattersonbooks

Follow James Patterson on Substack
jamespatterson.substack.com

Scan here to visit JamesPatterson.com and learn about giveaways, sneak peeks, new releases, and more.